# WITCH SILENCED IN WESTERHAM

*Paranormal Investigation Bureau #5*

## DIONNE LISTER

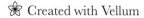

*To one of my best friends, Debra D. Has it really been that long since we finished school together? Thanks for sticking by me and reading my books. You're awesome. Text me. I think it's time we had another catch up and coffee.*

# CHAPTER 1

The cloying odour of disinfectant did its best to overpower the stench of human waste lurking somewhere in the building. Somewhere close. The smell forced its way past the inadequate protection of my vigilant hand. I had to remind myself I was here to support Will, and running back the way we'd come wasn't what a good support person would do. It wasn't even the behaviour of an adequate support person, and surely, I could at least be adequate. *That's the spirit, Lily. Aim high.*

Will's fist hovered in front of the door before dropping to his side for the third time. His inability to knock on the door was starting to worry me. I squeezed his hand but didn't offer any words. I'd never been faced with the tragedy of having a loved one with Alzheimer's, and I had no right to tell him it would be okay. If it were easy, we would have been in with his grandmother already, rather than standing in the corridor of the Saint Catherine Laboure Care Home for over five minutes, breathing in its unfortunate bouquet.

I took my hand off my nose and mouth. "Do you want me to go in and see how she is first?" Argh, the stink. I was such a baby. I put my hand back again before I gagged. It was hard having a sensitive nose.

"No. I'm sorry. It's just... I have no idea how she'll be. Two weeks ago, she knew who I was, but last week and a month ago, she thought I was her husband." He sighed. "My grandfather died twenty years ago." I'd learned a lot about Will in the six weeks we'd been dating, and even though I hadn't met his parents yet—I was putting that off as long as possible—he insisted I meet his gran, which made sense because who knew how much longer she'd be around. She was ninety-two, after all.

This time, I left my hand over my nose and mouth and mumbled through it. I was sure he could see the emotion in my eyes. "I know it hurts, but even if she doesn't know who you are, at least you've made her happy. She probably enjoys having company, even if she doesn't really know who it is. You'll regret it if you don't go in and make her happy."

Will looked down at me and snorted. "You're such an idiot."

I widened my eyes in fake horror. "Oh my God, who told you?"

He laughed, which meant my work here was done. I hated seeing him sad. "Okay, then. Let's get you out of this corridor before the fumes kill the few brain cells you have left." He knocked on the door and opened it without waiting for a "come in."

The room was small but not tiny. It was what you'd expect if you walked into a hospital room: white walls, a metal bed, a side table that looked like a mini filing cabinet, and two metal chairs with beige vinyl over the seat and back —not very attractive, but if someone had an accident, the chair would live to see another day.

His grandmother was a slender, long-limbed woman. Sitting on top of the covers of her neatly made bed, her legs were stretched out in front of her. She watched the TV that hung on the opposite wall. Her bedspread broke with the clinical theme of the room and added a splash of colour with blue and yellow flowers and multi-coloured butterflies. She wore light-grey slacks, with a distinct straight crease down the front, a fuchsia button-down shirt, and a stylish scarf around her neck with more vibrant butterflies.

As soon as she laid eyes on her grandson, her face blossomed with joy. "Oh, Frank, you came to see me!"

Will's shoulders sagged, but he quickly turned his frown into a tight smile, his forehead lines firmly in place. I guessed today was not a good day for her. "Of course I came to see you." He went to the side of the bed, leaned down, and kissed her cheek.

She gently patted his face. "I get so few visitors. It will be wonderful when I can get out of here. I'm so glad you could come." She turned to me. "And who's this?"

"This is my friend, Lily. We work together. Lily, this is Edith." He probably couldn't introduce me as his girlfriend because Frank, whoever he was, was probably married. We didn't want to upset her.

"Hi. Lovely to meet you." I gave her my brightest smile. Her skin was wrinkled, her hair white, but her eyes were the same blue as Will's, albeit a bit duller.

She returned my smile. "Please, have a seat." Other than not recognising Will and thinking she was going to leave here soon, she seemed fine. Her accent was suitably British and refined, her speech clear. She picked up the TV remote and switched the TV off.

Will sat in the chair closest to the bedhead, and I sat in the chair next to him. Edith fussed with the scarf. "So, Lily, what do you do at the factory? Are you Frank's new secretary?"

"Ah… yes. I am. He's lovely to work for, when he isn't grumpy." I winked at her. She laughed, and Will gave me a "you're going to cop it later" look. I did wonder if Frank was his grandfather or a cousin, maybe an uncle.

She turned to her grandson. "How are Elspeth and the boys?"

"They're doing well, thanks. What about you? Have you been okay?"

"Other than the terrible food, and the ward against magic use, I'm fine. I don't know why they won't let us use our magic. And why can't I go home? They healed my pneumonia as soon as I got here."

"They're worried it might come back. The weather's

been terrible, and so many illnesses are going around." He avoided answering her question about the ward against magic use. I could just imagine the disasters a bunch of demented witches could conjure. It was sad she didn't even realise why she was here. Or maybe that was a good thing. Ignorance could be bliss.

"How are Elspeth and the boys?" She smiled.

Will and I shared a glance. I gave him my sympathetic face. I wished I could give him a hug because he definitely needed one, but I didn't want to upset her, although she'd probably forget "Frank" and his secretary were having an affair the moment we left.

Will forced another smile. "They're good, thanks. How was your art class yesterday?"

She looked at him blankly. Alzheimer's was brutal. My heart broke for Will and his grandmother. Will leaned over and took her hand. "They must have called it off."

Edith stared into space for a moment. "Yes. They had to call it off because Queen Elizabeth visited."

Wanting to give Will a break, I said, "That must have been exciting. Did you get to meet her?" Why not play into the fantasy, if that made her happy? The truth didn't matter.

She smiled again. "Oh, yes. But only for a moment. She gave me a chocolate. Apparently she gave everyone one for being good patients. She also said that one day soon, witches will be able to announce they're here. We won't have to hide anymore. Won't that be wonderful?"

"That would be incredible." I smiled.

Her smile vanished. "But after the Queen left, Arnold came into my room to play cards, and before we had the game set-up, he collapsed. They came and took him away and won't tell me what happened to him."

Will turned to me. "Arnold is one of Edith's best friends here. They play cards quite often." He turned back to Edith. "I'll find out what happened and let you know. Okay?"

"Thank you, Frank." She shut her eyes for a minute, then opened them again. "Do you mind coming back later? I'm tired."

"Of course." He stood and bent to kiss her forehead. "I'll see you soon. Get some rest." He blinked, his expression soft, eyes glistening.

She gave me a sleepy smile. "It was lovely to meet you. Do you work with Frank?"

I smiled again, but my heart weighed a little bit more than when I'd come in. I couldn't help but wonder if James and I would have had to go through this one day if my parents had still been around. Having more years with them would definitely be worth this pain, not that I'd say that to Will. His despair was valid and hard for me to watch. "Yes. It was lovely to meet you, Edith. I hope you have a good nap."

Will put his hand on the small of my back and guided me to the door. Once we were in the hallway, he dropped his hand and shut the door. I started down the hallway, but only one set of footsteps tapped against the floor. I stopped and turned. Will stood in front of her door, staring at the ground. Should I go and comfort him, or did he need alone time? We'd only had a few dates since we'd decided to try things together because the PIB had been crazy busy after the Piranha disaster. I didn't know him nearly as well as I wanted.

He looked up and gave me a close-mouthed attempt at a smile. I tilted my head to the side. "Ready to go?"

"Yes, but just give me a minute. I'll find out what happened to Edith's friend." He approached me, and I went with him to the lift. Will punched the six-number code into the keypad. The care home was almost as hard to get in and out of as a prison.

I sighed.

"What's up?" Will was such a sweetie. He had enough to worry about, yet he was still tuned into me.

"Nothing major. It's just sad that people's lives, everything they've done, all the relationships they've had, are wiped, reduced to nothing, as if it never happened. They lose their freedom and who they are. It's like they die before they're dead." I frowned. "Dementia's horrible. I'm so sorry you're going through this." I stared into his eyes. "I wish I could take your pain away and make your grandmother better."

The elevator dinged and opened. We stepped in.

"Trust me. Beren's tried. But this stuff is beyond healing. Magic doesn't work on it."

The doors closed, and the lift descended one floor to ground level. "Why not?"

"We have a theory, but it's too complicated to explain in two minutes. We can talk about it another time if you like."

I shrugged. "Sounds good to me."

He stepped out of the lift. I followed him down the corridor to a green door that had Manager on a golden metal plate on the front. He knocked.

"Come in," a male voice called out.

Will opened the door and gestured for me to enter first —such a gentleman. I walked into a utilitarian space, which didn't exactly scream "manager". Grey vinyl floors, cream-coloured walls, a brown desk with three square-looking purple fabric armchairs. A purple pen holder sat between a purple stapler and a purple coffee cup on his desk. The purple piece that grabbed most of my attention, however, was the Great-Dane-sized Dino the Dinosaur sitting to his right. The cartoon character stared at me over the desk.

That was unexpected. I got my face under control— stunned mullet was not a good expression when meeting someone for the first time—and smiled at the short, slender man sitting next to his dinosaur. He stood, his wavy salt-and-pepper hair dishevelled and in stark contrast to his wrinkle-free white shirt and peacock-blue tie.

He removed his glasses and let them dangle from a purple chain around his neck. Someone had a favourite colour. I bet if we got him to take his trousers off, he'd have purple undies. I tried to contain my laughter and ended up executing a half snort.

"Can I help you?" His tone was filled with all the enthu-siasm of a sports-hating introvert who'd been told they'd have to attend a victory party for the local cricket team.

There would be only drunk cricket fanatics at said party, except for the sport-hating introvert who didn't drink.

Will stood next to me. We were too far from the table for him to reach over and shake the manager's hand, so he placed his hand on my back. You wouldn't hear any complaints from me. "I'm William Blakesley, Edith's grandson. This is my friend Lily."

I smiled. The manager raised his eyebrows. I dropped my smile and furrowed my brow. What the hell was his problem? Sheesh.

Will stood straighter. "My grandmother mentioned one of her friends wasn't well yesterday, and I told her I'd find out if he was okay."

"And who was this friend of hers? Not an imaginary one, I hope." He finally smiled—well actually, it was more of a smirk. What a di—

"No, it's a real person. Arnold."

"Ah, yes, Arnold. He died last night. It happens. They're all very old. Now, if there was nothing else you needed, I have a mountain of work to get through."

Other than the purple paraphernalia, his desk had a computer on it and two sheets of paper. It didn't look like there was a mountain of anything in here, except his crummy attitude, and the colour purple.

Will was more gracious than I would have been when he said, "Thanks for your time." He turned and went to the door, opened it for me, and followed me through before shutting it firmly.

"Wow, what a horrible little man."

"I know. I should have warned you. He took over this job a year ago. He's all about efficiency and cutting costs. Gran still seems to be getting everything she needs, and she's happy enough, so we've kept her here. Plus, there aren't many nursing homes for witches. There's one in London, which is always full and has a waiting list, and then there's one at Brighton, and that's popular too. They're the closest." We made it to the front door, and Will put in another code. The doors slid open, and we went to his car.

"But why does that matter? You can travel there and back."

"You have to go to an 'in area' one. We had those three to choose from, and it was the one she could get into first that she ended up at." He opened the Range Rover door for me, and I got in.

"But what if they're all full? What do you do then?"

He got in, shut the door, and started the car. "Make the best of it until you can get a place. It's not that bad. You can look after them at home using magic, and there are ward spells you can use to keep them contained."

"Still, that's not an ideal situation."

He pulled out into the street. "No, and those spells take a lot of energy. The care home pays eight witches. It takes two to keep the spell intact, and they do ten-hour shifts."

"When are you going to tell Edith her friend is dead?"

"Next time I'm there, but she might already know by then." He sighed, and my phone rang.

I pulled it out of my bag. Angelica's name flashed on the screen. "Hi. What's up?" She never called just to say hello, and now that she was pretty much running the PIB after Drake was killed, she was all about work, not that she hadn't been before, but if she'd had ten minutes a day to talk about other stuff, she didn't now.

"Meeting at James's tonight, seven sharp. Please tell Will and bring Olivia."

"Will do. Is that all?"

"Yes, dear. See you then. Bye."

William glanced my way before concentrating on the road again. "Anything exciting?"

"Meeting at my brother's tonight about my parents. You're included. It starts at seven *sharp*."

He grinned. "I'll be there on time. How *are* you going with that? Sorry I haven't been around to help."

"That's okay. You have enough to do. Witchface left a mess at headquarters." Dana had made changes at the PIB that had to be undone, and the crime she'd helped perpetrate—turning people into violent lunatics with contaminated tea—was still costing time and resources. Every assault had to be documented and witnesses interviewed so they could present the full list of crimes to the court when the time came for Gabriel to go on trial. A warrant was out for Agent Lam's arrest, but she'd disappeared, probably being hidden by the same group who'd tried to kidnap me when I first arrived in the UK, the same group we think orchestrated the disappearance of my parents.

My best friend, Olivia, was helping the PIB team deal with it. It was her first assignment since starting her new job. She liaised between the non-witch police and the PIB. And now she was going to help us find this super-secret witch group, I hoped.

"Tonight's our first meeting." I bit my fingernail and looked out the window. It was such a bad habit—biting my fingernails, that is, although when I was at school, looking out the window daydreaming was something I also got in trouble for. When I was nervous, biting my nails was my go-to thing. I figured if that was my worst habit, I was doing okay.

"Good luck. If you need anything, let me know."

I smiled and turned to him. "Thanks."

He glanced at me with a smile, and my stomach did a flippy thing. I hoped I never lost that feeling with him. Everyone said the "honeymoon" period ended after a year or two, and when I watched romcoms, I couldn't help but think after the end that they weren't going to be so damn happy five years down the track, but who knew? Maybe happy ever after did exist for some people.

Will dropped me at home and gave me a chaste kiss on the cheek before I got out of the car. We hadn't had a proper first kiss yet, which seemed ridiculous—we were both adults, and neither of us were virgins, surprise, surprise, but we'd only gotten together for jogging or café day-time dates —nothing romantic. I hadn't asked him why he was holding back, but I figured other than us agreeing to take things slow, he was like me: I wanted our first kiss to be special, something to remember for all the right reasons. As I got out of the car with my cheek tingling, I hated myself for being a closet romantic. If our first kiss didn't happen soon, romance would totally get chucked out the window. A sweaty kiss after jogging couldn't be that bad…could it? And, hey, it would be memorable for being super unromantic.

I let myself into the house, and as I shut the door, my phone rang. Wow, Angelica calling me twice in one day. Maybe tonight's meeting was called off? "Hi. Long time, no speak." I grinned.

"Yes, dear. Ten minutes is a long time, especially in dog years." Her dry tone was interlaced with a hint of a smile.

Oh my God, she'd made a joke, and it wasn't even gory. I laughed. "So, what's new?"

"I need you to come in and take professional photos of James and me. The powers that be are insisting. James held his previous role for three years, and I'd held mine for ten. They want updated photos to coincide with our new positions for our files and the portraits where they work."

"Where the 'powers that be' work?"

"Yes, dear. They operate out of a super-secret location that even I don't know about."

Well, that was weird. But then again, what did I know? I was so low down the food chain in the witch world, or any world, really, that the comings and goings of those who ran things were way beyond my notice. And I was sure that's how they wanted it. "Sure. I can do that. When would you like me to come in?"

"Is now too short notice?"

"Um, no, that's fine. I just have to get my gear, and I'll be there. Are these going to be indoor or outdoor shots?"

"Indoor."

"Okay. Thanks. See you soon."

I hurried upstairs and grabbed my knapsack and camera equipment. Most of it fit in the bag, except the tripod. I chuckled, remembering the day Will had to pretend to be my assistant at Olivia's engagement party. I'd made him carry a lot of unnecessary gear just to see him suffer. Ah, those were the days.

I made my doorway and travelled to the PIB reception room, my heart racing. I'd only been back twice since the whole Dana Piranha disaster, and it wasn't getting any easier. The bad memories of this place were really piling up.

I didn't even have to buzz to have the door opened— James was waiting for me, thankfully. He knew this place still gave me the creeps. "Hey, sis."

"Hey. This is good service. Couldn't wait to see me?" I grinned.

He smiled. "Yeah, nah. I was passing by, and Angelica messaged me about the photo shoot, so I stopped. Let me take that." He reached out and grabbed the tripod.

"Thanks." As far as brothers went, he was definitely a good one. That made me a lucky girl. I took a few calming deep breaths as we walked along.

We went to the lift and up one floor. When we alighted, James turned right. At the end of the corridor, he took a dogleg right that kept us travelling north, as far as I could tell. There were no windows, and I always got confused. This was a way I'd never gone before. After three minutes, we came to a hallway that had four white doors opening off it—two on either side. He knocked on the first door on the left. It turned green, colour leaching into the white until there was no white left, the way a chameleon changes.

Wow.

James opened the door and went in. I followed and shut the door behind me. The large room was divided into an entry area with an office behind. The same dark grey carpeting ran through both areas, and the walls were painted light lavender blue. Two three-seat Chesterfields faced each other in the entry area, an end table next to one of the couches holding a glossy-green indoor plant. I wondered if it were real or plastic. Unable to resist, I went over and touched a leaf. Damn. It was fake. I didn't know why that was so disappointing, but it was.

"Lily, when you've finished caressing the potted plant, we can start." Angelica stood behind her large mahogany desk, smirking. Two large windows at her back revealed the park-like garden outside. The empty wall to her left had a large square of darker paint.

"Is that where Drake's portrait was?" I asked.

"Yes. And that's where mine is going, if it ever gets taken."

Pushy much? They were paying me, so I guessed I'd just have to suck it up.

"Ha ha. So, are you after something formal or informal?"

"Formal. Sitting at my desk would be best." She sat in her black high-backed plush chair and ran a palm over her immaculate bun.

"Okay, great. I just have to get set up."

James unfolded the tripod while I fished my Nikon out of my bag and changed to the 35 mm lens. The windows behind provided good backlighting, but we needed some natural light on her face. I turned off the office fluorescents —ugly things—and got James to hold the silver reflector just out of shot.

I attached the camera to the top of the tripod and got to work. I was already taking the second shot when I realised I'd forgotten to turn my magic off. I had the terrible "talent" of being able to see if people were going to die through a camera. Whether it was my Nikon or the one on my phone, it didn't matter. If someone was going to die soon, they appeared faint, almost see-through when I looked at them. Thank God Angelica was as solid as the table she rested her clasped hands on. I heavy sighed my relief and kept shooting.

When I'd finished with Angelica, James and I went to his office and repeated the process. When we were done, I looked at my phone. The whole thing had only taken forty minutes, and it was just going on twelve thirty. Lunchtime! One of my favourite times of the day.

I packed my gear away, grabbed the tripod, and slung my bag over my shoulder. "See you tonight."

"Bye, Lily." James waved as I made my doorway and stepped through, my mouth watering. The leftover shepherd's pie in the fridge had my name on it. The way my life had gone ever since my twenty-fourth birthday, lunch might be the highlight of my day, so I was totally going to enjoy it.

I needed to appreciate each happy moment for the gift it was because the scary or sad moments had been outnumbering the good ones lately.

I shut all that out of my mind and savoured my lunch.

And it was a good thing I did.

# CHAPTER 2

After dinner, I travelled Olivia with me to James's. I knocked on the reception-room door, which set their dogs to barking. They were big dogs but total softies. Olivia stared at me, her eyes wide. "They're not vicious, are they?"

I smiled. "No. They just get excited. Don't worry. Are you normally scared of dogs?"

"Not really, well, maybe big ones, and ones that sound like that." She jerked her head in their direction.

The door opened, and she jumped behind me and put her hands on my shoulders. Millicent stood there dressed in a simple, loose yellow dress that showed her baby bump off to perfection. I grinned and stepped towards her. "Hey, Mill. You look gorgeous, and so does the bump."

She smiled and pulled me in for a gentle, if not awkward, hug where I had to stick my bum out to avoid the bump. "It's so great to see you." She stepped back and looked over my shoulder at Olivia. The dogs had quieted and were sitting at her feet looking up at us expectantly, their tails wagging. "What's wrong, Olivia?"

"She's scared of the dogs."

Millicent laughed. "They're just big softies. They never bite."

"That's pretty much what I said."

"There's a first time for everything." Olivia squeezed my shoulders harder. *Ouch.* I wanted to pry her fingers off, but what kind of friend would I be? I could take a bit of pain for my bestie.

"Wait here a sec." Millicent left the hallway and went towards the kitchen, where their back door was. "Come on, puppies. Come on." They followed her, tails still wagging. Olivia's grip loosened, but she was still holding my shoulders.

"You big scaredy cat." I turned around and shook my head. "I would never put you in harm's way. You can trust me. You know that, right?"

"Yes, I know, but when my phobias come on, I'm help-less. Rationality doesn't come into it."

"What are your other phobias?"

"Spiders and moths."

I gave her a quizzical look. "Moths? Those soft butterfly-like light-bulb worshippers?"

She nodded.

"But they can't hurt you. How can you be scared of those?"

"They could get stuck in my hair or up my nose, in my ears." She shuddered.

I tried not to laugh, but it came out anyway. I had no control. "I'm sorry, but moths? Also, I'm pretty sure one wouldn't fit up your nose." She had a pert little nose that was definitely narrower than the wingspan of even the tiniest moth. "Anyway. Next time we come, Mill can shut the dogs out back before we arrive. But I can't promise anything about the moths."

She looked around, maybe checking for moths, her eyes wide.

"You're such a nut. Ooh, I know. Do you want me to find a spell to cure your phobias?"

Her face relaxed, and she even managed a small smile. "That sounds like a great idea! But would it potentially harm part of my brain?"

"I have no idea. I'll research it and let you know." I faked a witchy laugh and rubbed my hands together. She rolled her eyes.

Millicent returned. "Are you okay? I'm sorry. I didn't know you were scared of dogs."

"It's just the big ones. Sorry to make you put them outside." Her caramel-brown cheeks darkened in a blush.

Millicent grabbed her hand. "Not to worry. The dogs like being outside anyway, as long as it isn't snowing." She laughed. "Let's go through. Everyone's waiting." She dragged Olivia with her, and I followed.

We walked through their lounge room, with the huge TV on the wall surrounded by white bookshelves filled with paperbacks, and into the dining room. James and Millicent's timber dining table was extended to its full ten-seat capacity. Angelica sat at one head, James at the other. Beren sat to Angelica's left, Will to her right. Millicent sat to James's left, and I went around to that side of the table and sat next to Will, his delicious, subtle aftershave chasing coherent thought away. I resisted the urge to shut my eyes and savour the moment.

Will smiled at me, and I returned it, but there was no kiss on the cheek, not with everyone watching. My face heated, just thinking about everyone watching us be affectionate. I didn't do PDAs, especially when we were on such new ground with each other. Maybe it would be different when I was more comfortable with *us*.

Olivia sat next to Beren and pulled a notebook and pen out of her bag. Beren grinned at her and said hello. She blushed again. Aw, they were so cute.

Angelica waved her arm in an arc. She cleared her throat. "Welcome, everyone. We have our bubble of silence. I want to remind everyone that what we're about to discuss is top secret. You will all be required to swear an oath of secrecy. What we discuss in these meetings must never be discussed with anyone else until such time as we've captured this rogue witch group. Make no mistake—they're operating against laws set up hundreds of years ago, and they're not only dangerous to us. Groups like this often have a bigger agenda. The safety of everyone here, and possibly around the world, is at stake."

I took a deep breath. Things were getting serious—well,

more serious than they'd been. I figured it was just me and my future niece or nephew who were in the most danger, but pursuing this group would put everyone in harm's way. But not chasing them would be worse.

Angelica clasped her hands on the table in front of her. "We're here to find and destroy the group Dana works for— the same group who have been trying to kidnap Lily. Before we swear our secrecy on the Witches Wellspring of Knowledge, I must warn you all: trust no one." Her tone hinted dire consequences for anyone who didn't heed her words. The solemn faces around the table indicated she'd made an impact. "Trust not the man, woman, or child in the street. Trust no one at the PIB. You can only trust each other. If you're not fully committed to this cause, please leave now." She turned her head and stared at Olivia. "If you swear to this cause, any misstep could lead to your death. Are you willing to take that risk?"

Olivia swallowed, her eyes huge. She looked at me, then at James and Millicent before turning back to Ma'am. "Yes, yes, I am. I've done a lot of thinking, and it's clear that whoever they are, controlling Lily isn't their only objective. Whilst they're out there somewhere, I have a feeling everyone is in danger... including non-witches."

I nodded. She and I felt the same way—this wasn't just about my safety anymore. They wanted me for a reason. If they didn't, I had no doubt Piranha would have killed me. And if I was the means to an end, what was the end?

Angelica gave a nod. "Your summation is correct, Olivia. If we're all good to swear in, let's get started. Once we've done that, I want to discuss our objectives." Angelica held her left palm upwards. A bell dinged, and a small golden book, just larger than her hand, appeared. Its smooth surface gleamed—it was the shiniest, most immaculate object I'd ever seen. I leaned forward to get a better look.

The cover seemed to be solid metal with an ever-diminishing pattern of squares pressed into it. None of the squares were complete. Just before the fourth line of each square reached its brother, the line started another, smaller square. But that wasn't the incredible part.

The book emitted the sound of running water, almost a babbling-brook type of happy, relaxed-summer-day noise. I turned to Will. "Can you hear that?"

He smiled. "Yes. It's the book."

"I know that, Captain Obvious. I just wondered if you could hear it."

"No need to get so testy, Miss Crankypants." He tapped my nose with his finger.

I raised a brow and smirked. "We've just started dating. I'm not taking your name."

He looked at me, confused, and Olivia giggled.

"Okay, children, if we can focus. This is neither the time or place to make jokes."

I swallowed. "Sorry. I was just thrown by the book's noise."

Angelica placed the book in the middle of the table where it hovered about four inches above the tabletop on a bed of golden light. I sucked in a breath. Wow. Magic still had the ability to surprise and awe me. Olivia wore an amazed expression similar to what mine probably looked like.

Warmth radiated from the small tome. I held my palms towards it, as if I was warming my hands in front of a fire. I shut my eyes and enjoyed the balmy energy soaking into my skin. The pleasant heat trickled through my veins and up my arm. Golden flecks winked into existence in the darkness behind my eyelids. One by one they appeared until a stunning golden Milky Way shone for me alone. The sounds of running water had changed from bubbling serenity to a whooshing roar. Somewhere in the distance, someone was calling out.

"Lily! Lily!"

I was shaking. No… someone was shaking me. I opened my eyes and dropped my hands, the warmth and twinkling golden lights disappeared. Instead, six people stared at me, mouths hanging open, eyes wide. Will still gripped my shoulder—he must have shaken me to get me to come back from wherever it was I had zoned out to. His face had drained to white.

"Lily, are you okay?" The book's warmth was nothing compared to the heat penetrating my forearm from his hand.

Why was everyone so worried? "I'm fine. What's wrong with all of you? I just shut my eyes for a minute. The book's like a little heater. I was just enjoying it."

Angelica stared at me as if not sure what to say, which was totally a first for her. She shared a glance with my brother before turning back to me. "Lily, you were sitting there unresponsive for five minutes. We were calling your name, but you ignored us."

Okay, so that was weird. Was she joking? "I couldn't hear you."

"What was going on?" Will asked.

I explained the golden stars and the sound of a rushing river. "I'm fine. Honestly."

James leaned forward, placing his palms on the table. "Lily, look at the book."

Weird request, but I complied. It was still where it had been before, but something had changed. "It's not glowing as brightly. Is that it?"

"Yes, but it was even fainter before, when you were in that trance. Watch. It's getting brighter."

And so it was. "What does that mean?"

James shrugged. "I have no idea." He looked at Angelica. "Do you know?"

She cleared her throat and glanced down at her hands, then back up again. "I have an idea, but we don't have time to discuss it here. Lily, don't do that again, okay?"

"Ah, sure." But what had I actually done? Everyone except Angelica and Olivia still gave me worried glances. Will had dropped his hands from my shoulder and forearm, and I patted both sides of my neck. Phew! I hadn't grown a second head. With everyone staring at me like they were, that wouldn't have surprised me.

"You'll all swear on the book. It will come to you, one at a time. When it does, place your hand on the cover and repeat after me. Olivia, you'll hold my hand and swear an oath that I will make binding."

"Yes, Ma'am." Olivia nodded, her face solemn.

Ma'am's lips moved, and the barest hint of sound rustled out, autumn leaves pushed by the wind, sliding and tumbling against each other. The book left the middle of the table and floated towards me. Of course I'd have to go first —the person with the least experience and probably the most scared person here, other than Olivia.

Would this hurt? And what would I be asked to sacrifice if I couldn't uphold my promise?

I placed a sweaty palm against the cool metal cover.

Angelica's voice was deeper than normal, even, and commanding. "Repeat after me, Lily. I, Lily Katerina Bianchi, swear to uphold the utmost secrecy in regard to the investigation into the group known as Regula Pythonissam."

As I repeated her words, hot air surrounded me, swirling faster and faster, the breeze like a scorching summer wind coming off the desert. The type of gust that was the opposite of refreshing. The hair in my ponytail stirred, fluttering against the back of my neck.

Ma'am continued, "If I discuss anything related to this case with anyone other than those currently in this room, I will forfeit my magic. My failure to keep this secret will result in me becoming a non-witch. Permanently."

Olivia's intake of breath was loud enough to reach me. Holy hell, that was pretty severe. But then again, what was I really losing? If my magic disappeared, I'd be safe again, and I'd just go back to my old life, because surely the group after me wouldn't need me anymore. But then again, Millicent had once explained how bereft I'd feel, and whenever I blocked my magic to stop weird things appearing in my camera, I suffered an emptiness that was hard to describe. It was as if a huge part of me was missing. Being honest with myself meant admitting I would miss my magic as much as I would miss my right arm. Also, that group's goals wouldn't change just because they couldn't use me. Maybe me having no power was just what they wanted?

I took a deep breath and repeated her words. The whirlwind picked up speed, slapping strands of my hair into my cheek.

"… becoming a non-witch. Permanently." The air spun faster until it was hard to breathe. I shut my watering eyes. Then it died all at once. I opened my eyes.

The book quietly drifted to Will, as if nothing had happened. The process repeated until everyone, including Ma'am, had sworn on the magical tome. Then it was Olivia's turn. Ma'am placed her hands on my friend's shoulders, and Olivia had to swear on her ability to walk. That was harsh, but I was relieved she hadn't had to swear on her life—none of us were risking our lives, just an ability, so it shouldn't have been different for her.

Ma'am waved her hand over the book that hovered in front of her. It disappeared. "Now that's done, we can get to work. I'm sure we all have ideas on how to move forward. I want everyone to write them down and bring them to the next meeting. We'll sift through them and formulate a plan. We'll meet here at seven tomorrow night."

Will's phone rang. Ma'am raised a brow—he probably should have had it on silent for the meeting. I'd switched my phone off, although I rarely received calls anyway, but I figured it would be rude for it to ring during the meeting.

Will looked at the screen. "It's my grandmother. I need to take it."

Ma'am nodded, and Will answered the phone. "Hello, Gran…. What? Slow down. Say that again."

We were all staring at Will. I guessed it was what happened when you took a phone call during a meeting. It didn't help that he sounded worried.

Will's brow wrinkled. "I know, but it happens. I'm sorry, Gran…. No! Don't worry. You'll be all right. I promise…. Of course I can come and see you. I'll be there soon. Bye."

"What happened?" I asked.

"Another one of her friends died. Everyone there always says these deaths come in waves of three. She's worried she'll be next."

"That's nonsense." Ma'am shook her head. "You go and comfort your grandmother, Will. You can make up the time tonight."

"Thanks, Ma'am." He stood and looked down at me. "Want to come for a drive? She seemed to like you last time. Maybe having you there will help calm her."

I stood. "I'd be happy to."

We said our goodbyes and left. I had an idea, but I wasn't sure if Will would agree, and to be honest, it scared me. As we drove, I placed my hand on my tummy to quiet the nerves and broached it with him. "Do you want me to take a photo of your grandmother? That way you'll know if she really has anything to worry about."

He stayed quiet, maybe considering my offer. After a few minutes, he said, "No, thanks. I'd rather not know. It's not like we can prevent it. She's old. Whether her time is tomorrow or in a year, it's coming." He frowned.

"Fair enough."

We arrived at the nursing home, and the night staff buzzed us in. While we waited for the lift, a scream echoed down the hallway, and a groan followed. "What are they doing to them?"

The lift opened. Will ushered me in. "Nothing. They're demented. The other day when we came in, it was unusually quiet. Normally, it's much noisier than tonight. At night, they drug the residents so they'll sleep."

"They do what?" My eyebrows climbed up my forehead.

"Not like that, Lily. Some of them have insomnia. It's part of caring for them, giving them sleeping pills. They don't all get them, of course. Normally Gran is asleep by now."

It was only about eight thirty. Sheesh, they had an early bedtime. When I was old—hopefully I'd get there and not die young—I would hardly sleep. Not having much time left should make you want to do stuff. And that was the other thing—old people drove so slooooow. I'd be speeding everywhere. God knew that they had no time to waste.

When the lift opened to the upper floor, crying reached us. Someone yelled, "Be quiet! Go to sleep." A door slammed. An old man in a dark blue dressing gown ambled down the dimly lit hallway towards us, his slippers scuffing along the floor, making a swooshing sound.

A woman in a blue nurse-type uniform hurried after him. She grabbed his arm and led him back the way he'd come with only a quick glance our way. I swallowed. What a horrible existence. I hoped I never had to experience this for myself.

When we reached his grandmother's door, Will knocked. "Who is it?" came from inside.

"It's me, Gran. Will." He turned the handle, but he couldn't open the door.

"Just a moment." After a minute, the screech of a chair scraping across the floor made me wince. The door opened a crack, and his grandmother peeked out. She opened the door further, leaned out past the doorframe and Will, looked both ways, then pulled him in. I followed. She shut the door quickly once we were in.

What the hell was going on?

She looked at me as if she'd never seen me before. She pointed a crooked finger at me. "Who's this? It's not a friend of the Queen's. Is it?"

"No, Gran. She's my friend Lily. She was with me when you called, so she came with me."

Will introduced us again, and I smiled. "Lovely to meet you, Edith."

Her eyebrows drew down, and she pursed her lips. This didn't seem to be the friendly Edith of this morning. Meeting her seemed as if it had happened a week ago, not less than half a day. And she didn't even remember me.

That was sad, but at least she recognised Will was her grandson this time.

She stood opposite William and grabbed his arms. "My friend is dead. That's two this week. They're coming for me next. You have to get me out of here."

"Who died?"

"Beryl… my Australian friend. She moved to London because she married one of us. She's been here for forty years, but now she's gone. They did it, William. They killed her."

"Who's *they*?"

She looked around, and when her gaze came across me, she scowled. She leaned towards William and whisper-shouted. She obviously didn't think I could hear. "She could be a spy. Make her leave, and I'll tell you."

"Gran—"

"Will, it's okay. I'll wait outside. Goodnight, Edith." I quickly left and shut the door quietly behind me. The only person outside was a woman carrying a tray with dirty dishes. She was passing Edith's room as I stepped out. She didn't glance back but hurried to the lift and pressed the button. Someone down the hall groaned, but it was fairly quiet otherwise.

I looked at Edith's door. She'd been so nice this morning when she thought I was someone else, and tonight…. Will must be happy she knew who he was, but now she was agitated, paranoid even. But what if something was going on, and it wasn't just an overreaction to the loss of her friends? Hmm. I decided to go for a walk.

I turned and walked past Edith's door, in the opposite direction of the lift. I had no idea what to look for, but it couldn't hurt. A young dark-skinned man hurried past, carrying a garbage bag. He gave me a nod, and I smiled. Further along, moaning came from a room to my left. The door was ajar. I stopped. The moaning continued, the tone of what I'd expect a ghost would have, not that I believed in ghosts. I glanced up and down the hallway—no one was around. I carefully opened the door a bit more and peered in.

The room was dark, so I couldn't see much. I tried to reach for the flowing river of magic to make a small light, but it was like grasping at air. An invisible barrier stopped me from reaching my magic. An uncomfortable sensation skittered along my brain—the precursor to panic. Sweat slicked my forehead and the space between my nose and mouth. I finally remembered that they blocked magic here to protect the residents. I took a deep breath and blew it out quietly. Phew.

I pulled my phone out and turned on the torch. Yay for technology. I shone the light on the floor—the reflected light would be enough to see what I needed. The groaning hadn't stopped.

An elderly man lay in bed, the covers up to his armpits. He was on his back, his eyes and mouth open, and he was staring at the ceiling, emitting that terrible sound. My light hadn't snagged his attention. The dirge stopped only long enough for him to take a breath. Then it continued. It was almost physically painful to hear. I pulled his door ajar and kept going.

There was no way I could work in a place like this. I totally respected the selfless employees who cleaned and cared for these people. I knew they were paid, but they were doing the worst types of things for people they had no history with. Poo was not my forte. I'd be gagging half my shift.

I finally reached the end of the hallway where there was a door to the left and one to the right. Both were closed, and I wasn't going to invade someone's privacy in that way. The door that had been slightly open was different, at least in my mind.

As I stood contemplating what to do next, the door on the right opened, and a woman hurried out, scaring the crap out of me. I started, my hand flying to my chest. The woman, who was about five foot three, had short wavy hair and looked to be about sixty. There was something familiar about her, as if I'd seen her before. Maybe I had this morning and it hadn't registered?

She stared at me; her dark blue eyes narrowed. Her tone was short. "Are you lost?"

"Um, no. I'm just waiting for someone, and I thought I'd go for a walk because I was bored."

"Well, walk yourself the other way. Visiting hours are over. You shouldn't even be here." She folded her arms and stood there, obviously waiting for me to do as ordered. Why couldn't people ask things nicely? She had no idea who I was or why I was there. I could have been the relative of one of the recently deceased residents. She really should be politer. Meanies like her made me hate people. Although, maybe she was just upset about the deaths too? It was likely she'd gotten to know the patients fairly well if she looked after them.

"Sorry. I'll go and wait back where I was. We're just here to comfort one of the residents who was upset because her friends died. Are you upset about it too?"

Her eyes registered surprise, then incredulity. Sadness didn't factor into it. Maybe she was just a rude b—

"I'm a professional. The people here are old witches. It happens. They've all had fantastic lives. If I were to get upset about everyone who died, I'd be crying 24/7. Now get back to where you came from, or I'll have to ask you to leave."

She was missing her empathy centre. Didn't that make her a psychopath? And why did she want me out of there? It wasn't as if I was doing anything. She raised her brows and tapped her foot. Gah. The best thing would be to turn and leave, and surprise, surprise, I did exactly that. I didn't need another showdown with a psychopath—I was still recovering from the whole Dana Piranha disaster.

Angry care-home lady followed me.

When I reached Edith's door, Will was exiting. The care-home woman wore the ghost of a smile when she saw where I'd stopped. In case she got any ideas about being mean to Edith, I squinted my eyes and radiated a "just try it, lady" look. Hopefully she got the message and didn't think it was because I was constipated or had a stomach ache.

The door clicked shut. Will looked at me, his forehead a puzzle of creases. "Where'd you go?"

"Just for a walk." I lowered my voice so the woman who was now almost at the lift couldn't hear. "I ran into that horrible woman on the way. She's not in the least upset that people are dying. That's her over there." The lift dinged, and she stepped in.

"She doesn't look that horrible. Besides, the people here are old, and it's expected."

"How would you feel if your grandmother died?"

"Upset, but I know she had a good life, and she can't live forever."

"But would you still cry?"

He looked at me as if I was stupid. "Of course."

"Well then. The people who work here get to know the residents. You'd think you'd at least spare a sad thought for them. They don't have robots working here. Do they?"

"No. But maybe you have to tune out; otherwise, it would be too hard to come in every day."

"Hmm, maybe." I wasn't convinced. That woman gave me an unpleasant feeling. Maybe I was just too judgemental? "How's your gran?"

"I finally got her calmed down enough to try and sleep. She's still worried they're coming for her next."

"Who?"

"The Queen." He shook his head. "She's been having delusions the last few weeks, and I thought they'd gotten them under control with medication, but this morning and tonight prove she's still off with the fairies, so to speak." He sighed.

"I'm sorry." My heart could hurt all it wanted for him, but there was nothing I could do. "Let's go. There's not much you can do right now."

"I know. It just scares me how quickly she's gone downhill. Her delusions were smaller before—it was more calling people the wrong name, thinking I was my uncle or whatever. But now she thinks the Queen keeps visiting, and she's killing her friends."

As we ambled to the lift, I wondered: what if there was some truth to Edith's ramblings after all?

# CHAPTER 3

W ill dropped me off and went back to work—crazy man. I went to bed soon after because the whole swearing on the book of magic tired me out. During the night, I dreamt of Queen Elizabeth, Prince Charles, and Camilla. They were dressed in designer threads—as usual—and they were wandering through the nursing home. Every now and then, the Queen would order someone knighted, and then she'd order Prince Charles to behead someone. He carried out her orders as Camilla laughed. I woke up the next morning feeling horrified.

I dressed and ambled downstairs to make my coffee. Once it was done, and I was sitting at the table inhaling the heady scent, it came to me—where I'd seen that woman at the care home before. *Thank you, brain*!

I hadn't actually seen her before, but she looked a hell of

a lot like Queen Elizabeth II. Did that mean Will's grand-mother had been talking about her? Had that woman killed the patients, or did Edith just think that because she was around every time it happened, which made sense since she worked there? Gah, brain. Stop! Just because two old people died, didn't mean anyone had killed them. Now I was buying into Edith's delusion.

But what if it wasn't a delusion?

I finished my coffee and stood. Maybe Olivia could help me nut this out or tell me I was being stupid and that my imagination was just trying to get attention. It was only 7:30 a.m., so she wouldn't have gone to work yet. I made my way to her room. As I was about to knock on her door, my phone rang. I raced into my room to grab it—the phone company I was with never let it ring long before it would go to message bank, which was supremely annoying.

I panted to catch my breath as I answered. "Hello?" I'd been in such a hurry that I hadn't looked at the screen to see who it was.

"Lily."

My heart thudded hard, and my stomach dropped. His voice was tight—the tone of voice one used when delivering life-changing bad news. I swallowed. "Will, what's wrong? Are you okay? Is James okay?" I held my breath, waiting for his answer. *God, please don't be James.*

"I'm fine. It's my gran." He paused, maybe trying not to cry. "I just got a call from the care home. She's dead."

The silence expanded, seemed to fill the whole room, pushing on my chest, making it hard to breathe. I hardly knew her, but Will's pain was my pain. My heart broke for him. "What do you need? I'm here, Will."

"Can you come with me to the care home? My parents can't make it. I need to collect Gran's things and… identify her."

"Did they say why she died?"

"They said it was a heart attack."

I had a gazillion questions, but now wasn't the time to ask. "Do you want me to meet you at the PIB?"

"I'm still at home. I'll swing by and get you in ten minutes."

"Okay… bye." I'd never been to Will's house. I didn't have the coordinates to his reception room, and I thought it too forward to suggest I meet him there. It irked me a little that I'd never seen where he lived, but we agreed to take it slow. I sighed.

I knocked on Olivia's door. "Come in." I did. She was sitting at her desk putting stuff into her handbag. She saw my frowny face. "What's up?"

"Will's grandmother just died. I'm going with him to the care home to finalise things."

"Oh, no. That's so sad. Is he okay?"

I shrugged. "Sort of. He's doing what needs to be done, but he's upset."

"How old was she?"

"Ninety-two. She wasn't unwell though, other than her mental state. She had dementia, but she could walk, get around by herself. She wasn't overweight, didn't smoke, didn't look overly frail. I don't know if I'm being silly, but it seems like her death was sudden, considering."

"By sudden, do you mean suspicious?" She had an eyebrow raised. She knew me so well.

"Yes. Am I being paranoid? She worried she would be the next to die."

Olivia's brow furrowed. "What?"

"Two of her friends died. One died the day before yesterday and the other, yesterday. Will thought she was being paranoid, but the more I think about it, the more I think she was right. Maybe someone didn't like what she'd been saying. She might have said something to others, not just Will and me."

"You think they were silencing her?"

I nodded. Poor Edith. We needed to get to the bottom of this, even if it was just to make sure nothing horrible was going on.

The doorbell rang. Huh? I didn't know Angelica had a doorbell. Everyone usually knocked. "That must be Will. I'll see you later. I'll let you know what happened."

"Okay, cool. I'm going to be at Kent Police Station today." She grinned. "Orientation. I've been at the PIB the whole time, but now I get to check out what happens on the other side."

"That's right! Good luck. I know you'll do well. We should make sure to eat dinner together tonight, and we can swap stories."

"It's a date."

I grabbed my bag and went down to the front door. Will

stood there, his back to me. He turned when he heard the door open. His eyes were red, and his face sad. I stepped up to him, wrapped my arms around his neck, and pulled him in close. We didn't speak. He slid his arms around me, and we stood like that for a couple of minutes.

"Thank you," he whispered. He stepped back and turned towards the car. I got the hint and followed. We were quiet for the first half of the ten-minute ride to the care home. But then I couldn't hold my questions in any longer. I was a total failure when it came to patience.

"Just tell me if you don't want to talk, but I have to ask a question." I studied him for a reaction. He nodded slowly but didn't take his eyes off the road. "Will they do an autopsy?"

He swallowed, his Adam's apple bobbing. "There's no reason to. She was old, and her health was deteriorating. They said a doctor confirmed a heart attack."

"She seemed okay last night... physically, anyway. She didn't look like someone who was about to, you know.... Sorry, but you know me—if I'm thinking it, I have to say it."

"Yeah, well, this isn't the time, Lily." His tired-yet-cranky tone was a warning to drop it. But when did I ever heed warnings?

"When is the time? When she's been buried or cremated? When any evidence is gone?"

He jerked his head around and glared at me, then gave the road his full attention the rest of the way. I stared out the window, frustrated more than upset. It wasn't my intention to make him feel worse, and I didn't actually have any evidence. Was I wrong? Hmm, I had my phone with me. Maybe I could take some candid shots? Would my talent work within the confines of a magic-free zone?

On arriving at the care home, we headed straight to the manager's office. The little man was already standing when we entered. His tie was yellow today, but his shirt was all about his favourite colour—purple, which matched the cord his glasses dangled from, creating the amusing illusion that his glasses floated, unsupported, in front of his stomach. "Mr Blakesley, so nice to see you. I'm sorry for your loss."

What a surprise! He was actually being considerate.

Will walked to his desk, leaned over, and shook the manager's hand. "Thank you. I'm here to collect the paperwork and her things."

"There's also the small matter of identifying her body."

Small matter? What the hell? It may be a common occurrence for this guy, but what about some sympathy for the bereaved?

"Yes, of course. I'd like to do that straight away."

"The sooner, the better. You'll also have to arrange for the funeral home to come get her. We're not a morgue."

My mouth dropped open; he definitely missed empathy 101 at care-home school. I turned to Will. "Do you want me to get her things while you're saying goodbye?" I had no desire to see another dead body, and I was sure he might have wanted to do this alone, say goodbye for the last time.

"Yes, thanks." He gave me a wan smile. "The lift code is two, four, six, eight." Hmm, that wasn't too tricky. How had the oldies not figured it out?

"Um, thanks."

We exited the office, the manager turning right and leading Will away. I turned left. At the lift, I punched in the code and pressed the call button. The lift was as slow as a stooped-over, shuffling old person. Maybe they didn't want to startle them if they had to go in it. I snorted. That was considerate.

Eventually it arrived and took me to the first floor. The hallway was livelier today. Two short old ladies, both with white hair and walking frames, slowly clacked along. One wore a scowl, the other a manic grin. That would be an interesting conversation to listen to. Who was annoying who? I snorted again. I could totally see Will and me here— me the manic one, and him cranky as hell. He had that look perfected, and he used it so often that his face would prob- ably set that way eventually.

A young male care-home employee pushed an elderly man in a wheelchair. The elderly man had his chin slumped on his chest, his eyes closed. Was he even awake? I smiled at the care-home guy, and he gave a nod. Gah, I hated that! If I smiled at someone, I expected reciprocation. I wanted to take the smile back, dammit. He didn't deserve it.

Moaning ghosted down the hallway, but I couldn't tell if it was the same man from last night. At least the poo smell was gone.

Edith's door was ajar. There was no reason to knock, so I opened it and went right in. "Oh, I'm so sorry." Looked as if they filled beds around here before they were cold.

An elderly man with pale skin covered in age spots lay in

bed, a middle-aged woman sitting in a chair next to him. "Can I help you?"

"I'm sorry to intrude. I didn't realise anyone would be here." My cheeks heated. "I'm just here to grab Edith's things—the lady who was in here before."

The woman gave a gentle smile. "Of course. I think that's her stuff there." She pointed to the floor below the window. A small, black suitcase sat there. I blinked. That was the sum of her life—at least the tangible belongings that would last longer than her children and grandchildren. The only thing left of her was one suitcase's worth. My shoulders sagged. How depressing.

I grabbed the handle and elongated it so I could wheel Edith's meagre possessions out. Before I left, I looked around the room. I took my phone out of my bag and turned to the lady. "I just need to take a photo before I leave… for her grandson."

The space between her brows formed two lines, and her mouth opened slightly in a perplexed expression. "Do you need us to leave? We don't want to be in the shot."

"No, that's fine. I'll take it from here back to the door." She probably thought I was weird, but whatever. She wouldn't be the first and definitely not the last.

I whispered, "Show me who killed Edith." A cool vacuum met my grasp at the power, and I sighed. I clicked the photo of the empty doorway anyway because I didn't want the woman wondering why I hadn't taken the picture. Damn. Had it not worked because she died from natural causes, or was it because my talent was stymied?

As I dejectedly wheeled Edith's bag down the corridor, a woman dressed in black and about my height sprang out of her room and wrapped her pudgy fingers around my arm. Her crazy eyes met my startled ones. She said nothing but pulled me towards her room. I only half resisted. What should I do? Maybe she just wanted company because no one ever came to visit. Would it hurt me to give her some of my time?

Once she had me in her room, she shut the door. The click of it shutting made me think of a tomb door closing for the last time. A cackling laugh accompanied her tooth-less grin. Yikes. She was the embodiment of how witches were usually portrayed—with the exception of Sabrina, and Samantha from *Bewitched*. Some stereotypes were there for a reason.

"Um, it's lovely to meet you, but I have a friend waiting for me."

She latched onto my arm again and tried to stop me leaving. Bloody hell, she had some strength for an oldie. My heart beat faster because even though it was unlikely she would hurt me, she just might. I hated being touched at the best of times, let alone by a loony, silent-except-for-cackling witch.

She gripped the arm that had Edith's bag. I leaned past her and opened the door with my other hand. I pried her death grip off me and hurried out. Apparently, I was no good at this hanging out and being nice to old people thing. Not that I didn't like old people, but these were strangers, and unhinged ones at that. I hoped I never had dementia. I would hate to burden anyone else, and to have care-home staff shower me and see me naked—oh, and to change my nappies. Nope. No way. No how. Why did some of us have to revert to baby state when we aged? Nature had a sick sense of humour that I didn't appreciate. Why couldn't we go back to being eighteen or twenty? That would be way more useful and fun.

Once I was out of there, I looked back. She appeared at the door, her thin white hair sticking up and making her look even nuttier. She grinned and nodded, ambling towards me in slow motion. Yikes.

I speed-walked to the lift, punched in the code, and pressed the call button with a shaking finger. The old lady had commandeered an accomplice—an elderly man, also grinning sans teeth. He was taller than her and skinny, but he had the same zombie gait she did. They were slow, but their pace still ate up centimetres of corridor faster than I would have liked.

Where was the damn lift? *Hurry. Hurry.* I shifted from foot to foot, my attention shooting from them to the lift doors and back again. My heart raced. Oh my God, a third person had joined them, limping behind. There were only a few metres left, and they would be on me. I was in my own mini zombie apocalypse, or at least, that's how it felt.

They weren't allowed into the lift, so would I have to try and stop them? A visual popped into my head, and it wasn't pretty. It started off like herding cats and ended with me surrounded on the floor with the zombies grinning and dribbling over me before they pulled my limbs from my body. *Get a grip, idiot.*

They were a metre away, almost close enough to touch. Their wide eyes shone with excitement. I listened intently, but no one was saying, "Brains, brains." Thank. God.

The lift dinged, and the doors opened. The saying "saved by the bell" now had a special place in my heart—the place that feared zombies and care-home residents. As I stepped in, someone moaned, and someone else said, "Nooooo."

I repeatedly smashed my finger against the G button—wow, that was close to G spot. How had I never noticed that before? Maybe that's why it was called a spot and not a button. Imagine the confusion that could arise. Lifts were already known as places where inappropriate behaviour happened. If the G spot were a G button, it would be so much worse.

As the doors started to close, the woman who had dragged me into her room reached out. I shrunk back. Her hand languidly moved towards me. The doors were still partly open. Her hand got closer and closer. I released Edith's bag and held my hands up, ready to push the woman away.

The old woman smiled, maybe thinking she'd made it.

The doors closed.

Oh. My. God. I didn't breathe again until the car descended. When it reached the ground floor, I gasped. I'd survived. But never again. I was never traipsing care-home hallways without someone there to protect me.

Will, waiting for me in the corridor, watched me step out of the lift. "Are you okay? You look like you've seen a ghost."

"If you change ghost to zombies, then yes, I have. Here's your grandmother's suitcase."

His fingers brushed mine as I slipped my hand off the handle, and he grabbed it. This wasn't exactly romance central, but a heart-stopping zing shot through my fingers and up my arm. What would it be like when we finally kissed? When would I find out? I hoped it was before my thirtieth birthday. Six years was a long time to make a girl wait.

"So, what happened up there?"

"Well, this isn't what scared me, but they've already got someone in your gran's bed."

His eyes widened. "They didn't waste any time." Was that a growl?

"No. Now about what happened. It was nothing, really, just me overreacting, but those old people were like zombies. I thought they were going to swarm and eat me alive. I managed to escape. The lift doors closed just in time."

He cocked his head to the side and regarded me with his brows drawn together. "You're such a weirdo, Lily." He shook his head. "Let's go."

"But what happened with—"

He whipped his hand up and placed his finger against my lips. "Shhh. We'll talk later." I nodded and stared into his eyes. The way the butterflies were destroying my stomach, I would have done anything he asked me in that moment. And he knew it. He smirked and put his hand down. "Let's go."

⊛

As we drove, Will asked, "Did you see anything unusual in Gran's room?"

"You mean other than the old guy in her bed?"

He shook his head and sighed. "Yeah, other than that."

If he was asking, he probably wasn't going to get angry that I'd done my best to find a clue without being obvious or going against his wishes. Okay, so he hadn't expressly told me not to investigate, but he had been annoyed at my line of thinking. "I tried taking a picture with my phone, but nothing showed up. I'm not sure if that's because nothing happened in there or that my talent couldn't work without access to any magic."

"Good try, though. I'll have to teach you how to use your talent when you're cut off from the main source of magic."

Whoa! "Why hasn't anyone told me before? Is it really a thing?"

He smiled. "Yes, it's really a *thing*. No one's told you probably because it's rare that you'd need it. Also, you have to be careful not to draw too much power because it's all coming from you."

"In other words, I could kill myself?"

"Yep."

"If it's possible, how is it the oldies don't accidentally kill themselves?"

"As witches age, their talent all but disappears if the mind goes. It would be extremely rare for any of those dementia patients to be able to access their talent. Losing your talent when you're old can be an early sign of dementia."

"Oh. What was your gran's talent?"

He smiled. "She was really good at encouraging plants to grow. Her vegetables always won prizes at agriculture shows."

"Isn't that cheating?"

He shrugged. "It made her happy. Plus, there was never any money involved—there were tons of blue ribbons, though." He chuckled.

"Did you find something suspicious?"

"A small chunk of her hair was missing."

"What?" I sat up straight and stared at him.

"Underneath all her other hair, at her nape. A thin line of hair where it meets bare skin had been cut off at the scalp. You would have to look closely to find it."

"What made you look so close?"

He turned to briefly look at me. His awkward smile was what I would class as chagrin. "I thought more about what you said. I also thought about how she'd been acting lately, and as much as she'd had delusions, she was never panicked. What I'd seen in her eyes last night was fear." He blinked and pressed his lips together. "I didn't take her seriously, and look what happened...."

"It wasn't your fault. And maybe she wasn't murdered,

but I just think it doesn't hurt to investigate to make sure."

"Yes, well, I've arranged for Beren and James to pick up the body and take it back to the PIB for an autopsy. They're going to use the PIB's mortuary ambulance, which has no signage. It will be perfect. They're pretending to be from Magic & Co Funeral Homes."

I would've laughed, but the whole thing was sad when you thought of why they were doing this. Was there really a witch funeral home called that? I'd have to google it later.

"Now what?"

"I'll wait for the autopsy results. If they find anything, I'm going to see if we can get an agent in there undercover."

"Sorry, but I'm not volunteering."

"Yeah, you're loony enough, but too young."

"Ha ha, thanks. But seriously, I'd have to be loony to fall for you." Ah, crap. Why did I have to say something sappy? Best way ever to get a guy to run the other way—admit to strong feelings, or any feelings, really. My cheeks heated. I turned my head and found some interesting grass and stuff to stare at. Where were the sheep and cows when you needed a distraction?

He rested his hand on my thigh, and my heart rate went from sixty beats per minute to three hundred, which should mean I was dead. Yep, dead and in heaven.

"For the record, Miss Crazypants, Mr Crankypants has fallen for you too."

I slowly turned my head, almost afraid to look at him. He spared me a quick glance. His full lips were in a wide grin, and his dreamy eyes told me everything I needed to know. My smile almost pushed the apples of my cheeks into my eyeballs. Goofy much? I was lucky he was back to looking at the road.

"I reckon Angelica would make a good patient." I snorted. She'd be the worst patient ever. I'd love to be a fly on the wall when that horrible Queen Elizabeth lookalike locked horns with her.

He imitated my Australian accent, "I reckon." He resumed his normal sexy British accent. "She'd make a fantastic patient, as long as the carers enjoy bossy, stubborn patients." We laughed.

Instead of dropping me home, Will turned down the road that led to PIB headquarters.

"Why are you taking me to work?"

"If this thing with my gran needs to be investigated, we'll want to chase as many leads as possible. I'd like to interview you about everything that happened with the staff and what you remember Gran saying. I need descriptions of staff and patients you've seen, especially from last night." He drove into the PIB entry and buzzed security.

"Great to see you, Agent Blakesley," said the voice through the intercom.

Will gave a quick wave to the security camera as the gates slowly swung open. We passed through, and he parked in the outside parking lot near the building entrance. Doing this the non-witch way was so much more involved and tedious. We'd have to go through a security check. I hadn't realised exactly how much I enjoyed having witch privileges.

"Hey, how come there aren't any security checks when someone comes in via the reception room?"

We hopped out of the car, and he locked it with his fob. "We have facial recognition surveillance in there. If you're not programmed into the system, you won't be admitted without a full security check."

"That makes sense."

"Glad you approve." He smirked, and I gently punched his arm.

"Smart arse."

"You know it."

After the rigmarole of going through the metal detector and checking in weapons—Will, not me—my name was recorded in the book as a visitor, and we made our way to the lift. "Why don't they computerise sign ins here too?"

"When you came in through the reception room, you were always here for a work meeting. You're here as a witness today."

I didn't see there was much difference, but whatever. It wasn't necessary to understand bureaucracy to be inconvenienced by it. And I'd spent enough time going through their motions today—my brain wasn't going to waste any more effort on the whys.

Will led me two floors up to his office, which was a cosy room. Eggshell-blue walls complimented the charcoal-grey carpet and white timber bookshelves. Two framed degrees hung on the wall to the left of his desk. The wall to the right had three framed photos. I wandered closer to have a good look while he sat at his desk and watched quietly. He had switched his face to poker mode, so I had no idea what he was thinking.

There was a photo of a forty-something-year-old Edith with a dark-haired man. They both wore formal clothes and gentle smiles. The man in his dark suit and white shirt reminded me of Will, except he had bright-blue eyes. They shared the same defined jaw and straight nose, even the way the man in the picture held his head with chin tipped slightly up was familiar. "Your grandfather?"

He nodded and smiled. "He was a kind, gentle man. Me, my sister, and brother used to stay with them in school holidays. He always took time off work to do things with us. He died about ten years ago. Gran was never the same. They were as happy as you could expect to be after fifty-five years of marriage."

"Wow, that's a long time." Hang on. Had he said "siblings?" My gaze shifted to the other pictures. A young Will, his sister, and a boy who was a bit bigger than Will stood in front of a man and woman who must be his parents. "How old are you here?"

"Seven. That's my older brother, Ian. He was nine there. He died two years later."

"What happened?"

"Drunk driver. We were walking to school, and this guy mounted the grass verge and ploughed into him. Missed Sarah and me by inches." He hung his head for a moment, then met my gaze. "He'd been dawdling behind us, and I gave him a hard time, told him to hurry up, so being the cheeky sod he was, he ran ahead. That's when it happened."

The pain in his eyes eclipsed what I'd seen at the nursing home.

My heart broke for him the second time that day.

I walked to his desk and cupped his face in my hands. "I'm so sorry. It wasn't your fault, you know. You weren't driving that car drunk. It was just stupid bad, terrible luck— wrong place at the wrong time. I bet if Ian were around now, he would tell you the same thing." He shut his eyes, and a tear wobbled down his cheek and onto my hand. I pulled him to me and cradled his head against my stomach. We stayed that way for a few minutes.

He pulled back. "Thanks, Lily. The guilt will never leave. It's my fault. If I hadn't—"

"Please don't say that. I won't ever think differently. It wasn't your fault." I bit my tongue to stop my own tears. The stuff people carried around that you couldn't even guess at, stuff that could never be fixed or changed, stuff that could weigh a heart down so much that it almost stopped beating. I knew how that felt, when each step was like walking through molasses, when you couldn't get enough air, when each moment of joy was tempered with melancholy.

Somehow, I'd find a way to heal him, take away the guilt. I couldn't bear to see him suffering.

Even with my good intentions, it was time to change the subject. I looked over at the third photo—Beren and Will standing next to each other grinning and holding out their PIB badges to the camera. "Graduation day?"

"Yep." He was understandably still subdued.

"I didn't know you carried a badge. It's not like you can show it to everyone."

"Would you like to see my badge?" He smirked. Ah, there he was, the Will I lov— ahem, adored.

"Is it a big badge?"

"Big enough. It's impressed all the witches I've ever shown."

"I'd like to make up my own mind. Whip it out. Let me see." I tried to keep a straight face, but it was no use. I snorted.

He reached into his drawer, took it out, and handed it to me. I hefted the black triangle in my palm. "Weird shape. It is nice and smooth though." I ran my finger over the slick metallic surface that had his name engraved into it in golden script with the words "Agent of the PIB" after it. I grinned. "It is kind of pretty, with the sparkly golden writing."

"No one's ever called it pretty before." He pulled a mock-offended face, then grinned.

I handed the badge back, and he stuck it in his pants pocket. "Do you want to get the interview done now?" I sat in one of two black guest chairs that faced his desk.

"Good idea." He took a small black square out of his middle desk drawer. The object was about the size of a fancy make-up compact. "This is a recording device. I'm going to turn it on and confirm your name and date of birth, then give you a disclaimer about the evidence being used in court and that giving us false information is a crime. We'll get into the questions after that. Any questions?"

I shook my head. "Let's do this."

# CHAPTER 4

Sitting between James and Will at James's dining table, I yawned. It had been a long day, starting with the visit to the care home and ending in a meeting for our little group. We'd just started. Everyone sat with a notebook in front of them and either a cup of tea or glass of water.

Angelica created a bubble of silence and brought the meeting to order. "First on the agenda is naming this secret operation. I've made an executive decision and called it Operation Snakecatcher."

"Nice!" I couldn't help but voice my approval. Those evil witches were snakes, and we were definitely going to catch them.

Angelica had the hint of a smile. "I'm glad you approve, Lily. We're going to go through the roles and chain of command. I'm the boss, obviously, and I will be making all the important decisions, with consultation, of course." She nodded at James. "James is second in charge, and he'll keep me updated with the more important details as he sees fit. We'll have a meeting here once a week where we'll go over the information we've found and assess how to continue. Millicent and Olivia are going to be collating information from the office and doing any research, setting up any special support we may need. Our agents on the ground are William, Beren, James, and Lily."

I put up my hand.

"Yes, Lily?"

"I'm not an agent, Ma'am."

"Do you want to join the PIB?"

"No, sorry. Other than helping out sometimes and getting to the bottom of what this group is up to, I don't have any desire to be doing this 24/7. I really would prefer to work in my photography business." I'd had a few good jobs lately with two weddings, an engagement, and various corporate photo shoots. I'd even worked for large companies based in London. I loved that every assignment was different and temporary. I didn't have to like the people I was photographing, and I'd never have to see them again if I didn't want to. Not that I hated anyone in the PIB. I knew I definitely didn't want to be married to the job, which everyone else around this table was.

"Then you're a consultant and support staff in the field. You will defer to any agent you're in the field with at the time. You must follow orders, Lily. Am I understood?" She raised a brow. I couldn't blame her for making the point. I tended to operate on gut instinct, and I'd ignored requests before. I never intended to, but it sometimes just happened. Kind of like when you expected the day to be sunny, and the rain came. Maybe I was English weather in a previous life. I snorted.

"Yes, Ma'am."

She gave me a beady-eyed look. I must have snorted at the wrong time.

I straightened my face further and put my right palm, fingers pointing to the ceiling, in the air. "I promise on my coffee machine." She had to know I was serious.

"Hey, I gave you that machine. I'm not getting you another one. Just so you know." Will was so cute when he was cranky.

"Yes, I know. I will do as ordered." I almost said, "No questions asked," but that would be a lie, and they'd never believe it anyway.

"Next item on the agenda is where we're at today. What evidence do we have? I'm going to hand out information sheets. Once you've read them and you don't need them, you are to touch the paper—it doesn't matter if it's a whole hand or just a finger—and direct a trickle of magic to the paper. It will set off a return-to-file spell. This sensitive information is held in a secret location protected by numerous spells. If you want to access these papers again, you'll need to put in a request with either Olivia or Millicent, and they'll see that you receive the papers, which you can only read whilst here. We've created additional protection spells around this house. It would take a witch army to get through. If there is ever an attack, you are to come here immediately. Am I clear?"

We all nodded. Beren said, "Yes, Ma'am."

I turned to Millicent. "Are you okay with people popping in whenever? I mean, the baby'll be here soon, and you'll need privacy."

"This situation is temporary, so don't worry. Angelica and James are scouting out locations for a more permanent base. We would use the PIB offices, but we may not have weeded out all of Dana's informants yet. If things get too crazy, I can go to my parents', but to be honest, I feel safer here with all the extra protections, and I love you guys. You're always welcome. Once the baby comes, if we're still operating out of here, we'll arrange something for when I'm asleep or feeding the baby." She smiled. It was so true that pregnant women glowed. Apparently, the hormones did awesome stuff to their skin. There had to be some benefit to carrying a parasite, didn't there? Just joking. I already loved this baby, and it wasn't even mine.

A small pile of paper appeared in front of each person. It took me ten minutes to read through it. It had a profile report on Dana, her history, everything the PIB knew about her. A breakdown of the key points of the tea-and-violence incident. Interviews conducted with the witch caught and imprisoned for the crime. (He was yet to stand trial, but the judge declined bail, which was common with witch cases since witches could disappear with the wave of a hand.) It even included pictures of the snake tattoos found on both men I'd killed, photos of those two men, the limited information we had on them, and printouts of the photos I'd taken at the warehouse of Dana's partner. The label under the photo said, "Name Unknown."

So this was our starting point. We had a ton of work to do.

As daunting as it seemed, a little tumbleweed of excitement rolled through my stomach. I could accomplish a lot with my Nikon and witch-given talent.

Angelica waved her arm. A massive whiteboard appeared. It hovered in the air to the right of Angelica. She got up and stood next to it. A photo of Dana's gorgeous but ugly—because someone that evil would never be beautiful in my eyes—face was in the centre of the board with lines drawn outwards. One line went to the man we thought was her partner, and another line went to a picture of Gabriel's face—the witch who would spend life in prison for his crime of poisoning Kent's tea. A line went from the guy with a snake tattoo to a picture of the other thugs with the same tattoo.

Angelica swirled her finger in a circle, and a red circle appeared around the picture of Dana's tattooed friend. "His image hasn't shown up in any international PIB or UK police records. We've been in touch with the New York office, and they said Dana was single, as far as they knew. We couldn't send them the photo because we shouldn't have any photos of him, and if she has accomplices over there, they'll know we're onto them."

Hmm. "He looked kind of rich. He had that arrogance,

and his clothes could pass for designer. I wonder if he's ever appeared in social pages or on the Internet?"

"Great idea, Lily." Angelica turned to Olivia. "That's a job for you, dear. I want you to scour the Internet for any images."

"Yes, Ma'am." Liv grinned. It was awesome that she was enjoying the job so far.

"Millicent, I'd like you to search PIB records for any other hotspots for witch crime in the world. Make a note of the places and crimes and report back to James, please."

"Yes, Ma'am."

"Does anyone have anything they'd like to add?"

We were supposed to have told Olivia about my mum's diary ages ago. In fact, it had been planned for the night the violence in Westerham started, but we had to cancel because James and Millicent were called into work, and Olivia had to help her father transport her mum to hospital after she'd taken a violent turn. Now was the time to dive in. Who knew: the diaries could be crucial to this investigation.

"I do."

Angelica sat and flicked her hand. The whiteboard disappeared. "Yes, Lily?"

I looked at everyone in turn, James last. He gave me a small nod. This was the last private thing we had of Mum's. Once I tossed it into the ideas pile, it would never truly be ours again, and her words wouldn't be private anymore, but she wouldn't have minded—I was sure of it. I acknowledged the tingle of potential tears in the back of my nose and mouth but pushed on. "My mother left James and me her diaries. There are four. They have some mundane stuff, like normal daily things"—I smiled, remembering some of the days she'd chosen to record—"but there are also entries that paint a picture of where she and my dad were whenever they came here."

Angelica interrupted to clarify. "Lily's parents worked for us—her father as her mother's bodyguard. Sorry, please continue."

"In the last few weeks, I must have read them each a hundred times." James and I shared a smile. He'd read the diaries over and over again too, and many of the memories were good ones. "When I first went through them and figured out my witch talent with the camera, I decided to go to places Mum had mentioned in the diary. So when I went to the National Gallery and had that meltdown, Liv, it was because I'd seen my parents through the lens, standing in front of the Canaletto." Everyone but Olivia knew about what happened that day.

Her mouth dropped open. "Oh, my goodness! No wonder you were a mess."

"Yeah." I half laughed. "I couldn't tell you the truth, or you would've thought I was a nutter. I took photos again when we went to Churchill's house. So far, I haven't come up with much, but there was a Porsche they'd driven. I took a photo of the number plate. Then, the other week when I felt like we'd been followed to the tea place your mum had been to, I got you to read out the number plate on the other Porsche. They're different numbers, but I'm wondering if we can get them checked, see who they're registered to."

Angelica pursed her lips. "Hmm, that's a bit of a long shot, but Millicent can run them through the system."

"Anyway," I continued, "I've narrowed down a list of places I'll need to photograph. Maybe I'll see what happened to them or pick up a trail that's been cold for ten years."

Will slipped his hand around mine and gently squeezed. "I know that can't be easy, Lily. You don't know what you're going to see. I'll be with you every click of the shutter button, okay?"

He really was a sweetie. My gut had been right. "Thanks. I appreciate it." I was scared of what I might find, but this needed to happen. James and I craved answers, and whoever took my parents should be punished. The price I'd pay would be worth it. And who knew how many other people we'd save by taking them down?

James's gaze was kind—he knew more than anyone how hard this was for me. "Where do you plan on going next?"

"The Ritz Restaurant at the Ritz Hotel."

James nodded, likely recalling Mum's diary entry that had described having lunch there with Dad the year before they disappeared. They'd been to London that March for two weeks.

"I'm going to have to book a table. I can't see any other way I can get inside and have time to take enough photos otherwise. They're likely to not let me in, in the first place, or kick me out before I've been able to get anything."

Will smiled, his dimples slaying me. "Allow me to book us a table, and I'm paying. I'll get us in as soon as possible for lunch. How does that sound?" How was it this man liked me? He could have just about anyone. Wonders would never cease.

I smiled. "That would be perfect. Thank you. I can't let you pay though. I'm happy to pay, but isn't the PIB covering it?"

Angelica cleared her throat. "No. I'm afraid not." She shared a meaningful glance with James. She licked her lips and took a deep breath through her nose. "James and I have reason to believe that the infiltration of the PIB may have gone further than the staff and agents who are lower level. We can't afford any unusual expenses triggering curiosity from my bosses."

My eyes widened. Was she saying the people running the PIB could be part of the group or at least helping them in some way? Anger burned in my chest and warmed my face. I shook my head. "Bastards! Why is it the same with any big organisation or government? They're only ever in it for themselves. They're supposed to be there to help people, not run their own agenda."

"Calm down, dear. I don't know for sure, but it's not a chance we can take. We could all lose our jobs over this, so I'm being extra careful. We're investigating something privately. When I suggested to one of my bosses that we needed to find Dana, he was adamant it would be a waste of resources. He said he would handpick two agents to follow up when they had time. That was all I needed to know to be suspicious. One of their best agents has gone rogue, and they don't even want to pretend to look for her or care? She's tied up in a major crime—that should be enough to have them do more than what they've done." She clenched her jaw. Okay, at least I wasn't the only one upset over this.

"I'm booking and paying, Lily. Besides, we haven't been on a proper date yet. I'd hardly call jogging and hanging out at care homes wooing you." Will laughed.

He had a point. I shrugged. "I'm sure I've had worse dates. I just can't remember. I've probably blocked them out. Oh, that's right: tennis with a murderer, and you and James on the court next to me giving me death stares."

"Hmm, I'd definitely class that as the worst date ever," said Millicent. "James has taken me to the Ritz for dinner before. You'll enjoy it, even if you are there for a different reason. I'd leave taking the photos for after dessert, so you can enjoy yourselves."

"That's a great idea, Mill. I'll definitely do that. You know I love my dessert."

She grinned.

Angelica looked at her nephew. "Beren, I'd like you to keep your nose to the ground at head office. See if you can weed out any Dana sympathisers or spot anyone with that tattoo. I doubt they'll have the tattoo uncovered if they have one, so be vigilant. If you find anyone, pull their file and send it to me at home. I'll send it onto the security facility. At this stage, I don't have anything else for anyone to do. We don't know enough about this group's goals to dig deeper or profile their members. Barring anything else happening, we'll meet here again same time in a week." Her gaze circled the table. "Any questions?"

Everyone shook their head. Angelica stood. "If you haven't already disappeared your papers, please do. I'll see you when I see you." She made her door and left.

I pinched the corner of the pile of papers in front of me between thumb and forefinger and trickled a few droplets of power into it. It vanished. Neat.

Millicent yawned and rubbed her rounded belly. Would it be a boy or girl? They weren't going to find out until the day, which irritated me. I wanted to know, dammit! If I ever had kids—which may never happen because I wasn't that enamoured with them—I'd find out as soon as possible so I could buy the right stuff. Apparently boys and girls had different types of nappies. I supposed men and women wore different types of underpants from each other... most of the time. I snorted, thinking that some men probably loved wearing women's lacy knickers, and it was normal for women to have "boy-leg" ones. Ah, the crap that filled my head when I let my guard down.

"I'm off to bed. Night." Millicent waved at us and gave James a hug and quick kiss on the lips.

"Bye, bro." I gave James a quick hug.

"See you later, alligator."

I smiled at him. Our dad used to say that, and we'd reply with the "in a while, crocodile." I sighed as melancholy slid over me like the shadow from a storm cloud passing the sun.

Will embraced me and placed a lingering kiss on my

cheek. "I'll text you when I've booked lunch." He stood back and smiled.

"Can't wait. And let me know what happens with the autopsy."

His smile fell, and he nodded.

After Beren and Olivia said their goodbyes, I grabbed Olivia's hand. As I made my doorway to take us home, a prickle of unease skittered along my nape. I had a feeling trouble was coming, and it would be here sooner rather than later. There were too many sharks circling. Eventually one would strike. The question was: would we be ready for it when it did?

# CHAPTER 5

The next day after lunch, I chilled at home, reading a cosy mystery on my iPad. Everyone else was at work. It sure had been quiet lately, and I missed Olivia's company. I didn't have any photography jobs booked for the next couple of weeks, which was fine because I'd been paid for all the work I'd done with the PIB to crack the tea-and-violence case. Angelica had been in charge and had given me a bonus, which really equated to danger money because of the night at the warehouse. My only expenses were my phone and food since Angelica wouldn't take any rent, so I had plenty saved for a rainy day. Actually, over here, that would be for a sunny day. I snorted at my own joke.

My phone dinged. I started, and my arms jerked up, almost launching the iPad across the room. Gah, could I be anymore high-strung? I clutched the iPad to my chest while I got myself together. I slotted the iPad carefully and safely between the chair arm and myself, then grabbed my phone from the little round table between the armchairs.

Ooh, it was from Will. I grinned. *Hey, My Little Aussie Witch. I've made reservations for lunch :). We're booked in at 12:30 p.m., Friday the 12th. I'll pick you up at 12:15 p.m. Always, your Crankypants.*

Was he sweet or what? And had he given me a pet name? I texted back, *Yay! I can't wait. And thank you, Your Little Aussie Witch.*

Happy warmth spread through my stomach. I couldn't stop smiling. Yeah, I knew I was such a dag, which meant dork in Aussie-speak. The technical meaning was gross, matted wool around a sheep's bottom, and sheep didn't use toilet paper, if you got my drift. Okay, so Aussies were a strange lot, but that was my normal.

So, I only had ten and three-quarter days until we went on our first real date. How was I going to not spontaneously combust from the excitement? Why did almost everything require patience I didn't have? Oh, yeah, the universe's stupid sense of humour.

My brain intervened, making sure to temper my joy. Had Will gotten the autopsy results yet? I didn't want to ask. If he had them, he likely would have said, and it would surely take longer than one day. They were witches, but how much of the investigation could be done magically? I figured at least some of it had to be done the normal human way.

Well, that was sobering. I put my phone down and went back to reading on my iPad. The time flew by, as it did when you can't stop turning the pages. About three hours later, my phone rang. I quickly grabbed it, just in case it was Will.

Angelica's name was on the screen.

"Hi. Is everything okay?" She didn't normally call me to chat. Okay, she'd never called just to chat.

"Hi, Lily. We've just gotten the autopsy results back. I'd like you to come in for a meeting."

Oh no. That must mean Edith had been murdered. I sighed, my whole body sagging into it, sad for Will. "But what can I do? I can't use my talent at the care home because magic use is blocked."

"Will's requested it, dear. Now hurry up. We haven't got all afternoon." She hung up. Well, if he wanted me there for moral support, say no more. I magicked my iPad up to my room—Angelica did not like mess, and I was prone to it. It was easier now that I could tidy using magic, but I sometimes got distracted, walked off, and forgot to come back and remove my stuff.

I walked towards the front door and stopped halfway, remembering I wasn't going somewhere in the car. Being a witch wasn't always automatic for me yet. I wondered if it ever would be.

I stayed where I was, made my doorway, and stepped through. Gus was there to open the door. It was always nice to see this particular face. He was such a calm, amenable person. As we walked to the conference room, I avoided all subjects that could lead to vomit or poo. Except, it was harder than I'd thought.

"Seen any good movies lately, Gus?"

He rubbed his chin. "I saw part of a good movie last week, except halfway through, I felt sick. Must've been the takeaway fish and chips I'd had for dinner. I only just made it to the restroom in time, if you know what I mean." He shook his head.

I wasn't sure if he meant vomit or diarrhoea, and I was not going to ask. Nope.

"Wow, that's not good," I said as we reached the conference-room door. I was going to have to learn to walk faster, so there'd be less time to chat. "Thanks, Gus."

"My pleasure, Lily." He opened the door and stepped back, letting me through.

My brother sat to the left of Ma'am. He gave me a chin tip in greeting. Ma'am sat at the head of the table, her expression serious and her posture straight-backed, ready to get down to business. I took the hint and hurried to the closest chair, which happened to be next to Beren, who sat to Ma'am's right. "I got here as quickly as I could." I was pretty sure Ma'am wasn't angry with me, but I felt the need to defend myself.

"That's fine, Lily." Her voice was calm but devoid of emotion, as if we were about to discuss the budget for the next financial year.

Across the table from me, next to James, Will was not looking so calm. His furrowed brow overshadowed sad eyes and a clenched jaw. "Thanks for coming, Lily."

"Whatever you need, Will. I'm here." I gave him a sad smile. Argh, there was nothing worse than seeing someone you cared about be miserable. Why couldn't emotional pain be the kind of pain we could take away, never to return, like a splinter or a headache that was banished with tweezers or a tablet? Self-medication for emotional pain only lasted as long as the alcohol or pills were in your system, and even then, it was still there waiting to pounce. It made perfect sense to just face whatever it was, revel in the horror, then move on. Avoiding it only prolonged the suffering.

Ma'am magicked some papers into her hand. She held them up. "This is the autopsy report on Will's grandmother Edith. I've already spoken to Agent Blakesley"—she gave him a quick glance and turned back to Beren and me—"as I thought it prudent to give him time to digest the news. The autopsy findings conclude that she was murdered. The cause of death was a heart attack brought on by air bubbles in the blood. The injection site was on her neck and into her jugular."

"So that's really a thing? Dying by air bubbles." I'd thought it was an old wives' tale. I mean, weren't there little air bubbles in drips? I had my appendix out when I was ten, and I remember being freaked out at some bubbles in the clear tube going to my arm, but the nurse reassured me it would be fine. I'd assumed after not dying that it wasn't actually something that could kill you.

"Yes, Lily. If enough air is injected, it will cause a heart attack. Whoever did this probably assumed no one would bother getting an autopsy on an elderly person with dementia who had clearly had a heart attack, and they may have been right if they hadn't picked the grandmother of an agent."

"Are we ordering autopsies on Edith's friends, the two she said died recently?" Beren asked. Will must have filled him in.

"Not right now." Angelica shared a look with James. They had obviously worked out a plan already. "We don't want the care home to get wind of our investigation. They don't know we've autopsied Edith. To get access to the other bodies, we'd need to find out where they went after the care home. And we don't want irate relatives going down there and threatening them. Also, we don't have enough evidence to start a proper investigation. They could say it was an accident, and by then, the culprit would be alerted. If the murderer is a witch, they'll disappear, and we'll likely never find them."

"So how are we going to investigate?" I thought gathering evidence was par for the course. And now that we couldn't go and visit Edith there, it would be hard to find anything else out.

"I'm going undercover as a patient."

My mouth dropped open. Ma'am, as a dementia patient? I guessed she had the cranky face mastered, but still, I couldn't imagine her letting herself be subjected to other people showering her and telling her when to go to bed and when to eat. And what if something happened to her while she was there? She wouldn't have access to her magic.

"Being an agent, you know self-defence, right?"

She smiled. "Of course I do, Lily. You don't get to my position within an organisation like this without being good at everything."

Hmm, well, that ensured I'd never be the boss of anyone, which was fine since I didn't want the responsibility.

"I'm also going to have a listening device with me at all times."

I still wasn't convinced. "Where are you going to hide it? I mean... what about when you're in the shower, or they're brushing your hair? It might be tricky." I figured she'd have to find one place to put it, and then it had to stay there.

A grey teddy bear appeared on the table in front of Angelica. She picked it up. "This has an audio-visual device hidden in the teddy's eye, and I'll be wearing fake hearing aids, which will also transmit sound to nearby agents who will be listening 24/7."

I pressed my lips together to stop a smile. Angelica with a teddy bear? That was something I had to see. I looked at Will, and his mouth curved up on one side.

"Ma'am and her teddy?" I asked.

He nodded, his smile growing.

"Well, if you two are finished laughing at me, we'll continue." She raised a brow. Exaggerate much? Surely, she could see the humour in this? "Lily, I'll need a photo for my care-home ID. Would you mind taking one now? We can just do it with your mobile phone."

"Ah, okay. But you're in your PIB gear."

She stood, mumbled a few words, and a bed and bedside

tables with forest-green lamps on them appeared behind her. At the same time, her clothes had changed into pyjamas, and her hair had gone white, wispy, and hung loose to just below her shoulders, which were newly stooped. She had aged fifteen to twenty years in a matter of seconds.

Ma'am hobbled to the bed and got in. She arranged the pillows so she could sit up. She settled back and laid her arms on the outside of the covers. "I'm ready when you are."

I stood next to the bed, slid my mobile phone from my pocket and switched it to camera mode. "Do you want to give me a vacant, child-like smile?"

"Oh, good idea." She did just that, and I laughed. I wasn't the only one. Multiple chuckles came from behind me.

"Is this what I have to look forward to when I visit my decrepit aunt when you're ninety?" Beren asked.

Her serene expression vanished, and she narrowed her eyes. "Just for that, I promise to stay sane and annoying as long as is witchily possible." She smirked and resumed her docile smile.

I snorted. Poor Beren.

I lifted my phone, pointing it towards Angelica.

Oh God, no! It couldn't be. I shut my eyes tight and then opened them again. I swallowed, my heart thumping hard. "Um, I think there's something wrong with my phone. I just need to restart it." I held the button down and waited for it to turn off.

James started a conversation with the guys, but I couldn't hear what was said over the whooshing in my ears. I turned the phone on and waited. While it powered up, I turned my gaze to Angelica. She met what was probably my terrified look with one of calm. I didn't have to say anything: she probably already knew from my face.

*Please don't be real. Please don't be real,* I chanted while I pressed the camera app again and held it up.

My stomach dropped faster than a meteorite. I snapped the shot and tried not to cry. I lowered the phone, and Angelica held out her hand. I passed her the phone so she could see for herself.

Her face paled—she wasn't as stoic as I thought.

"What's wrong?" Beren's voice held a note of worry, and he got up and hurried to the bed. They all knew my special talent, and Beren had probably already guessed what was up.

"Apparently," Angelica said with a firm voice, "I'm going to die." There was a sharp intake of breath from either Will or James, and Beren shook his head.

She turned my phone around so Beren could see the image on the screen—the image of a see-through Angelica.

There'd been times I'd hated my magic in the past— when I'd been confronted with images of my parents—and this was up there with that. But I refused to believe it. Surely there was something we could do to change things?

But by the looks on Beren's and Angelica's faces, there wasn't.

"Can you just not go undercover? Surely that's why you're see-through." I didn't want to say, "going to die." That was too final.

Angelica handed Beren the phone. "We need a photo that's not see-through."

I might have gotten a normal photo—it had happened before at a wedding I'd photographed where the bride's father was see-through, then wasn't. He still died. But it would be quicker if Beren took it. But why would she still insist on going through with being in the care home?

Angelica assumed the demented patient position, but this time, she kept a slack face—no smile. And who could blame her? Beren pressed the button, and my phone made the click noise.

"Please, Ma'am. Reconsider. Surely someone else can pretend to be old and not all there?" I winced. Bad choice of words.

"I'm one of the oldest here, dear." She swung her legs over the side of the bed and stood. With a flick of her wrist, everything she'd conjured disappeared, and she was back in her PIB uniform. "There are two other agents who are older than me, but one is on light duties after sustaining injuries in an explosion, and the other has a wife and children. His youngest daughter has just moved back home with her two babies after a messy separation, and she doesn't have a job. He's supporting the whole family. I won't risk his life."

"But that's his job. Isn't it?" I tried to keep my tone even, but frustration sharpened the edges of my words.

"I won't change my mind, Lily. And who knows? Maybe that's not why I'm going to die. Maybe I'll be in a car accident on the way home from work."

"You don't drive. You magic yourself everywhere." I wasn't going down without a fight. "What if we have the intention of putting him in your place, and I take his photo? If he's see-through, we won't send him, and if he's not, we do?"

James and Will had joined Beren and me. We stood united against her death wish. "Aunt— Ma'am, Lily has a point. Please let us at least try?"

James stared at her, his gaze calm but unrelenting. "I'm not ready to run the PIB. You know they'll call someone else in from New York. All the years you've worked to get to the top, and you'll throw it in for some other idiot to take over and maybe send us back to being inefficient? What if one of the You-Know-Who clan sneaks someone in to replace you?" He must be talking about the snake people who were after me—Dana's people.

"I won't let you." William had stepped past me and was staring down at Angelica.

"I think you'll find, young man, that you can't stop me. It's not your place." Ma'am folded her arms and looked up at him, anger flickering in her gaze.

He shook his head. "If you die, it will be my fault. I'll carry that with me forever. And what about Lily? Do you want her to suffer with guilt forever too?"

"If I die, it won't be your fault."

"Yes, it will." I hoped my eyes conveyed the full horror of what losing her this way would feel like to me. "I have a chance to stop you. We've been forewarned. If I don't do everything in my power to stop this from happening, it will be my fault." She stilled, and I wondered if we had almost convinced her. She might need another nudge, just to get her over the line. "I've already lost my parents. I can't lose you too. You're like the aunt I never had… one I sorely need. And you're the only one who knew my parents. Who else can answer James's and my questions about them? We need you. If Mum were here, she wouldn't want you to risk yourself this way either." If only I had the power of persuasion. I was immune to it, but I'd never tried it. And yes, it was illegal unless it was for an extremely good reason, but I didn't see what a better reason could be than saving a friend.

Ma'am looked over my shoulder, to a far-off place where she stayed for a couple of minutes. No one said anything. It was as if we held our breath in unison, waiting for the axe to fall. Will slid his hand over mine and gently squeezed. I squeezed back and enjoyed the comforting feeling of having someone who would be there just for me. I had James, and nothing could come between our brother-sister bond, but he had Millicent and their future baby to worry about and be there for. His other family had to come first, and I appreciated that. It was nice to have my own person to lean on if I needed to. The thought of grieving someone was horrible—it was just a little less so if I could do it in my gorgeous man's arms.

Ma'am gave a small shake of her head and eyeballed

each of us in turn. "All right. We'll do it your way. I hereby appoint Agent Gryffith to go undercover at the care home. But if his photo is ghostly, I'm going undercover." She placed her hands firmly on her hips. "I don't want to hear any arguments. Any agent, or Lily, who argues will be off this case. Understood?"

"Yes, Ma'am," we answered. The lump of worry that squished my chest eased only slightly. I wouldn't take a deep breath until I'd taken that agent's photo. Could I turn my magic off and take it? I sighed. As much as I wanted to, I couldn't deceive Angelica like that. Then she'd live with the guilt of sending him in, and I'd live with the guilt that I'd lied. Why couldn't life be simple and safe?

Angelica magicked a phone into her hand. She put it to her ear. "Agent Gryffith, Ma'am here. Can you come to the main conference room, please? Yes. Now." She pressed the screen, and the phone disappeared. "Everyone, sit."

We resumed our seats, but Will sat next to me this time. I leaned towards him. "How are you?" I was pretty sure he'd know what I meant—how are you feeling after finding out your grandmother was murdered?

"Angry, sad, so disappointed I could kick myself. I should have listened to her, Lily. If I'd taken her fears seriously, she might still be here." His breath huffed out of his nose like an angry bull.

"How could you know? She wasn't exactly making sense when we went to see her. I didn't take her seriously either." Guilt slid fingers around my wrist, but I shook it off. This wasn't our fault. "You know that's how they get away with things for so long."

His brows drew together. "Who?"

"People who kill people in nursing homes. They would know no one takes the patients seriously. How can they when their relatives know they're living in a fantasy world? Paranoid delusions are probably common with people who aren't in their right mind."

"I know. But still…."

The door opened, and a tall, fit man walked in. He filled out his suit in a way suggesting he was muscular without being a mountain, and he moved with the power and grace of a panther. I wasn't expecting him to look so, well, young. If he was older than Ma'am, that put him at late 50s, early 60s, but he actually looked younger than Ma'am. He stood tall, his thick wavy hair dark and luxurious. I hit my palm against the side of my head, protesting my brain's annoying tendency to use words I didn't like. His hair wasn't a Ferrari, a five-star hotel room, or a mega yacht. Why did people use luxurious to describe hair? Stupid other people putting that idea in my head.

"Thank you for coming on short notice, Agent Gryffith. We're testing new software on the iPhone. I just need you to stand there for a moment."

His brows raised the tiniest bit, but he nodded. "Of course, Ma'am."

"Lily, if you wouldn't mind taking a photo."

"Of course." I flicked my phone into camera mode again. I took a breath and held it, lifted the camera, and clicked. Crap. "Um, looks like the software isn't working. What a huge disappointment." My shoulders slumped.

"Thank you, Gryffith. You may go."

He gave her a small bow, turned, and left via the door. I guessed he was going to another place in this building that he didn't have coordinates for. Ma'am put her hand out. "May I?"

I sighed and handed it over. He was as ghostly as could be. Stupid magical ability.

"Well, that settles that, team. I'm going in." She turned to Beren. "Obviously Lily and Will can't be involved in any care-home interaction or visits. Beren, you'll have to make all the arrangements. Use these identities." Two pieces of paper appeared in her hands, and she gave them to Beren. "I'm Angelica Prestons, and you're my son, Preston Prestons."

I snorted. "What kind of a mean parent are you?"

She grinned. "One who likes to have a little fun at the expense of my offspring. My diagnosis is early onset Alzheimer's. Make the arrangements today. Tell them it's urgent. From what Will said, they have a fairly high turnover, and in light of what we now know, I'm not surprised. And, Beren, I'll have to get you to take a photo of me for the care-home ID."

Beren nodded, and I was pleased that he didn't do a damn thing to hide his frown. At least I wasn't the only one who hated Ma'am's idea. I still couldn't believe she was really going through with it. And what if we were doing this for nothing, and she died, but we still didn't catch the culprits?

Will said, "Ma'am, how will Lily and I be involved?"

"You'll both take shifts in the surveillance van that will be parked down the street. While I'm undercover, James will take my place running this operation and the PIB."

James gave a single sober nod. He exuded confidence. Was he really feeling it, or was it for the benefit of Angelica? "I won't let you down, Ma'am."

She smiled. "I know. You're one of the best agents we have. I've always seen the potential in you, James."

My heart lurched to the right as if to break out of its cage and jump to its death. It knew what pain was coming and didn't want to face it. Neither did I. It seemed as if she was telling James something she'd always thought but had never said—something she wanted to make sure he knew before she…. "Isn't there any other way? I mean, is it worth losing you to catch the killer? Maybe we should just order autopsies on the other bodies."

Angelica pinned me with her stare. "What did I say before about arguing?"

"I was just asking a question." I sunk lower in my seat.

"Well, don't. I've made up my mind. And even though your magic has predicted death in the past, that doesn't mean it's always going to be right. I have a job to do, and nothing will stop me doing it. Danger is ever present in what we do. Do you understand me, Lily?" She held her gaze on me until I nodded— sullenly, I'd admit, but it was a nod. I also bit my tongue. Pointing out that my magic had never been wrong before was obviously not going to help, and if anything happened to her, I didn't want one of our last moments together spent disagreeing.

Satisfied I was going to toe the line, she turned back to James and Beren. I tuned out as they discussed the finer points of the sting—there was only so much time left for me to figure out how to save Angelica. And I had a feeling I was going to need every second.

# CHAPTER 6

The next morning, just after 9:00 a.m., I sat at the kitchen table, yawning and cradling my cappuccino when Olivia walked in looking as tired as I felt. She was dressed in a black T-shirt with a white Siamese cat on the front with the words "I'm Feline Purrfect" and red tracksuit pants. Okay, so her T-shirt wasn't telling the absolute truth, but it made me smile.

"Good morning. I missed you last night."

She turned on the kettle. "I got in late. I worked some overtime and got a handle on the computer system. It's taken a bit, but I'm really getting the hang of it now."

"That's awesome because we're going to need all your skills to track down Dana and her evil associates."

She put a teabag in her mug. "Not only that, but Ma'am's asked me to pull some info on that care home Will's grandmother died at."

That was a good sign—she wasn't just going to go in there totally blind. "What kind of info?"

The kettle boiled, and the switch clicked off. She poured the water into her cup and sat next to me. "Well, you're lucky you have clearance, so I can tell you."

"How do you know if I have clearance?"

"When Ma'am gave me the request, she put a list of people I could share the information with. You're one of them."

"Oh cool. Otherwise, I'd have to magic it out of you." I wiggled my fingers at her.

She gently slapped them away. "Ha ha, very funny."

"So, what do you have to research?"

"The notices the care home has sent to the Care Quality Commission. Every time there's a death, they have to provide them with paperwork. Then I'll have to try and find info on everyone who works there and look into their history. It's not going to be easy. I mean, the first part will be, but trying to find who works there without asking them directly is going to be a pain in the bum." She jiggled the teabag up and down, grabbed milk from the fridge, poured some into her cup, and sat down again.

I swallowed the last of my coffee and acknowledged the panic storm lurking on the horizon. "Did Angelica tell you what happened yesterday? About the photos I took?"

Two small vertical lines appeared just above the bridge of her nose. "No. What happened?"

"This is confidential, of course."

"Of course."

I knew I could trust her, but I had to say it, just in case. The less people not in our immediate circle who knew about my talents, the better. "After Angelica agreed to go under-cover at the care home, I took her photo. It came back with her looking see-through." I blinked back tears. "She's going to die." I shook my head, still in disbelief about the whole thing.

Olivia's face slackened—it appeared she was as dumb-founded as me. "Are you sure?"

"When has my talent ever been wrong?"

She shrugged. "I have no idea, Lily. I haven't known you the whole time you've had your powers. Please tell me there's been at least one occasion."

"I'm afraid not." I told her about the bride's father and the woman at the airport in Paris, both of whom died shortly after I'd seen them as ghostly images through my lens.

She blew out a loud breath. "Does she know?"

"Yes, of course she knows, but she refuses to back out. I've lain awake all night trying to think of what I can do to change things. But I haven't come up with anything. We need to find out what we can as quickly as possible. Do you think you can start those searches after you finish breakfast?"

"Definitely."

"Thanks. Is there anything I can do to help?"

She pressed her lips together, thinking. "Hmm, there is something you could try. Do you think you could put a spell on my search that helps me find stuff quickly?"

Could I? "There's a good chance I can. I just have to figure out the right thing to say, although it's a fairly simple request." I smiled.

Olivia grinned. "That's my Lily. You're awesome. You know that?"

"And so are you."

"How much time do you think we have before Angelica goes undercover?"

I scratched the back of my head and yawned. "Um, I'm not sure. At least all of today. Beren had to apply to get her a place at the care home, and if there aren't any spare beds, she'll have to wait. Who knows? It could take a week or more. I have no idea how often people die and a bed becomes available, or how long the waiting list is." Except at least three people had died there in the last week. It would have been great if the wait was two or three weeks—the longer, the better.

"Okay then. After breakfast, we'll head into the bureau."

"Oh. We can't do it from here?"

She shook her head. "My laptop's not powerful or secure enough. We need the PIB system. I'll just check with Millicent, and then we'll be good to go."

Millicent was her direct report. Olivia had to confirm everything with her first. I was so glad my sister-in-law and best friend got to work together. I would have hated if Olivia had been stuck with some demon boss. Someone like Dana, for instance.

Olivia texted Millicent and got the okay. Then we had

toast for breakfast. Olivia looked at mine, slathered with butter and Vegemite, and pulled a disgusted face.

"Mmm, Vegemite." I grinned.

"That looks disgusting."

"Have you ever tried it?"

She shook her head. "No way. Ew."

I rolled my eyes. "Wussy baby. I guess everyone can't be as tough as us Aussies."

She raised a brow. "Is that so? Okay, then. Let me have a bite, and I'll prove that I'm as tough as you, and that it's disgusting."

I handed her a triangle and smirked. She would likely hate it—most people did if they hadn't been brought up eating it—but I'd enjoy watching her squirm. She bit into it, her face pensive until her eyes widened, and she squished her eyes shut tight, stuck her tongue out, and gagged.

"Oh my Lord, this is terrible." She swallowed and put the rest of the piece back on my plate. "You Aussies are sickos. You know that?"

I grinned and bit into my toast. "Mm, mmm. Sick and loving it."

She shook her head.

After breakfast, we changed into PIB-issue uniforms—I figured I'd stand out less if I was dressed like everyone else there—and I travelled us to the reception room. Good old Gus was there to open the door.

"Hey, Gus," said Olivia as she walked into the hallway. "How's the puppy?"

Wait, what? Noooo! I'd forgotten Olivia was probably

here more than me now and had been getting to know people. If only I could have warned her not to ask any dog-related questions.

"Good morning, ladies. The dog's good, thanks, Miss Olivia. But you should've seen him yesterday." Gus held his hand on his belly and laughed. As his laughter subsided, he shook his head. "On our walk, he decided to roll in the grass, only it wasn't just grass, if you get my meaning." He pinched his nose between thumb and forefinger. "It was a massive pile of shit, all matted into his fur with a few twigs and leaves, for good measure. I was off to work, so my Mrs had to bathe him." He laughed again.

I gagged and could swear I smelled dog poo. I lifted each foot and checked under my black sneakers. Of course there wasn't any—I hadn't worn these shoes outside for ages, since I tended to *travel* everywhere, and I had a different pair for jogging. I looked down at Gus's shoes. Hmm…

"We'd best get a move on, Liv. We have lots of work to do." I smiled at Gus. "See you next time. And thanks for answering the door."

"It's my pleasure, Miss Lily, and it's my job." He winked. I chuckled. He was a lovely guy, but I was starting to associate him with things that smelled horrible.

"Bye, Gus." I hooked my arm through Olivia's and dragged her down the hallway. "So, where's your office?"

"This way." She continued towards the lift. "And why were you in such a hurry. I enjoy chatting to Gus."

I gave her a worried side-eye glance. "I don't want to

talk about poo… or vomit, or black pudding. Spending my day with nausea is not my idea of fun."

She laughed. "But you eat Vegemite."

"Ha ha ha. Very funny."

"He he, I know. But actually, you're right. That's the third time he's grossed me out with a story about his dog."

"And you'd think you would have learned your lesson. From now on, don't ask him about his dog, at least not when I'm with you."

"Fine." She snorted.

We took the elevator to the floor above, and she turned right, then went left at the T-intersection. I hadn't been down this corridor before. She opened the second door on the right, which led into a reception area. It had a two-seater pale-blue fabric couch, and the receptionist's desk actually had someone sitting behind it. The old lady—she must have been sixty-five in the shade—looked up and smiled. "Can I help you?" she shouted.

I started, not expecting the loudness.

"Sally, it's me, Olivia. I'm working with Millicent. Remember?" Olivia had raised her voice as well. Was the old lady deaf?

Sally smiled and patted the white bouffant that stood atop her head. It was a two-storey hairdo—it rose two head heights from her scalp. That type of hairstyle was quite rare and must have required an entire can of hairspray to maintain. Thank goodness the PIB was a smoke-free zone, or she'd be at risk of catching fire. "Oh, yes, Olivia! How could I forget? And who's your friend?"

"This is Lily, Millicent's sister-in-law. She's helping me out today. Lily, this is Sally, Millicent's secretary."

"Lovely to meet you, Lily," she yelled.

"Lovely to meet you too."

"What?" Her white brows drew down.

Oops, I forgot to yell. I pitched my voice louder. "I said, nice to meet you too!"

She smiled. "You can go on through. Millicent's not here at the moment, but you know where your desk is."

When we got into Millicent's office and Olivia shut the door, I whispered, "I didn't think Mill had a secretary."

"She didn't until two weeks ago. You know Tim, head of our IT department?"

I nodded.

"His dad died a few months ago, and his mother has been at a loose end. She was suffering from depression. She used to be a secretary, so Tim thought if he could get her a job doing simple things like filing and running errands around the PIB, it would give her a sense of purpose. She'll only be here for a few months."

"But she's deaf. Should she have a hearing aid? How's she supposed to answer the phone?"

"We don't get landline calls. Anyone who wants Millicent just calls her mobile."

"Fair enough."

"So, let's get to work." Millicent dragged a chair from in front of Mill's desk and placed it next to an office chair in front of a second desk, which had two monitors on it. "We'll sit here."

Olivia sat in one seat, and I sat in the other. She turned on the computer. Once the programs were up and running, she turned to me. "So, great witch, please cast a spell and give me quick searches."

I looked around and back at her. "Um, I don't see any great witches here."

She rolled her eyes. "Oh my God, you're so funny today. Did you put a spell on yourself giving yourself an awesome sense of humour?"

"No, but I put a spell on you taking yours away." I poked my tongue out at her. She laughed.

"Seriously, though. I have to think. Maybe get started, and I'll chime in as soon as I can."

"Sounds like a plan." She got to work, and I rummaged around in my brain. It was messy, and none of my thoughts were where I wanted them to be. This was going to take a while. I bit my fingernails and stared off into space.

"Ooh! I know." I had only taken ten minutes, but I'd finally come up with something. "I'm ready to make magic."

"Yay! Just in time, too, because it's taking me ages to get the reports on how many witches have died at that care home recently and who they were. I hate to think how long digging for the other info is going to take."

I shut my eyes, pictured the golden river of power, and reached my thoughts towards it, imagining I was dipping my hand in. Tingles vibrated across my fingers and up my arms. "My friend Olivia is searching online, for information to solve a crime. She needs speed to get results fast. Help her get the right answers within two minutes of starting the search." I opened my eyes. "Done."

She had her lips pressed together, her eyes shining with barely contained laughter.

"What?"

She sputtered as her self-control waned, and she gave into the guffaws she'd been holding back. Eventually she stopped laughing. "Oh my God. You can't rhyme to save your life. Hilarious!"

I shrugged. "Yeah, yeah, I know. Apparently spells don't have to rhyme—that's just to make them easier to remember. By the way, has anyone told you lately how ungrateful you are?" I folded my arms and glared at her.

She bit her bottom lip, still wearing a cheeky smile. "Sorry, hon. It was just funny. That's all."

I sighed and smiled back. "I know. I sometimes laugh at myself. I was only joking about being upset."

She shook her head. "So, it should be faster now?"

"I have no idea. I hope so." I snorted. "Give it a go and find out."

She typed away and hit Return.

Within seconds, a list of document links appeared on the screen. "Wow, nice!" Liv clicked on one of the links, transferring her to another screen filled with information on the last person who died at the care home: Agnes Porter. It stated she'd died a month ago.

"What the hell? It looks like they haven't been reporting properly. This makes the manager look pretty damn guilty. Can you save that and look at the rest?"

"Of course." Olivia went through each document and saved and printed them.

I got up and collected the twenty sheets from the printer. I sat down again and looked through them all. "The earliest one we have is from fourteen months ago. Peter Klein. Cause of death listed as heart attack. Then a month after that was Catherine Hayden. Cause of death: food poisoning." One by one, I read out the names and causes of death. By the end of it, there were two food poisonings, one complication of the flu, and all the rest were heart attacks. "Can you google what percentage of elderly people die of a heart attack?"

Liv tapped out the request on the keyboard. "It's not very detailed. They talk more about people with heart disease. Hang on.... Hmm, here we go. It's around 35 percent for over 75s."

"Wow, so the percentages are way out at this place. Why don't we check other care homes in the area?"

Olivia searched for the other care homes and then pulled up their death notices. After looking into details for five other care homes, whose statistics fell in line with the 35 percent, I could only draw one conclusion. Except... "Liv, those were all non-witch care homes, weren't they?" I knew witch care facilities were few and far between after discussing it with Will before.

"Yes. There aren't many around."

"Can we do a search of the other two near here? There's one in London, maybe more, and one towards the coast. I can't remember exactly where. Maybe being a witch gives someone an increased risk of having a heart attack?"

"Maybe. Let's see."

I gathered all the new printouts and sat. "Hmm, they seem to be in line. Actually, they're a bit under. The London one is around five in seventeen deaths over the same time period, and the other one is four in eighteen. Most of the causes of death seem to be Alzheimer's. I didn't know that was an actual cause of death."

"I supposed if someone deteriorates and their body finally gives up, it's because of that rather than being fairly well and dying suddenly."

"True." The unreported deaths worried me, though. "The other thing we need to find out is how many deaths occurred that were unreported. And can you check how many residents each of the three care homes have?" Those numbers would be crucial in figuring out if there was an unusually high rate of death and could help us prove our case later. It would at least give us a stronger reason to be investigating the whole thing.

Olivia looked at me. "I think I need another cup of tea to think this through. Do you want a coffee?"

"Cappuccino? I can't drink the instant stuff." I shuddered.

She grinned. "Yes, Miss Coffee Snob, I know. I was going to order from the PIB café."

"Yes please."

Olivia put the order through, and within five minutes, our beverages had arrived. The office smelled so much homelier with *eau de café*. Hmm, maybe someone should make a perfume that smelled like freshly brewed coffee. Or, I could just dab some coffee onto my wrists each morning. I chuckled.

Olivia gave me a "what's so funny now" look and shook her head. "Do I even want to know?"

"Probably not, but I'll tell you anyway. Coffee perfume! Why has no one invented it yet?"

"Because it's a terrible idea. Seriously, stick to your day job." She laughed.

I rolled my eyes in mock offence. "Why do people have no vision? I'm surrounded by idiots." I grinned, and it was Olivia's turn to roll her eyes.

Olivia had a couple of sips of tea, then put her cup down. "I've got an idea, but I'm not sure if I have the skills to do this. We may need to get Tim's help."

"Which we'd need to clear with James first. I'm not sure how secret this investigation is. Are you sure it's not something my magic can help with?"

"I honestly have no idea. We'll need to hack into the care home's database, see what residents they had and now don't have. And if someone died, they would have at least recorded it on their own system because they can't keep getting the benefits, and the family of the deceased would have notified authorities, surely."

"I'll call James." I rang and updated him on everything.

"I actually had all that on my to-do list, but I've been caught up with a different case that has escalated quickly. I'll call Tim now and have him come down. Don't give him all the details of the case. Just ask him to do this specific search."

"Won't he be curious?"

"He's used to it. I have to go now, but give everything to Mill once you have the results. Bye, Lily."

"Bye." I turned to Olivia. "He's sending Tim to help us. We aren't to elaborate on what we're doing. Just ask him to search what we need, and that's it."

Her brow furrowed. "Okay, cool."

Within five minutes, Tim was walking through the door, his grey hair pulled back into its usual low ponytail. "Hello, ladies. I hear you need some hacking help." He grinned, his smile standing out now that he'd shaved off his beard. He looked so much younger without it. I would have pegged him as being in his fifties when we'd first met, but I wouldn't be surprised if he was ten years younger than what I'd thought.

I stood and sat in Millicent's office chair. Olivia scooted over to where I'd been sitting, and Tim took her seat.

Olivia said, "We need you to hack into the Saint Catherine Laboure Care Home database and get a printout of all the residents who have died in the last twelve months. We may need to go back further eventually, but for now, that's it."

He nodded slowly, likely thinking about how to go about doing what we wanted. "Righto, then. This may take a while. Is it urgent?"

"Super urgent. Sorry. Also, we need details of every staff member—name, address, whatever's in the system." I tilted my head to the side and pressed my lips together in the universal sign for "I'm sorry to ask but not sorry enough to retract my request."

He smiled. "Okay. I'll get to work. You ladies may want to find something else to do for a couple of hours. Unless I get very lucky, this is going to take some time."

"Not a problem. Thanks for helping." Olivia stood and looked at me. "Is there anything else we can do while we wait?"

"Shopping in London?" Now that I was stronger, transporting both of us to London would hardly put a dent in my energy. And even though I wasn't okaying this with anyone, if anyone from Dana's evil crew was following me, they'd never know where I'd popped off to.

"Sounds good. I need a new pair of boots." She grinned.

I texted my plans to James, so he'd know where we were, and grabbed Liv's hand. "Ready?"

She nodded.

"Harrod's toilets, here we come."

# CHAPTER 7

We returned to Millicent's office just over two hours later. Liv had found herself a gorgeous pair of high-heeled ankle-length leather boots, which we dropped at home first. Millicent was sitting at her desk when we walked in, two piles of papers in front of her.

"Hey, ladies. How was shopping?"

"Good for some." I jerked my head towards Liv. I hadn't seen anything I liked, at least nothing I wanted to pay a gazillion dollars for. There were a couple of lovely pairs of boots, but they would have set me back four-hundred quid each. I wasn't into spending stupid amounts of money on clothes or shoes. Maybe if I was rich, I could justify it, but my wages were so sporadic, I had to be sensible. I'd just live vicariously through Olivia, who was used to the finer things in life—not that she didn't earn it, but she had her parents for backup if anything went horribly wrong.

"Did Tim get the information we needed?" Olivia sat at her desk, and I took the chair next to her again.

Millicent smiled. "He sure did. He finished about half an hour ago. Apparently, it was easier than he anticipated. That nursing home needs better online security."

"Lucky for us." I smiled. "So can I have a look?"

She handed Olivia one pile of paper and me the second pile. "Olivia, I'll get you to go through the death records. Crossmatch the care-home records against the official ones; then give me the ones that haven't been reported." Mill turned to me. "Lily, I'd like you to start by going through these employee records. Make notes on any staff you've met. Once you've done that, you and I will go through all of them and put them in order of who would have had the easiest access to Will's grandmother. Then we'll need to dig deeper online—previous jobs, social-media pages, school records, etcetera. We want to draw as complete a picture for each employee as we can. Anything that needs hacking, we can refer to Tim."

"Sounds good." I started leafing through my pile, and Olivia did the same. Millicent made a few phone calls as we got stuck into the work.

After thirty minutes, I'd done all I could. Out of the thirty-two employees, I'd met two, and just seen one other. So, the boss, the guy who loved purple—what did I think of him? Did he seem like the kind of person who would be killing the elderly residents? He wasn't the friendliest of people, and he would have the run of the place and be able to falsify records and lie to patient families. But why? Wouldn't the high patient-turnover rates look bad on his resume? Except he could lie about it and already had, according to what we'd discovered so far—Olivia had handed fourteen sheets back to Millicent. Fourteen unreported deaths over the last twelve months.

I stood and moved to sit opposite Millicent at her desk. I slid the manager's information across to her. "That's the care-home manager, Mr Hyde. Will said he's all about cutting costs, so maybe that's some kind of motivation for killing residents, but I have no idea how. He wasn't very friendly. When we dropped in to see him, he wanted to get rid of us as quickly as possible. I'm not sure if he has something to hide or if he just hates dealing with patients' families. On a scale of one to ten—ten being guilty—I'd put him at around a six. He has access to all residents and can change records to suit himself. I'm just not sure on a motive, plus, he wasn't very nice."

"Okay, fine. What else have you got?" She held her hand out, and I passed her the second piece of paper.

I took a deep breath. "This woman gives me the creeps."

"Elizabeth Phillips. She's been working there for two years. Why does she give you the creeps? She looks normal to me." Millicent leant back in her chair and rested her hands on her pregnant belly. It seemed to be growing by the day. I couldn't wait to meet the little cutie inside. Would it be a girl or a boy? And what would they call it? I still had to get

Millicent a baby shower gift. I really should check with James and see what she needed. "Lily? Hello, Earth to Lily. Come in, Lily."

"Oh, sorry." I smiled and shrugged. I needed to work on focussing on the moment, especially when I was at work. I told her what happened when I'd wandered off in the care home, and she'd found me, then told me to get back to where I was supposed to be, or she'd kick me out. "For a short woman, she was scary. And she didn't seem upset at all about the recent deaths."

"Well, everyone who goes there ends up dying, pretty much. You'd get used to it. It doesn't mean she wasn't sad. Some people are really good at hiding their feelings."

"She didn't bother hiding how cranky she was with me. She had no reason to be." I folded my arms. "Anyway, I give her an eight out of ten. She definitely has the knowledge and opportunity, and if she's always that cranky, the motive. She'd probably kill someone for not eating their rice pudding, considering how angry she was with me wandering the hallways."

Millicent raised an eyebrow. "Don't you think you're being a little bit harsh? They probably worry about security. Maybe you were there to rob the elderly patients or steal drugs? Nothing's impossible."

"Rob them of what? Their false teeth and slippers?"

"Some of them have valuables locked in their bedside drawers. My great-grandfather died ten years ago. He had dementia and was in a care home in London."

"I'm so sorry. I don't know much about your past—

before you were with James." What a rotten sister-in-law I was.

She smiled. "It's okay. We weren't that close, but Mum took me to see him a few times, and she'd always check his gold watch was in the drawer. They left it there because it was the only thing that could calm him sometimes."

"Okay, but she didn't accuse me of stealing anything, and she certainly didn't search me." I knew Millicent was just looking at every angle, but that didn't change the fact that I didn't like that woman.

"Right. We'll check her out, but what's the last page you have?"

"This is an orderly, according to the sheet." I handed it to her. "He was pushing a patient down the hallway when I was there. I said hello, and he gave me a nod. I would think he's a one or two out of ten. He didn't seem angry or dodgy." I shrugged. "I'm only giving him a rating because he's there and has opportunity, but nothing about him screamed 'murderer.'"

"They don't always have a murderer tattoo on their forehead." Millicent laughed. "That would make our job way too easy." Millicent picked up her desk phone and dialled. "Hi, Tim. Yes. I need everything you can get me on these three." She waved her arm, and all the sheets of paper disappeared. "I'll have more for you later, but that's it for this afternoon. If you can get the lot on them, I'd appreciate it…. Okay… thanks. Bye." She hung up.

"What about this pile?"

"I'll rank them in order of importance based on what

they do at the care home. As far as your work here, I think you're done for today. You can go home if you like. Will's going to call you later about tomorrow. He's going to run you through protocol and operations in our surveillance van."

My heart rate kicked up, and it was nothing to do with being alone in a van with Agent Crankypants. Ma'am was going undercover soon, and she was going to die. My forehead tensed.

"Hey, it's going to be okay, Lily." Millicent gave me a reassuring smile. "Ma'am can look after herself, and your magic may not be telling you the whole story. There's probably a good explanation for the photograph." I could tell by her falsely happy tone of voice that she didn't believe her words either.

I shook my head slowly. "I don't like this one bit. We have to do everything we can to make sure she's not in there a minute longer than necessary."

Olivia looked up from her work. "I'm working as fast as I can, and I'm sure everyone else is too. Try not to worry. There's no use stressing, at least until she's in the care home. She's fine right now."

What if I was wrong? What if she wasn't going to die in the care home. What if she didn't even make it that far? My eyes widened.

Millicent wrinkled her brow. "What's wrong, Lily?"

"What if she dies in a car accident, or on another assignment before then? My magic is never wrong." I swallowed. This was horrible. My magic was more trouble than it was worth. There was nothing I could do. Tears scalded my eyes, and I gritted my teeth. Feeling helpless sucked big time.

No one answered, but by the look in their eyes, I knew they felt just as I did.

"I need to go for a run. I'm going to go home and get changed, then I'm going to travel to Brighton and jog along the coast. I'll call you when I'm back home in about forty minutes."

"Are you okay without protection?" Olivia asked.

"Yes. If I travel, whoever's after me won't have any way to track where I've gone."

Olivia looked at Millicent.

"Yes, Liv. Lily will be fine." Millicent turned to me. "But I will send someone to look for you if you don't call in at"— she checked the time on her phone—"four. Okay?"

"Done. I'll see you later." I travelled home, changed into my running gear, and grabbed a bottle of water and earbuds. Next was to travel to the public toilets closest to Brighton Palace Pier. I built my door and set my coordinates. Within two seconds, I was there. I switched my music on and hurried out.

Ah, the sea air. The familiar salty tang soothed my nerves, and I soon got into a pleasant rhythm: one, two, three, breathe in; one, two, three, breathe out. I passed the pier and kept going.

The sun shone through the high, fluffy white clouds. It was the perfect afternoon for a run, and I grinned, momentarily pushing thoughts of Angelica's potential demise away.

How was it that I could travel from place to place within seconds? What a miracle that I could be in Westerham one moment, Brighton the next, and even Paris if I wanted. I'd already taken Olivia there once for lunch, but it tired me out a fair bit, so I wasn't going to take her again until I was stronger. Plus, the further from home I went, the harder it would be to get help if the snake people managed to figure out where I was and came after me.

I savoured each beat of my joggers against the concrete... until ten minutes later when my music cut out, and my phone rang. Damn.

I pressed the button to answer it, slowing my legs to a walk. "Hello," I said on an exhale before sucking some air into my greedy lungs.

"Hey, Lily. It's Will."

"Oh, your number didn't come up on my phone."

"I'm calling from the PIB landline. Sounds like I've got you all worked up." He snickered.

"Ha! You wish. I was just running. You're interrupting my sanity-retrieval time."

"That's what they all say." I could hear his smirk. I rolled my eyes. It was a shame he couldn't see it.

"Yeah, yeah. Dream on." I grinned. He probably wasn't far from the truth—if I hadn't already been running, he would have at least caused my heart rate to increase. But I would never admit that to him. His head was big enough as it was. "So, why are you bothering me this afternoon?" It was my turn to smirk.

"Bothering you? Oh, I thought you enjoyed hearing

from me." Gah, was he pouting? I swear his voice was the most expressive one I'd ever heard.

"Of course I do. I was just joking. But seriously, why did you call?"

"Ha! I knew it. I was just joking too. I know you love hearing from me. I'm awesome."

"You idiot." I shook my head and wiped sweat off my brow with the back of my hand. "Please just tell me why you called, or I'm going to have to hang up so I can get back to my run. I have to be back at work soon."

"That's why I'm calling. Millicent asked me to show you the surveillance van this afternoon. Things are moving quicker than we thought."

My pleasant afternoon went to hell, and my stomach dropped. I didn't want to ask, but I had no choice. "When does she go in?"

"Tomorrow morning."

And just like that, everything I'd wanted to forget came rushing back.

# CHAPTER 8

After going home and showering, I was back at the PIB in a lift with Will as it descended into the bowels of the organisation. Who came up with that description anyway? Like anyone wants to go into stinky poo-covered tunnels that end in getting squeezed out of someone's—

"So, I'll show you how everything works. It's really neat equipment."

"Ah, yeah. Sounds good."

We stepped out into an underground car park, the grey starkness broken only by white parking-space lines and over-head fluorescent lighting. Yep, it was a car park like any other. About thirty metres from the lift sat a white van. That was a surprise. For some reason, I imagined it would be black. Probably because everyone wore black uniforms, and in the movies, spy cars—and bad-guy cars, come to think of it—were black. But white made more sense. It had Brian's Plumbing on the side in blue text, the apostrophe in the shape of a drip. Nice.

Will pressed the button to unlock it, and the blinkers flashed. He opened the side sliding door. "After you, m'lady."

I grinned. "You're such a gentleman." I stepped inside.

It was empty, except for a large toolbox and a handful of pipes along the opposite side to the door. It really was a plumber's van.

"What the hell? Does the surveillance comprise of us looking out the window? Because if that's the case, I know why Ma'am's going to die." I almost choked on the last word. Dammit! Why wouldn't she listen and do this a different way?

"Patience, young grasshopper. All will be revealed." He jumped in and shut the door. As soon as it closed, desks, three fixed chairs, keyboards, and several monitors appeared, and the pipes disappeared. The toolbox, however, stayed.

I started, my hand flying to my chest. "Holy Witchnan-nigans, Batman! Where did all that come from?"

"It was here but invisible. It's a spell that hides the van's contents for when we're getting in and out. It's not much of a surveillance van if passers-by can see all our equipment."

"What's in the toolbox?"

He gave me a wary look. "Stuff that you can't touch. It's for the other agents in the van. There will probably be four of us at any given time." He pointed at the yellow and black box, and the lid opened, revealing four handguns and ammunition. Holy hell.

"Ah, yeah. Can you move it out of the way? I'm likely to trip on it and somehow shoot myself."

He laughed. "They're not loaded. We're not amateurs."

"Nice to know. So how does all this work?"

He sat in front of one of the monitors and indicated I should sit next to him. I conjured a notebook and pen because there was no way I was going to remember everything, and it was a good thing I had. For the rest of the afternoon, he ran me through the systems until I thought my head would explode.

"That's it." He must have noticed the horrified look on my face. He smiled. "Hey, it's okay. No one expects you to be an expert after one day, or even one week, and that's why you'll be observing, more than anything. You'll just need to be extra watchful. And alert one of the other agents if something's going down, and Ma'am's in danger." He laid his hand on mine and squeezed.

Was it hot in here? I swear someone had cranked up the heat. His hand was warm. The sensation of his skin against mine had my pulse racing. He cleared his throat and licked his bottom lip; his pupils dilated. At least I wasn't the only one.

"Why don't I take you out for dinner, Lily? It's been a long day, and tomorrow is going to be even worse."

"Oh my God! You don't think they'll kill Angelica tomorrow, do you?" The cosiness of moments ago disappeared, and it was as if the van was getting smaller in a claustrophobic, coffin way. I jumped up and hopped out. Then I started for the lift.

"Hey, it's going to be okay." He hurried after me and stood in front of me, stopping my progress. He put his large hands on my shoulders and looked down into my eyes. "Maybe whatever your magic is trying to tell you isn't what you think? I won't believe she's going to die until the moment it happens and there's no denying it. We live with the reality every day on the job, to be honest. You just have to block it out and keep going. Everything will be okay. I promise."

I shook my head. "You can't promise that, Will. I appreciate you for trying. I'm not really that hungry, but I could go for some sort of food; otherwise I'll be hungry later. Stupid stomach." I gave him a weak smile.

"That's my Aussie witch." He ran the back of his fingers down my cheek, and I inhaled a shaky breath. The things that man could do without even trying. I was in so much trouble. "I'll just shut the van. Then we'll go get some food."

As good as the company was, and as yummy as dinner tasted, it wasn't enough to stop the freak out from messing up my brain. Tomorrow, for good or ill, it would start. The beginning of the end for Angelica, and I didn't know how I would get through it. It brought back terrible memories of when my parents disappeared, the grief of their loss never truly disappearing.

Angelica was like a favourite aunt to me, and if something happened to her, it would break my heart. And as much as I knew it wasn't my fault, I would blame myself for not figuring out a way to stop her from going through with her plans. There had to be a better way, surely.

Will had taken me to a quaint pub for dinner—The Stanhope Arms. It was full, the raucous cheer of happily dining and imbibing patrons making it hard to have a conversation, which was fine with me; I wasn't much in the mood for talking. He'd taken me there because he knew the coordinates for the church next door. We landed on St Martin's Church Brasted, hidden by the stone crenellations surrounding the clock-tower rooftop.

Evening had dimmed the already-grey sky. Will had cast a no-notice spell on himself and peered over. When he was sure the coast was clear, we travelled to the ground behind the church. From there, it was a short distance past the gravestones to the pub.

After dinner, he paid the bill, and we wandered back to the church. Past the crooked gravestones. Normally, I'd be interested to read them, see how the people died, how old they'd been, but tonight, they just reminded me of death and the fact that Angelica would soon have one of her own.

Once we were behind the tower, out of sight, Will enveloped me in his arms. I sank into him, breathed in his scent, and took comfort. "It will all work out, Lily. And if it doesn't, I'm here for you. Okay?"

When I looked up at him, tears clouded my eyes. He wiped an errant teardrop from my cheek with his thumb. I tried to steady my voice. "Thanks. And I'm here for you too. I know this whole thing hasn't been easy, with your gran."

He said nothing, leant his face close to mine, and placed

a sweet kiss on my lips. Adrenaline shot through my system, warming my stomach. His lips were so soft and warm. I barely registered the croak of frogs that surrounded us as his tongue parted my lips. Oh, dear God. So this was our first kiss. Next to a graveyard, or were we actually in one? Funnily enough, that didn't bother me. I was too busy. And it didn't make it any less enjoyable. Did that make me a weirdo? Probably, but I didn't care.

He finally pulled back, both of us breathing harder than was normal. He grinned, and I couldn't help returning it. "Bye, Lily. See you tomorrow. You go first."

He obviously meant travel home first. That was the equivalent of a guy dropping you home and waiting till you went inside before he drove away. "Night." I made my doorway and stepped into Angelica's reception room, my head still floating from that kiss. Guilt bopped me on the head, bringing me back to Earth a bit. How could the most wonderful thing and the most horrible thing be happening at the same time? I mean, Angelica wasn't dead yet—that I knew—but the impending event cast darkness over every-thing. As much as I wanted to not worry till it happened, I knew my magic was never wrong. Stressing about a foregone conclusion was unavoidable.

I showered, set my phone alarm, and went to bed, the dread of tomorrow ensuring I didn't sleep much, so when I got up at 7:30 a.m. the next morning, my eyes were grainy, and I wanted to curl up on the floor and go back to sleep.

Angelica and Olivia were already at the table having breakfast when I walked into the kitchen. "Coffee, dear?

You look rather tired." A full mug appeared at my usual spot at the table.

I sat and inhaled before taking a sip. I enjoyed the sensation as it slid down to warm my tummy. "Thanks, Angelica. What time do you go in?"

She looked at her watch. "At nine. Beren's coming to pick me up, and we're going in the normal way because of the anti-magic shield on the care home."

"Is all your surveillance stuff ready?"

She nodded and pointed to her diamante earrings—a solitary diamond glinting out of each setting. Although they could have been crystal. It didn't really matter. "These transmit video, and the teddy will transmit video and audio. We did away with the hearing aids because getting video is more important." She held out her hands, and the teddy appeared between them.

Olivia finished her mouthful of cereal and said, "I hear you had dinner with Will last night. How did it go?" Her smile was mischievous.

"How did you know? Word travels fast around here."

"Beren told me. I was wondering where you'd got to. Angelica and I ended up getting delivery at the office."

"Delivery of what? Isn't the organisation supposed to be fairly secret?"

"Chinese." She grinned. "It was so yummy. There's a restaurant run by witches about twenty minutes away. They pop in and out via the normal PIB reception room."

"Wow, that's cool. Is there a list of witch-run businesses? You never know when that would come in handy."

A notebook appeared on the table. "There you go, dear," Angelica said. "That's just for businesses between here and London."

I flipped through the pages. "There's a lot more than I thought. Are there any clubs for witches to get together? What about dating sites?"

"No." Angelica drained her teacup of the last two sips. "It would draw attention to us. Also, non-witches might like to join since we can't say it's a club for witches, and they would be refused for no good reason. It would just create trouble."

"Bummer." I had another sip of coffee. "Have you got any last-minute instructions? Or maybe you've changed your mind about going undercover?" I tensed, waiting for her rebuke.

She shook her head. "What am I going to do with you, Lily? I have to do my job, and what kind of leader would I be if I sent my agents where I feared to tread? We know the risks of our job, and we face them willingly. Now, no more questions. James can fill you in on anything we haven't covered. I have to rehearse my Alzheimer's performance. I've spent the last two days reading everything I can and becoming acquainted with the person I need to be."

While Angelica zoned out, I poured myself some cereal and milk. I'd only half finished, but I couldn't force down another bite. I sighed. Olivia shook her head at me. "Hey, Lily, why don't you go get dressed? Will is expecting you in the surveillance van by eight thirty. Here are the coordinates." She pulled a slip of paper out of her pocket and handed it to me.

"Thanks, Liv. What are you doing today?"

"I'm backup at headquarters, and I'm still gathering all the info on everyone who works there. Tim's got stuff left to get too. When we're done, we'll send you everything. Once we've all had time to think about it, James is going to call a meeting." She patted my arm. "We're all doing everything we can. We're going to catch this killer, and Ma'am's going to be fine."

We both turned to look at her. Her vacant smile, as if she didn't recognise us but was trying to be polite, showed me she at least had some acting chops. "You're eerily convincing." I leaned back, away from her.

She laughed, a crazed cackle. Olivia and I looked at each other.

"Yeah, I think I'm going to get dressed. I'll see you both in ten. I want to say goodbye before I leave." I magicked my uneaten cereal into the bin, and my cup, bowl, and spoon into the dishwasher. Tidying was so awesome with magic.

By the time I came back down, Angelica was standing at the bottom of the stairs, a pink suitcase with black cat motifs all over it at her feet. I swallowed my tears. This was it.

I gave her a hug. We weren't massive huggers, but she accepted it with ease and hugged me back. I'd been expecting stiff reluctance. It was a nice surprise. "Stay safe," I said and stepped away.

"You too, Lily. Don't be worrying about me so much that you forget to stay alert for yourself. Okay?"

"Okay. Good luck." We shared a smile. Then I built my door, putting on the van's coordinates, and stepped through.

⚜

My doorway had taken me to a tiny black space. It took me a moment to realise it was an area surrounded by a black curtain. I opened it to see the rest of the van. Will and another guy stood there chatting. Will saw me first, as he'd been facing the curtained-off area. "Lily! Welcome to our mobile surveillance centre." He grinned but made no move to give me a hug. Disappointment descended until I remembered we were at work, and being all over each other would be totally unprofessional.

I smiled. "Hi. Reporting for duty, Agent Blakesley."

"Agent Cardinal, this is Lily. She's not an agent, but she's doing some contract work with us at the moment. She doesn't have weapons clearance, but she'll be great on the monitors."

"Nice to meet you." The redhead extended his hand, and I shook it. He must have been about my age and had blue eyes and freckles. He was a couple of inches shorter than Will, and whilst muscular, was a bit thinner. His smile revealed a gap between his two front teeth.

"Are you going to introduce me as well?" a female voice asked from the front of the van. Black curtains blocking off the two front seats parted, and a tall, ebony-skinned woman slipped through. Her broad shoulders were almost a match for Will's. She smiled, her straight white teeth glowing against her skin. Long lashes framed her warm brown eyes. Wow, looked like being a supermodel was a great way to get a job at the PIB. Most of the younger agents were gorgeous —I thought of Beren and Witchface. Okay, so Agent Cardinal wasn't my cup of tea, but Will wasn't into dudes, as far as I could tell.

"Lily, this is Agent Imani Jawara. Agent Jawara, this is my friend and a PIB contractor, Lily Bianchi."

She held out her hand, and I shook it. "Lovely to meet you, Lily. Are you James's sister, then?" Her English accent was more street than refined, but it was full of cool attitude. I'd bet she was fun to hang out with.

"Lovely to meet you too. And yes, I'm James's sister."

"Let me know if there's anything you need, Lily. And if you have any questions about how anything works, just ask. I'm here to help."

Wow, she was so nice. "Thanks, Agent Jawara. I will."

She waved her hand. "You can drop the 'Agent' business while we're in here. Call me Imani. And I love your Aussie accent." She smiled.

I grinned. "Oh, wow. Thank you, Imani. I was thinking yours was pretty cool too." Some of the tension left my shoulders. I realised that not only had I been worried about Angelica, but learning new skills and meeting new agents wasn't fun either. I didn't want to muck anything up, and who knew when I was going to come across another psychopathic agent, like Dana. It seemed as if this shift was going to be okay.

"You'll sit here, Lily." Will pointed to the middle seat

and monitor—one of four sets running along the driver side of the van. All of the monitors were on, but showing black screens, a white cursor sitting waiting for something to happen on each one.

I sat. "Do we have to wait for Ma'am to go inside before we get any feed?"

Will sat to my right. "Yep. And Beren's placing some cameras around the place as well, when he takes her in." He smirked, probably proud of how sneaky they were being. I couldn't argue, though—it was kinda cool.

We'd been chatting for about twenty minutes when Will said, "Lily, if something happens and we have to rush the place, you must stay here, contact headquarters, and keep watching the monitors. You'll be able to give them vital information. We're all wearing body cams we'll turn on in the event of an incident." He nodded at his comrades. "Okay?"

I nodded. "Definitely. I'll stay here, call HQ, and keep them updated on the situation." I knew I would hate waiting while they were in there trying to save Angelica—because that's what a "situation" amounted to—but if that was how I was going to be most effective, I'd take it.

The screen directly in front of me came to life, displaying a picture of the front entry of the care home. Imani settled into the chair to my left to watch. The view turned and paused on our van. Beren's voice came through. "No, Aunty. This way." They'd started the act outside, which made sense. The view must be from Angelica's earring camera.

One of the three screens to my right showed something greyish white. I squinted, trying to make out what it was. Then the grey became two steps. Oh, how funny. It must be the teddy bear. I chuckled. I could just imagine it dangling from one of Angelica's hands. It was a shame we couldn't see out of the van—the back windows were all blacked out, and the curtain blocked off anything visible through the windscreen.

All conversation in the van had stopped, and everyone stared at the monitor receiving the earring transmission.

The front of the property comprised a pretty, late-1800s brick home with bay windows, and the rear had been added maybe forty or so years ago and was much uglier but likely more practical. At least the uglier part wasn't visible from the street. The front door was getting closer and closer, until it filled the screen.

Beren buzzed the intercom. Within seconds, the door clicked, and he pushed it open. From there, they traversed a hallway and headed to the front reception area, where there was a middle-aged woman sitting behind a half-height wall, kind of like at the hospital. She smiled as Beren and Angelica approached.

Then the screen just to my left filled with a shot of skin. What was that? I tipped my head to the side, trying to figure it out. Then the view swung wildly, and the picture became a blur before stabilising on a wall with a print of a turquoise-and-black butterfly with the words "Time for our residence passes as gently and beautifully as a butterfly fluttering passed." How had I not noticed that last time? The spelling was a dog's breakfast.

"What's wrong, Lily?" Will whispered.

I blinked. "Oh, that picture on the wall."

"That's from Beren's wristwatch cam."

"No, not that. The spelling's wrong. They've spelled 'residents' and 'past' wrong. Seriously, it's in a public spot where everyone sees it. If their record-keeping is as shoddy as their spelling, they're in trouble."

"Lily, focus. And shh." Will shook his head.

"But you ask——"

"Shh!"

I inhaled a huge breath and blew it out loudly. Will pointed at the screen with a stiff, angry finger. I did the adult thing and kept quiet… whilst rolling my eyes. Imani smirked. I was pretty sure I was definitely going to get along with her.

"How can I help you?" the lady behind the counter asked.

"I'm here to admit my mum." He handed her some papers. "The doctor's reports are in there, and the forms are all filled in."

She quickly flicked through the papers and put them aside. "Just a moment, and I'll call someone to show you and your mum to her room."

"Thanks."

"What room? What's going on, Son? I thought we were going for ice cream?"

"Later, Mum. First we just need to do this. Okay?"

She was looking straight at his face, and Beren was doing a great job of looking anxious. His forehead wrinkled, and his eyes held sadness. Maybe he was thinking to a time when his aunt wouldn't be around. Even if he believed Angelica was going to survive this assignment, time eventually caught up with all of us, and he was likely to lose her one day rather than the other way around.

A short woman with a blonde bob haircut arrived. She wore the basic light-blue long-sleeved top and drab pants that most of the staff wore. It was hospital-style garb, which made sense because they probably got all manner of gross stuff all over them on a daily basis. The people who worked in aged care were angels... well, except for whoever was murdering the residents. Maybe they could be classified as dark angels—angels of death. Hmm, way to make myself feel better. Why did my brain always take the worst path possible?

The lady smiled at Beren. "Welcome to Saint Catherine Laboure. I'm Michelle Price, admissions manager.

"Hi, Michelle. Lovely to meet you. I'm Preston, and this is my mother, Angelica Prestons."

"Lovely to meet you both. Is it Mrs or Ms Prestons?" She directed the question at Beren.

"Mrs, but you can call her Angelica. She won't mind."

The woman smiled at Angelica. Her voice had a kind tone. It seemed as if she really did care and probably wasn't going to end up being the killer. Although, if it were that easy to tell, no one would need detectives. "Why don't you come with me? I've got a lovely room I'd like to show you. Your son can come too. Would you like that?"

The picture bobbed up and down—she must have nodded.

"Let's go, then." The woman led the way to the lift and punched in the code. They got out on the first floor and turned left—towards the room that had been Will's grandmother's, but they stopped two doors earlier. "Here we are." The room was identical to Will's grandmother's, except there was standard bedding—a cotton-looking blanket on top of white sheets, and two white pillows. There was no TV.

They all pottered around the room, getting Angelica settled. After ten minutes, it looked as if she was set, and she hadn't said a word the entire time. I texted Olivia. *Can you add "not likely" to the file on Michelle Price, admissions manager? She seems quite nice. The footage will be there tonight.* Everything recorded here was being saved on a hard drive, which would end up at the PIB at the end of each day. They didn't want to transmit anything in case it was intercepted. On change over, the hard drive would magic itself to a PIB safe, and a new one would pop into existence in the recording device. Magic meant no more dramas changing print cartridges either. They bought them in bulk and spelled them to change when needed. It was totally awesome.

Angelica put her teddy on the bedside table, and for the first time, I could see her. My breath caught in my chest as she sat on her bed, and nausea spiralled up my throat.

She was ghostlike on the video too.

"Lily, are you all right, love? You look like you've just seen a ghost."

I turned to Imani, who was leaning towards me. She placed her hand on my shoulder. I swallowed, speechless as I got my brain working again. My talent was a secret I couldn't let anyone else know about. Only those I totally trusted were privy to my secret, and with a price already on my head, the fewer people who knew, the better.

"Um, I'm fine. I think my breakfast doesn't agree with me."

"Do you need some fresh air?" she asked.

"No. I'll be fine. If I have to leave, I'll just pop home for a few minutes." Well, that was an added benefit of being able to travel—the comforts and privacy of your own bathroom was always only a few steps away.

"Okay, love. You do what you have to. If you need to rush away, feel free."

I smiled at her. "Thanks, Imani."

Someone tapped me on the shoulder. I turned around.

"Are you sure you're okay, Lily?" Will's brows were in their preferred wrinkly configuration, but I could tell he had guessed my sudden "illness" wasn't because of breakfast. I had to find a way to tell him in code.

"I'm sure I'll be fine. I just hope no one at the care home can see through Angelica's disguise like I can. I've never seen her so docile before." My short laugh came out strained.

Will nodded, his gaze softening. "I think she's doing a fine job. We'll catch those murderers before you know it."

"If anyone can pull off an undercover job, it's Ma'am," said Agent Cardinal.

I nodded and gave him a wan smile. If only I didn't know the truth. Whether she succeeded or not this time, the result would be the same.

She was going to die.

# CHAPTER 9

Our shift in the van finished at four thirty in the afternoon—there were three eight-hour shifts—after which, we travelled to headquarters. Agent Cardinal and Imani wandered off to their own offices, which left Will and me standing in the hallway. "What are you up to now?" he asked.

"I need to see Olivia and go through the employee files, so I can make notes on today's observations. What about you?"

"I'll come with you. We can pool thoughts, plus I want to ask you more about this morning."

I sighed, the tragic inevitability of everything like being smothered by a ton of manure—it wasn't just heavy and suffocating; it was crappy... literally. "Come on." He slung his arm around my shoulder, and I leaned into him as we walked to Millicent's office.

The reception desk was unoccupied, so I called out. "Mill, Liv, I'm back."

"Come through," Millicent said.

Olivia was at her computer. She looked up and smiled. "How'd it go?"

Will and I looked at each other before I looked back at Olivia. "Uneventful yet horrible."

Millicent frowned. "What happened?" A sea of paper covered her desk—it was far from the orderly space I'd left yesterday. I recognised a couple of the photos on printouts; one was one of the orderlies I'd seen wandering about, and the other was the mean carer. Millicent was obviously doing her best to crack the case before Angelica became the next victim.

"Angelica settled in well enough, and Beren deployed all the other cameras. Unfortunately, once I saw Angelica via video, my talent kicked in. She was a faded version of herself, and all I could think about all day was what's coming."

The sympathetic looks I got from both women almost had me crying, but I needed to be strong. I wasn't the only one who was going to lose Angelica, plus Millicent and Will had known her for much longer than I. And what about Beren? Gah. I was the only one being a huge baby about this—but then, maybe no one else really believed she was going to die.

"I'm sorry, Lily." Millicent's shoulders sagged. "We're doing all we can to stop it from happening. Who knows? Maybe tomorrow she'll be her old solid self again?"

I gave her a "what can you do" smile. "Maybe. You never know. If that happens, I'll let you know."

"And what about the extra cameras?" she asked.

Will answered, "Beren brought in a TV, so we have that camera. He also hid one in the common lounge area on the leaf of a plastic plant, in the dining room, and on the top of the door frame to Angelica's room. It faces the hallway. That way we can warn Angelica if we need to."

"Huh? How would you warn her?" Had they given her a phone? And if they had, would someone take it off her?

"The teddy is a two-way communication device. If we need to talk to her, the teddy will squeak, alerting her—it also has a built-in squeaker in case Angelica needs to make an excuse as to the noise."

Somehow, that made me feel slightly better, but then I realised it didn't change anything. Bummer.

"Did he manage to place one in the manager's office?" Millicent asked.

"Not today. He was meant to meet with the guy, but the manager cancelled because of another meeting. They're meeting tomorrow at ten."

Millicent nodded. "Okay. Great. I'll get that information sent to James. And now, let's have a look at these." She nodded at the sprawl of documents on her desk. "We're starting to get an idea of who each employee is—where they were born, where they grew up, other workplaces, whether they're single, married, divorced, have children, arrest records, etcetera."

Wow, that hadn't taken them long. "Have any of them

been in jail before?'" I would imagine it would be hard to get a job if you had a criminal record.

"Just one. One of the three chefs that work in the kitchen."

"Well, I would hope he's using his skills in the kitchen and not anywhere else." I laughed.

Olivia shook her head. "Your jokes are not funny."

I placed my hands over my heart. "Oh, how you wound me. I'll have you know that I'm hilarious. If you don't believe me, just ask me. I'll tell you."

She snorted. See—I was totally funny.

Millicent cleared her throat. "Okay, yes, very funny, Lily. But back to it now, please. He was arrested for drug possession, served his short time in jail, and has supposedly been clean ever since. They have to do annual drug tests to be employed at this nursing home. It's important because, of course, there are drugs on-site to treat the residents. Now, I've separated these into two piles—one was supposed to be for me to go through and one for you, Lily, but I'll hand mine to Will." She absently rubbed her belly, and I smiled. Soon I'd have another person to love, and I couldn't wait. Mum and Dad would have been ecstatic. A pang of inevitable bitter-sweetness squeezed my chest. "I want you two to look for any patterns or anything that seems unusual —quick job changes, moving around a lot for no apparent reason, that kind of thing."

I grabbed my pile. "On it."

Will grabbed his pile. "Do you mind if Lily and I do this in my office? It's a bit crowded in here with four of us."

"Be my guest. It's getting late anyway, and you two are back in the van tomorrow morning, so do what you can, and drop them here afterwards. You can pick them back up tomorrow afternoon. If you do find anything unusual, though, let me know straight away so I can arrange to follow it up ASAP."

"Consider it done," said Will. He turned to me. "Let's go."

We settled ourselves at opposite sides of his desk and got to work. After an hour of scrutinising my pile, I only had three employees who seemed to change jobs every year or two: another one of the chefs and two of the nursing staff. I marked them for further investigation. The chef was a Jamaican-born twenty-five-year-old male called Leroy, and the two nurses were women. One of them, Mary, was thirty-seven, a single mother of two kids, and had started there six months ago. She'd been at the job before that for six months, and the one before that for ten. Assuming the unusual number of deaths may have started more than six months ago, she may not be our suspect, but I wasn't going to discount her. All her previous jobs had been at care homes, so we'd have to question her previous bosses.

The last woman was twenty-eight, and this was only her second job in the field, but she'd been at her first job only a year, and this job a year so far—so the timeline fit. Her employment report showed she'd been handed two warnings at the last job for giving residents the wrong dosage of medication, which resulted in the residents almost dying. Could have been an honest mistake but could have been intentional. I'd have to chase those reports, see if it may have been the prescribing doctor's fault too—goodness knew doctors weren't infallible, even though many people thought they were. So far, she was my most likely candidate.

I finished making notes and looked up. "How's it going? Find anything?"

"Maybe. Is this the woman you ran into that night?" He held up an A4 sheet of paper. The photo taking up the top right-hand quarter of the page showed the carer I didn't like. She was smiling, but even so, she looked... cold. Her lips were too taut, her eyes devoid of warmth. If I had to put money on anyone, it would be her.

"Yes. That's definitely her." I leaned forward, hopeful. "Did you find something?"

"Not really. She's been at Saint Catherine Laboure for two years—so she started well before we estimate the increased number of deaths began. Her job before that was for a notable non-witch care home. She was there for ten years and left with high praise."

A stone of disappointment dropped into my belly. "So, why did you point her out?"

"I don't like the look of her. She has the stare of a psychopath. And trust me; I know what they look like." His grey gaze darkened, and his eyes narrowed. Was he referring to Dana?

I hated to concede my gut was wrong, but unless we could find some evidence to back up our feelings, I'd have to admit that she was innocent. "Maybe she's a psychopath who does a good job? Just because you have no empathy, doesn't mean you kill people for fun. Maybe that's why she doesn't get sad when they die? Maybe it lets her stay detached and do things by the book. If she gets paid well, which I can see from here that she does, why would you jeopardise it? Maybe she loves the money and doesn't mind the job. Maybe she kind of likes seeing people suffer through dementia? That could be all it is." That made her a shitty human but not a murderer.

He made a noncommittal grunt.

I shrugged. "So, what else do you have?"

"The only other one I can see who would raise a red flag is the manager."

"Granted, he wasn't very nice when we were there, but why else?"

"He started there a couple of months before the rise in death rates. He was fired from his last job, although it doesn't say why, and it wasn't with a care home."

"How did he get that job?"

"His sister was the previous manager. She received an internal promotion, so now she's district manager for that group of care homes—this company manages a few witch care homes in the UK. Both she and her brother are witches, but the company employs both witches and non-witches, since no one can perform magic on-site anyway. Every non-witch who works there has to swear on their right arm not to tell anyone."

Huh? "Is that like swearing on the Bible or on your mother's life? Because I'm sure people do that and lie anyway."

He smiled. "Ah, no. With a spelled swearing, they will actually lose that arm. It's usually to a flesh-eating bug that miraculously dies once it gets to the shoulder."

My horrified intake of breath echoed around the room. "What the hell? That's crazy. You witches are cruel!"

"Um, I hate to break it to you, gorgeous, but you're a witch too." He grinned.

Ooh, he called me gorgeous. My cheeks heated, but then I realised I was one of the crazies. "I would never do that to anyone."

"What if it were a matter of survival: you or them? What about if it were Dana threatening your life or the life of every witch you loved or cared about?"

Hmm, he made a fantastic point. I put my hands up in surrender. "You win. Flesh-eating bugs are fine. I guess threatening someone with armlessness is a way to make them harmless. Ha ha."

"You really need to work on your jokes, Lily. They're getting worse."

"Gah. Not you too. Have you been comparing notes with Olivia?"

He smirked. "I didn't need to. It's obvious."

"Fine. Since you both hate my jokes so much, I'm going to make more and more bad jokes, and they're going to get worse and worse. I have no pride to salvage anymore. It's liberating having nothing to lose. Don't you think so?" It was my turn to smirk. I'd make them both suffer. I did my best evil laugh. "Mwahahahahahahahaha."

His smile disappeared, and he put his hands up, palms facing me. "I surrender. Just don't make me suffer."

"Too late. I have no mercy. When you least expect it, expect it." I grinned, then let it fade. "Where was he working before there?"

"It doesn't say."

This was getting curiouser and curiouser, and yes, I knew curiouser wasn't a word, but it should be because it was awesome. "So, now what?"

He looked at his phone. "It's close to seven. I don't know about you, but I'm hungry. Want to grab some dinner, then call it a night?"

My stomach rumbled loudly. I looked at it and blushed. "Um, my stomach obviously agrees it's dinner time, so I vote yes to your suggestion."

We returned the paperwork to Millicent's office. She'd left, but Olivia was there, typing away. "I was wondering how long you'd be. Just put them on her desk."

"Want to join us for dinner?" I wasn't sure if Will would mind, but it wasn't as if he was taking me for a romantic meal—we were tired, and we all had to work tomorrow.

She looked at me, then Will. "Are you sure it's okay? I kind of feel like a third wheel."

Will smiled. "Nonsense. You're part of the PIB family now, plus Lily loves you, so you're always welcome. There's a nice Italian place in Tonbridge. We can drive. It won't take long. The prices are reasonable, and the food is good."

Olivia smiled. "I think I know the place. Pizza Express? Right next to the river?"

"That's the one."

"Yes, please. Mmm, I can smell the garlic bread already." She sniffed the air, and I laughed.

"Well, if it's that good, let's not waste any more time. I'm starving."

## CHAPTER 10

The next morning, we started in the van at the usual time—eight thirty. I'd had a restless night's sleep because I worried someone would kill Angelica while I wasn't watching—not that there was much I could do even if I had been in the van. But maybe if she died, someone could revive her. "Will, do we have a plan for if Ma'am is killed? Like, can we turn off the anti-magic shield, pop in and grab her and get out again? Is Beren on standby?"

He was sitting next to me, at the same monitor as yesterday. He turned his head to look at me. "Beren's on standby, but we can't switch off the shield. It's against regulations, and if any of the old people caused havoc, or killed someone by accident when it was down, we'd be responsible. Don't worry, Lily. We're across the road. If something happens, we'll be in there in sixty seconds."

"If someone kills her, every second counts if we want a chance at reviving her." I ignored the little voice that told me whatever they did to her might be something there's no coming back from. "The lift is slow, especially when you need it to come quickly." I shuddered, remembering the zombie-witch attack.

"She makes a good case." Imani, seated to my left, glanced at Will before looking back at the monitors.

"It's probably worth considering." Agent Cardinal thrummed his fingers on the desk.

"How would you propose we do it?" Will didn't sound keen, more like he thought it was a waste-of-time avenue to traipse down.

Agent Cardinal, sitting on the other side of Imani, turned to regard Will. "Leave it with me. If I can think of a way that doesn't leave us liable, I'll let you know."

Will gave him a chin tip but said nothing, then turned back to his monitor. Well, that went well. Not.

A quiet grumble came from our system. "I could die just from the food. It's awful. And it appears to be made for people without teeth."

Angelica! A burst of happiness showered my insides. It was good to hear her voice.

Last night, before I fell asleep, I vowed I wouldn't look at the monitors that showed her, for obvious reasons. I was focussing as much as I could on the monitor that showed what she could see. Sometimes her ghostly hands or arm would come into frame, but right now, I was looking at her bowl, which held watery porridge. At least I thought that's what it was.

The view panned up, showing she sat by herself at a table for two. The dining room held around fifteen tables: some were for two, and some were for four. Around half of the tables were occupied by elderly witches. Her gaze wandered the dining room. She was obviously showing us the set-up, plus who knew when we'd notice something unusual that could be a clue.

Angelica's gaze snapped back to her table and the chair opposite her. An older lady, but not too decrepit looking, sat down. Her brown eyes were glazed but fully open and bright enough to be assessing Angelica. The woman was obviously a patient: her pink silk pyjamas were a dead giveaway. She looked to be around seventy, and when she smiled, she had a mouth full of perfectly straight teeth. Hmm, too perfect. They were probably dentures. "I'm Elizabeth. I run things around here. Are you new?" What did she mean, she ran things around there?

Angelica looked left, then right. She was stalling her answer, maybe trying to seem as crazy as possible. She whispered, "I'm Mrs Prestons. But don't tell anyone. They're listening, you know." Ah, she was going for paranoid. I snorted.

Elizabeth leaned forward and lowered her voice too. "Who? Who is listening?"

"Them."

The other woman looked at Angelica as if she thought she was crazy. Ah, the irony. "Well, if they do anything to you, I can help. I'm a nurse." Wow, if she thought she worked there, she was just as crazy as Angelica pretended to be.

"Do you work here?" Angelica whispered before taking a loud slurp of her icky porridge. The noise was so gross. I probably wouldn't eat porridge for two years after that. It might have even ruined porridge for me forever. I couldn't stand people making noises when they ate.

"Yes. I take care of everyone. The other nurses aren't very nice, though. There's one who thinks she's me—the other Elizabeth. They'll tell you I don't work here and that my name's Penny, but they're just jealous because I get things done. I'm the manager's favourite—he treats my like royalty. And I have the best room." A smug smile slid onto her face.

Angelica nodded. "Which room is that?"

"Number four. It's the Asian number for death." Um, okaaaay. I would have thought the death room would be the worst room to have, but that's just me. "Give me your wrist."

Angelica's near-transparent arm reached across the table. The other woman grabbed it and proceeded to take her pulse. After a while, she dropped her wrist and said, "Nice strong heartbeat. You're very fit, or maybe you have a slow metabolism. Your heart rate is sixty-two beats per minute. I bet you have a nice strong heart."

One of the male carers, a young, slim Indian with short straight hair, came over. "Penny, are you behaving yourself? And where's your breakfast?"

Penny? So, her name wasn't Elizabeth—colour me surprised. The woman, whoever she was, waved a hand behind her. "Over there somewhere. I ate some. I'd like to go to my room now."

"Okay. I'll help you." The young man helped her out of her chair. Angelica's gaze followed them until they walked out the door.

Once they were gone, an elderly man arrived at the table. His thin frame was hunched over, and one side of his face drooped. He had trouble getting the words out when he said, "This is my usual table." He sat. Angelica was about to stand—the camera had wobbled, and the scrape of her chair came through, but the man raised his hand. "No, stay. I could use some company." He sounded sane enough. What was he doing in the dementia section?

"Okay, then. What's your name?"

"Winston Baker. I'm convalescing. The war was a terrible time, and I need a rest." That answered my question.

"I wouldn't worry, dear," said Angelica. "You did a wonderful job. We're all safe."

He smiled, only one side of his mouth curling up. "And what is a lovely lady like you doing here?"

Her voice conveyed a smile. "I'm not quite sure. My son says it's a holiday village, but there's not much sun or sea. I prefer to holiday by the sea. I just want to go home." She sighed.

He looked around, then met Angelica's gaze again. He lowered his voice. "I've been in the know for a long time."

He tapped the side of this nose. "Be careful of that Elizabeth woman. She's a sneaky one. I don't think she's really a nurse."

"Elizabeth?"

"You know, that woman who was just sitting with you."

"Ah, Elizabeth. I thought her name was Penny?"

"Is that what she told you? Once, she told me her name was Agatha Christie. Like I'd believe she was the famous author. Like I said, she's a slippery one. Anywho…." He stood. "I'll be off. I have a call with the prime minister shortly."

After he limped away, Angelica stood. She lifted her teddy—I hadn't realised she'd brought it. Maybe because its view had been of the floor. The poor thing had been face down under her chair. Yes, I knew it wasn't alive, but I still felt sorry for it. She said to her bear, "Let's go to my room and have tea. Maybe Preston will bring me some of those biscuits I like. The porridge was blech."

Will pushed a button on the keyboard and said quietly, "I'm sure he will." Angelica gave the teddy a ghostly smile and dropped him to her side again. It was reassuring that we could communicate with her, but her faded appearance was the reminder I didn't need that it was all a false sense of security.

Angelica went to the toilet on the way back. We all looked around awkwardly as the noise reverberated around the van—we couldn't see her, of course, but still…. She was a braver woman than me. Finally, she returned to her room, got into bed, and watched TV. Ooh, it was one of my favourite shows, *Location, Location, Location*, an English reality property show where the two happy-but-snarky hosts find someone the place of their dreams, or at least the place they could afford that has one or two of their multitude of criteria. I loved virtually walking through all the old houses, and the two hosts had fun chemistry.

Will picked up his phone and pressed a couple of buttons. "Hi, Mill. Yes. We need to add a suspect to the list."

What had I missed?

"Yes. No…. It's a patient. A woman whose name is Elizabeth or Penny. She's in room four." He listened for a minute. "Yes, Caucasian, around seventy, curly, short grey hair, about five foot five, English accent, may have been a nurse. Okay, thanks…. Bye."

The other agents looked at Will as if to say he was being nuts and way overcautious. He turned to me. "Lily, do you remember what my grandmother said when we visited her?"

Um, she'd said quite a few things, but I took my time and ran through it in my head. Oh, wow. "Yes! She said she'd met the Queen. You don't think she meant Queen Elizabeth, do you? And if she had been a nurse, she'd know how to kill people in hard-to-figure-out ways."

"Like injecting them with air," finished Imani.

"Exactly." Will turned back to the monitors. "I'll try and keep track of Penny, or whoever she is, while you concentrate on Ma'am. We can see her door from the camera on Ma'am's door frame. Maybe Beren can put another camera somewhere else so we can track her movements to the other patients' rooms."

"Could he manage a camera above her door frame, facing away from Ma'am's room?" I asked.

"Maybe, but they still have their security cameras around the place, and they might pick up on him doing that. At least if he's milling about his own mother's doorway, it doesn't look weird."

"Could we somehow hack into their system?"

Will looked at me as if I were a genius. I could get used to that. People didn't look at me that way very often—in fact, almost never. I didn't even have to wonder why. "Lily, that's a brilliant idea! I'll call Millicent again."

"What are you going to ask her?"

"If Tim can hack into their system. It would solve a lot of problems, and we'd have access to way more footage."

"You know what would be even better?" Now my brain was really on fire. "What if we got one of our people to replace one of the guys who monitors the on-site cameras? It might be harder, but then we'd have someone inside who could help Ma'am quickly if she needed it."

Will nodded slowly. "You're right: it would be more diffi-cult, but it would be better. If they hire out their security to a private company rather than employing in-house, we'll be in luck. James can influence them. It's all legal. By the end of the operation, they'll know why, but in order to keep it on the down-low, we'll do it quietly." He grinned. "Nice work, Lily."

"I do what I can." I smiled.

Will dialled Millicent and explained the situation. He took a few minutes convincing her, but in the end, she agreed to call James and run it by him. I had complete confidence in my brother to make the right decision.

The day passed fairly quickly. Beren visited Angelica with the biscuits she wanted, stayed for half an hour, then left. I checked my phone. With only twenty minutes to go on our shift, the woman I disliked came into Angelica's room. She held a chart and wore a kindly smile. Was this really the same woman I'd met the other night? Maybe she did like the old people. Although my gut was telling me otherwise. She had the hairs on my nape standing up.

"Hello, Mrs Prestons. I'm Elizabeth, nursing manager of the home. How have you enjoyed your first day so far?" She stood at the foot of Angelica's bed, holding the clipboard against her chest.

"Breakfast was terrible." Hmm, Angelica wasn't going for amiable. I snorted. Elizabeth's smile wobbled but stayed in place.

Elizabeth looked at her notes or charts, whatever was on the other side of the clipboard. "It says here that you had the porridge. We use organic porridge. Was that unsatisfactory?"

By the way the view moved, Angelica was shaking her head. She picked up the bear and cuddled it. "It was like watery sawdust; wasn't it, Mr. Teddy?" Angelica cuddled the teddy to her and dropped her face, so she wasn't looking at the nurse, but the teddy was. So we saw the look of frustration and the eye-roll that followed. Ha! I knew she wasn't all rainbows and sunshine.

Elizabeth made some notes on her clipboard paper. "So,

what would you like for breakfast tomorrow? Is there something you'd prefer?"

Angelica didn't look up and mumbled, "Eggs, sunny side up, and toast, please." I'd never heard her so timid before. She deserved an Oscar for this performance, but instead, she was just going to get killed. Argh. I was never going to be able to put it out of my mind.

"Righto. Tomorrow morning, we'll have two eggs, sunny side up for you. So, it says here your dementia's advanced to the stage where you have paranoia and aggressive outbursts, but you still recognise family. Is that right?"

Angelica didn't answer, but honestly, what kind of question was that to ask someone with the condition? She couldn't think straight to answer it, and maybe it would put her in distress. Was she trying to make her upset?

"Do you understand my questions, Mrs Prestons?"

"No." She looked up. "Can I have a biscuit?"

"I'll arrange to have one brought up if you'll answer a different question."

Angelica nodded.

"Do you remember what it was like to be a witch?"

"Yes. I could cook things when I wasn't even in the room. I could make my teddy walk behind me like a dog. It was wonderful." She waved her hand in front of her, then let it drop with a *bomp* to the covers. "It's all gone now." Dejection weighed in her tone.

Weirdly, Elizabeth smiled. "Ah, I bet it was wonderful. A bit disappointed, are we?"

Angelica nodded. "Where's my biscuit?"

"Don't you worry. I'll have someone bring it up in a minute."

The door opened, and Angelica's gaze must have cut to it quickly. A man put his head through. He looked to be about forty, with straight brown hair and a short, neatly trimmed beard. He grinned at Elizabeth.

Her face lit up. "Andrew. You're early. You may as well come in and meet Angelica. She's our latest... resident."

He slipped into the room and shut the door. After giving Angelica a quick nod, he grabbed Elizabeth and kissed her. With tongue and everything. Ew. Did we need to see that? Really? I almost laughed, wondering how Angelica felt, being in the same room.

Elizabeth finally swatted him off and giggled. "You know that's not allowed. I could lose my job."

"Well, we don't want that. You do such a wonderful job, sweet pea." They both laughed as if it was the funniest thing they'd ever heard. "Are you ready to go?"

She nodded. "My shift is over, Mrs Prestons. Have a good afternoon. I hope you enjoy your stay here. And try not to miss your magic. You should be grateful you ever had it—some of us aren't so lucky. Rest assured, I'll see you again... soon." Why did that sound like a threat? Meh, I was probably being paranoid. She left and closed the door quietly behind her. I wasn't quite sure what to make of the encounter. Why would she be trying to upset Angelica, or was she weirdly curious, or even just trying to get to know her better? I was sure Angelica had an opinion on what was going on; I just hoped she'd share it with us sooner rather than later.

At least Elizabeth was true to her word—the biscuit arrived within a couple of minutes, and there were two, in fact. After the overweight lady who'd delivered the biscuit left, Angelica's door opened again. The patient who had claimed to have been a nurse in her former sane life poked her head in. Her gaze took in the whole room before settling on Angelica. Penny—I was assuming the carer had called her by her proper name—slipped in and shut the door. She placed herself next to Angelica's bed and grabbed her wrist. By the way she was concentrating, I figured she was taking her pulse. The fact Angelica was letting it happen surprised me. She wasn't a touchy-feely person at the best of times, and this woman was getting creepier by the minute.

Finally, Penny dropped her wrist. "Your pulse was up a touch there. Sixty-five bpm." She put her hands on her hips. "I wish I had my sphygmomanometer. High blood pressure leads to heart attack. Did you know that? So many people die of heart attacks, especially where I used to work. So, so many." She shook her head. "People should look after themselves more."

I shared a worried glance with Will. "I know who we'll be researching as soon as we get back this afternoon," I said.

"At least they'll have gotten a start on it. Looks like James and Beren have a lot of interviews coming up." Will looked at his phone. "Shift change coming up." Within a minute of his statement, the black curtain shifted, and four agents came out, one after the other. Two women and two men. Everyone said hello, and Will updated them on today's events—it was evident he was the senior agent in our little group. He was so awesome, and he liked *me*. I smiled. I was one lucky witch.

We all said our goodbyes, and Will, Agent Cardinal, Imani, and I travelled to the PIB reception room. Will and I went straight to Millicent's office. Tim's mum wasn't in, so Will called out as we walked through, "We're back."

"Hey, you guys. How did it go today?" Olivia, seated in her usual spot, smiled. Millicent wasn't there, but her desk was full of neatly arranged piles of paper. It looked like she'd had a busy day.

"Lots of action in the home today. Angelica's made a new friend." I sat next to Olivia.

"The woman I've pulled up some info on? Penny who thinks she's Elizabeth?"

"That's the one," I said.

Olivia turned and grabbed some papers off her table and handed some to me and some to Will. "Her employment history, going back twenty years prior to when she stopped working. She's been retired for five years, in the care home for a year and a half. Her timeline fits, and there's some interesting death stats on the four hospitals she worked at in that time. She was at the first one for four years, the second for three, the third one for five, and the last one for eight. She worked on the cardiac wards."

Will sat in one of the guest chairs in front of Millicent's desk. We both got to reading. Olivia had done an amazing job with the research. She'd compared like with like, dividing the hospital death rates into departments and matching them against other hospital's individual departments—not just an overall comparison. A disturbing picture was emerging.

Beginning within six months of her starting a new job, deaths in her ward increased by forty percent. Death rates had been similar to surrounding hospitals but looked sickly in comparison while she worked there. As soon as she left, the death rates fell.

Holy moly.

I looked at Will; my brow furrowed. "Um, do you think we've found the culprit?"

"Maybe. The evidence so far is compelling, but we'll have to dig deeper. And until we can catch her in the act, we can't pull the plug on this investigation. Also, what if we think it's her, but it's not? Coincidence could be a factor. And if we call this too early, Angelica's cover will be blown, and they'll be onto us."

"Hmm, maybe." I wasn't convinced. If it looked like a dead fish and smelled like a dead fish, I was pretty sure it was a dead fish. But I had no say in how things were done, so I just had to go along with what others decided. Which was fine—I didn't want the responsibility either. Imagine making the wrong call and causing many more deaths. No thanks. "So, can we access the autopsy reports on anyone who died in coronary care while she was working there?"

"I don't know if it would make any difference. Assuming Penny did kill anyone at her old jobs, she could have done it any number of ways and made it look like an accident; also, don't forget she's a witch. She could have done it with magic, which wouldn't have been picked up on the autopsies. Any evidence would be long gone. If it was her, we'll have to catch her in the act."

Will had a point. Gah, why couldn't we just solve this now and get Angelica out?

The outer door to Millicent's reception room opened and shut. James walked in. "Hey, crew. How's everything going?"

Will, still in his seat, turned to look at James. "Hey, man. Getting there, sort of. What's news?"

"Millicent's gone home early. She's not feeling well."

I sat up straighter. "Is she okay? Do you want me to go and check on her?"

"She'll be fine. I think she's just rundown. She's been working late the last week or so, and the baby's been moving a lot at night, keeping her awake. Anyway, I thought it was time for me to come and have a chat and confirm our next move." He moved around the desk to sit in Millicent's chair. "Before we start, I wanted to let you know that Beren and I visited the security contractors for the care home."

Ooh, that was good news... I hoped. "What happened?"

"I had to influence them, but they've just hired Agent Cardinal. He's out of the van, but he'll be in the care home every night from seven. His shift will end at 5:00 a.m. If anything urgent transpires, he'll call Beren first. He'll travel to the van and Agent Cardinal will let him straight in. Beren, as you know, is our best healer, and of course, he has additional motivation to perform miracles because it's his aunt's life at stake."

"He won't be in any danger, will he?" asked Olivia.

James shook his head. "No. He'll be perfectly safe. Whoever is in the surveillance van will accompany Beren. We'll have more than enough agents to subdue our perpetrator. We're assuming it's one, or at the most two people, and none of them are black belts in karate." He grinned.

I snorted, thinking of the short, dweebie manager, petite Elizabeth, or elderly Penny. Yeah, it wouldn't take much to take any of them down… except maybe Elizabeth. She had a hard stare, and I would bet she'd be vicious in a fight.

Will handed his papers to James. "That's great news. Now, interviews. Where are we on those? And I don't know if Millicent had time to explain much, but this one looks like trouble."

James glanced at the information in his hand and met Will's gaze. "Yes, she did, but Olivia hadn't done all the research yet. Let me go through this first." He read through it. "Hmm. I think this would be a good opportunity to utilise Lily's unique skills. How do you feel about a trip to the hospital with your camera?"

That was unexpected. "Um, sure. What do you need?"

"I want you to take photos of Penny killing people."

"Oh, of course you do." That didn't sound like fun at all, but if my camera showed us what we needed, we'd know for sure if she was the murderer. "Okay. Can we go now? The sooner we get to the bottom of this, the better." I'd put a no-notice spell on myself, and I'd be able to wander in and out of whatever room I wanted.

"Will, can you go with her please?" James asked. "I've got way too much to do. I honestly don't know how Angelica keeps up with running multiple investigations at once."

"Of course I'll go with her. Someone needs to keep her out of trouble." He smirked.

"Just watch yourself, buddy. I can turn you into a toad, you know."

Olivia stared at me, mouth open. "Really? You could do that?"

I shrugged. "There's only one way to find out." I turned to Will and wiggled my fingers.

He folded his arms. "That's such a cliché, Lily. Try and be more original." The corners of his mouth twitched, ruining his serious façade. "Are you ready to go?"

"I'll just pop home and grab my camera."

"But you can just use your phone," said James.

"Yeah, I could, but the shot quality is definitely better, and I enjoy using my camera."

"But the phone is subtler to use. The no-notice spell should work, but every now and then, people can see past it, and if there are any witches there, they'll definitely notice you pointing a massive camera at people."

I pulled my phone out of my pocket and checked the charge. It had 60 percent. "Okay. I'm good to go. I will miss my camera though. I kind of feel naked without it." I placed my palm on my chest. It was so vacant.

Will pulled me in for a hug. "It's for a good cause."

I inhaled and sighed. He smelled almost as good as coffee. My face had a new favourite spot: his chest. It was firm, yet there was a slightly squishy layer on top, perfect for nuzzling into.

James cleared his throat. "Time's a wasting."

I looked at him. "You're just uncomfortable with us cuddling, aren't you?" I laughed.

He shook his head, then nodded. I snorted. "Always the big brother. Okay, let's get going. Oh, where *are* we going? I need the coordinates."

James sent the coordinates of the last hospital Penny had worked to both Will and me. I made my doorway, stuck the coordinates on the front, and walked through.

Before walking out of the cubicle, I cast my no-notice spell. A toilet flushed as I slipped out the door. I hurried through the hand-washing area and through the main door. The hallway looked like the typical hospital hallway from the seventies. The men's toilets were right next door to the women's, and Will came out at the same time as me. He grabbed my hand and looked down at me. It wasn't exactly the most romantic place, and we had a job to do, but the stupid butterflies in my stomach didn't know that. They were ready to party.

Will placed a soft kiss on my lips. "That's for good luck." He smiled.

"You know you don't need an excuse." I smiled. Using my magic to try and solve crimes was always a little nerve-wracking, but having him here made it easier. Agent Crankypants was fast becoming my rock.

"I know, but you do need luck. And it was killing two birds…"

I chuckled. Okay, I didn't like that word. Chuckling belonged in horror movies. Maybe it was because it sounded like Chuckie. A chuckle might sound like an evil laugh rather than a short, lesser-effort one. Hmm.

"Lily?"

"Um, sorry." I gave him my apologetic "whoops" face. It was one I used way too often. "So where's the cardiology ward?"

"I have no idea. We'll find the main hospital foyer, and there should be signs from there."

We set off down the corridor. One left turn, followed by a lift ride down one floor, and traversing two long corridors later, we reached the main entry.

Hospital visitors ambled in and out, some bearing flowers or teddy bears, others clutching each other and walking slowly. A few lucky people were leaving, newly released patients in tow.

A sign hanging from the ceiling, proclaiming Cardiology Ward, pointed straight ahead. It took us to a T-intersection where another sign pointed to the right.

The late afternoon hour meant dinner trays were being delivered. The fragrance of cooked meals wafted around me and made my mouth water. Crap. It reminded me that I hadn't eaten since twelve thirty. My stomach grumbled. I rubbed it. "Yeah, I know. I'll get you something when we're done here."

"What?" Will looked at me.

"Sorry. I wasn't talking to you."

His eyes widened. "Can you see actual ghosts now?"

I scrunched my face, my mouth in a *huh?* frown. "What?"

"Who were you talking to?"

I snickered. "My stomach. I haven't eaten since lunch, and I'm starving. That food actually smells delicious." I pointed to the trolley stacked with meals.

"When we're done here, I'll take you out, if you like."

Argh, the thought of going somewhere else after such a huge, and at times emotionally draining, day was more than I could bear. "What about we get Indian takeaway and go to Angelica's? I can ask Beren and Olivia if they want to join us."

Will smiled. "Good idea. Sounds nice."

"I'm already tired, and after using my magic for this"—I jerked my head towards one of the patient rooms—"the last thing I'll want to do is anything other than sink into the couch."

He rubbed my back, and I sighed. "I totally understand."

I took my phone out of my jacket pocket. That's one good thing that could be said for the PIB getup—pockets galore, even the women's suits. Someone got something right.

"I guess we're wasting our time taking any photos out

here. I'm going to have to go into the rooms. Will the no-notice spell be good enough? It's not like we're walking past in a public space where there are a lot of other people."

"It should be fine, unless we come across another witch, and then we may have some explaining to do, but if that happens, leave it to me. Okay?"

I nodded, nerves I didn't have much of before multiplying. I had to force myself to walk through the first door into a room containing four patients. I swallowed against the dryness in my mouth and pushed the door wider. Just inside the door, I shuffled to the side—I didn't have to go right in, but I didn't want to block the door. If anyone walked in, they'd crash into me, and I was pretty sure they would notice that. I tensed, waiting for one of the four patients to notice me. A nurse was taking someone's blood pressure. Phew. None of them looked my way.

I held my phone up, brought an image of the old lady at the care home into my mind, and whispered, "Show me Penny."

I started. She appeared right in front of me, on her way out of the room. One patient was in the bed nearest the door, to my right, but the other bed, closest to the window, had the curtain pulled. The other two beds were vacant. From the looks of Penny, it would have been at least ten years ago, probably more. She looked about sixty and walked with a straight back—nothing elderly about her here.

Okay, so I knew she'd definitely worked in this ward. It might have been tricky if they'd ever renovated and changed ward locations. We may have had to go through the whole hospital before finding where she'd been. I got in and out of the phone app to clear the screen. If she had killed patients, would she have put the curtain around the bed, or did she single out people in private rooms?

The more I thought about this, the more complicated it became. Wasn't that always the way? Why couldn't things just be straightforward for a change?

Hoping I wouldn't have to walk further into the room—to get on the other side of any closed curtains—I whispered, "Show me Penny killing someone."

In the bed closest to the window, but on the left-hand side, Penny stood with her back to me. I tiptoed closer to get a better look. The man in the bed clutched both hands to his chest. His face was contorted, his eyes scrunched shut, pain etched into his features. I took picture after picture as I neared. I reached the side of the bed and looked over the top of my phone—it wouldn't do to walk into the closed curtain. I edged carefully around it. There was a patient in the bed in real time.

*Please don't see me. Please don't see me.*

When I looked at my phone again, Penny's face was right in front of me. She looked even younger than in the last photo. Was this roughly the time she'd started working here?

She was looking down at the man, a satisfied smile on her face, her palms raised slightly facing him. Had she been performing a spell? Unfortunately, my talent didn't include picking up magic. But it was obvious he was in distress, and as a nurse, the least she should have done was help him, call someone, do something. But instead, she watched gleefully. I snapped the last of the photos, including one of the man's chart and the sign above his bed with his name, doctor, and procedure written on it, and lowered my camera.

The current occupant of the bed was eating his dinner and looking up at the TV screen mounted from the ceiling. *Phew*. He hadn't noticed me.

Ignoring the prickles on the back of my neck because I was exposed to everyone, I stood in the middle of the room. Again, I put in my request. I slowly turned in a circle, pointing my phone at each bed. And there, to my right near the window, she was again. Her greying hair was pulled back in a severe bun, and she grimaced, holding the slight old man down. Her palm pressed into his chest to stop him, it was clear he was attempting to sit up. Terror spewed from his eyes, no doubt giving Penny her fix. I shuddered. That poor man. I had no idea how she'd killed him, but I took the photos anyway and included a shot of his chart and of the whiteboard above his bed. Maybe Olivia could pull this patient's records, and we could piece together how she'd done it.

Will had quietly stepped into the room. He stared at me, his eyebrow raised. I pointed to the door, indicating we should go outside. I was pretty sure it was time to move into the next room. If we couldn't find anything there, we could come back here, and I'd ask that terrible question again. Goosebumps flamed across my arms at the thought of so many deaths in this small space. I mean, I knew people died in hospitals all the time, and that was creepy enough, but if your soul was dragged kicking and screaming to the afterlife, it was way worse.

Not that I believed in any of that, but still....

Back in the hallway, I inhaled deeply, as if I hadn't had a proper breath in hours. The constant fear of being discovered was like being held underwater, waiting for the wave to pass as you held your breath. Floating to the top and popping through the water to draw that first huge gulp of oxygen brought sweet, sweet relief.

"Are you okay?" Will's brows did that adorable wrinkly thing they did when he was concerned about me.

I gave him a small smile. "Yeah. I'll be fine. I just keep waiting for someone to see me. It's horrible. It's also icky and sad watching someone experience their last terrifying moments on earth. How can people get joy from killing someone? It's just... just...." I sighed.

He pulled me in for a hug and kissed the top of my head. "I know, Lily. But just think: because of you, we should be able to solve the murders of so many people. Not that it will bring them back, and I don't know if we can even punish someone with dementia, but maybe there's someone out there who needed answers to be at peace."

"But can we tell anyone? I mean, we can't show humans my photos. Maybe we could tell them our suspicions so they can begin an investigation, but are they going to rush to do it when it could mean millions in compensation to patients' families?"

He shrugged. "Let's not worry about it now. We need to save Angelica first."

"Good idea." I reluctantly stepped away from him and approached the next door. Stupid, evil witch. If it weren't for her, Angelica wouldn't be in danger, and Will's grandmother would be alive. This time, the door was wide open, revealing another room with four beds. Three were occupied by women—two looked to be in their fifties, and one was fairly young, maybe about thirty. That was way too young to have heart problems. The things people had to face that they shouldn't have to. I counted my blessings as I quietly walked into the room.

I whispered, "Show me Penny killing someone." I panned around the room, and there she was, again at the far end of the room near the window, at the bed on the right. This time, the patient looked to be asleep as she injected a syringe into his neck. Had she magicked him asleep? My heart thrummed a gazillion miles an hour as I approached the bed that was occupied in real time too.

I risked getting close so I could take all the necessary shots, including one of the extreme concentration on Penny's face. Even her tongue was sticking out in the universal sign of super focus. James came to mind. When we were young and we played video games, he would have his tongue sticking out half the time without realizing it. Normally, that memory would have made me smile, but not today.

When I was done, I went back to the door to make my

new request. I didn't want to be close to anyone while I was whispering, if I could help it, because they'd likely hear me.

"Show me the last time Penny killed someone in this room." My eyes widened, and my mouth dropped open. This… this was something I hadn't expected to see.

Oh my God.

There were three sleeping patients, oblivious to the murder happening in the middle of the room. Penny stood, her back to me. She faced another nurse, a young, slim woman, maybe in her thirties, with a straight dark fringe which settled above her distressed brown eyes. She clutched her chest, and as I clicked and walked to get a view from the side, it was apparent Penny was the cause of her distress.

Penny held her hands towards the nurse's chest. Her hands were in claw-like positions facing each other—it looked as if she was squeezing something. Something heart-sized. I kept pressing the button, taking as many shots as I could, until I lowered the phone and asked my magic to show me what happened five minutes after this scene. I'd never done that before, and I wasn't sure if it would work.

But it did.

The nurse lay on the floor on her back. Penny knelt on the floor next to her, along with another nurse and doctor who looked to be performing CPR, but I would imagine they were too late. The nurse's name tag was in my photos. I leaned over the scene: Rose. We'd have to check that out too, find out who she was.

I straightened. Again, I asked my magic to show me who else she'd killed in here, and when I was done, I'd move to the next room, and the next. All these people needed to have their stories heard.

By the time Will took me home, it was after ten, and I was too exhausted to eat. "Now that we're pretty sure it's her, is someone going to tell Angelica to be extra careful around her?"

"Already done. Beren's been keeping her up to date with our investigation."

I wasn't sure why, but I wasn't as relieved as I should've been. Angelica couldn't sleep with her eyes open, but at least Penny didn't have access to her magic.

Will gave me a squishy cuddle and a passionate kiss goodbye. I'd have to say that had been the highlight of my day, and I was reluctant to let go so he could leave. If only he could stay the night, but we were taking things slow. There was no way I was going to suggest it. I didn't want to look too desperate. Stupid dating conventions.

When I fell into bed, it was with a bruised heart and a head full of murder victims.

Now we just had to prove Penny was the care-home killer.

But nothing is ever that easy.

# CHAPTER 11

I slept in until eleven the next day. Will and I had an evening shift in the van. Before that, we were going into the PIB to have a meeting with James, Millicent, Olivia, Imani, Agent Cardinal, and Beren. It was funny; Agent Cardinal hadn't given me permission to use his first name, so I even thought of him as Agent Cardinal. Who knew I was so polite?

When I went down to make a coffee, there was a double-chocolate muffin on the table with a red ribbon around it. A note lay on the table next to it. *To my gorgeous Aussie witch. Thanks for all your hard work yesterday. I know it's not easy to see what comes through your lens, but it's appreciated. Will xx.*

Be still, my beating heart. I put my palm over said organ. Will was so considerate. What a sweetie. How had I ever thought he was just a cranky meanie? Oh, that's right:

because he had been. I chuckled. What a difference a few months made.

I magicked up a cappuccino and sat down to enjoy my brunch muffin. I sniffed the treat once before digging in. "Mmm." Heaven. I hadn't been to Costa for ages. When did life get so busy? It used to be that I wasn't allowed because I was in danger, and now I was still in danger, but I could look after myself a bit more. When I first got here, I was looking for things to do, but now time to relax and wander around had disappeared, like the muffin just had. I pouted. One muffin was never enough but not wanting to put on twenty kilos meant it was all I was having.

I dressed, grabbed my bag, and went to the PIB.

The reception-room door opened. "Hey, Gus, how have you been?" My shoulders tensed, waiting for a mention of poo or vomit.

"Very well, Miss Lily. Very well, thank you. How have you been?"

Phew! "Good, thanks. How's work going?" That should be a safe question. Not much gross stuff happened at work, and he wasn't allowed to bring his dog.

"Same old, same old. Oh! Except yesterday. The lads brought someone in—arrested some witch for making drugs and selling them to humans. They happened to arrest him when he was home, but he was only home and vulnerable because he had food poisoning. When I opened the reception-room door, oh my, the smell! He was covered in his own vomit, and so were two of the agents. I almost retched meself, I did."

I gagged and looked back the way I'd come, wondering if I should stop asking Gus questions altogether. There didn't seem to be a safe topic of conversation. He had a real knack for turning anything down the gross path. "In *that* reception room?"

"Ah no, we have another one, closer to the cells. Mainly used for bringing in the crims. When we're busy, they bring 'em up here. Anyway, you should've seen it! There were even carrot chunks." He shook his head and laughed.

Yeah, very funny.

"Oh, look, Gus. We're here already." I turned to him and smiled. "Have a wonderful day!"

He smiled. "You too, Miss Lily." He opened the conference-room door and stepped back to tip his hat at me. I hurried through.

As usual, I was the last to arrive. If this kept happening, I'd end up with a major case of paranoia. I checked the time on my phone—I was actually four minutes early. James sat at the head of the table. A pendulum of pride and worry swung inside me. He was doing an awesome job, but Angelica was in danger.

Beren sat on James's left, then Olivia next to him, and Will. Millicent sat on his right, then Imani, and Agent Cardinal. I took the other head of the table near Will.

"Hi, Lily." Imani waved as I passed.

"Hi, Imani." I smiled. She was so nice. Warmth shot through my chest at the thought that I might have actually found another person here who I really liked.

"Hey, Lily." Olivia smiled. I returned her greeting, then said hello to everyone else.

"Okay, that's everyone," said James. "I'm calling this meeting to order. First on the agenda, Agent Cardinal starts his first shift tonight watching the security cameras."

Beren nodded. "Nice work."

James continued, "Second on the agenda: Agent DuPree had a quick chat with Ma'am this afternoon. She said the most likely suspect is Penny, but she's not ready to call it yet. She's not convinced Penny has the steady hand it would have taken to administer the needle that killed Agent Blakesley's grand-mother. Third on the agenda is our review of the video footage. Penny wandered the hallway last night until she was caught by one of the staff and put back to bed. According to the records, most murders have happened at night, which is a prime time for Penny to sneak around." He clasped his hands on the table in front of him. "I'm in no way calling this investigation early, but together with other evidence we've found linking Penny to several unexpected hospital deaths a few years ago, it's looking like she's our main suspect. But we have to catch her in the act." Thankfully he didn't mention how they got that evidence. But how long would it be before my secret got out?

I put up my hand.

"Yes, Lily?"

"Can't we just leave our cameras in there and get Ma'am out?"

James shook his head and gave me a firm look. "We've been through this, Lily. There is no other way. We can't get cameras in other people's rooms without risking being caught. Ma'am has the only cameras that make it into a room. I'm afraid we'll need to keep her in there till we catch the culprit."

Millicent looked at me, a sympathetic expression on her face, but she didn't say anything. As an agent, she knew whatever James decided, went. Besides, once James or Ma'am made up their mind on something, that was the end of discussion. James had been like that growing up too. Especially if he thought it was for the best, there was never any way to influence him.

"Fourth, we're crossing one of our suspects off the list. The manager was only on-site when two of the assumed murders were committed. Most deaths have occurred at night or early in the morning. His hours are from 8:00 a.m. to 6:00 p.m. All employees use an electronic system to clock in and out, so it's easy to prove. I also don't think he has motive. The care home doesn't benefit financially from having a higher turnover. Unless he's a psychopath who enjoys the kill, there's no reason he would want his residents dead."

James had a good point, and to be honest, after all the photos I'd just taken at the hospital, he was pretty much off the hook. I mean, what were the chances of more than one serial killer being at the same care home? Oh, crap. "Um, James."

"Yes, Lily?"

"What if we're dealing with a team... like more than

one killer? It's probably unlikely two serial killers are there together, but it's possible."

Millicent and James looked at each other, and everyone else looked at me, surprised faces slowly relaxing to thinking. Beren said, "Hmm, that's a possibility. But who would you peg for the other killer? Also, it's not really a crime that needs an accomplice." He scrunched his nose and shook his head. "Nah, I'm not really seeing it. It was a good suggestion though, and I guess we could keep our options open in that regard."

James looked at me. "I agree with Agent DuPree. I think it's unlikely, but it's not impossible, and who knows; maybe you're right, Lily."

"Don't worry. It was just a suggestion. You didn't have to agree." I shrugged. I really wasn't worried. It just popped into my head, and I was the queen of saying random stuff that just popped into my head, usually and unfortunately without thinking whether it was appropriate or not. If only my magic worked in the care home, all our problems would be solved. Although, they wouldn't really. I mean, we'd know who it was, but we wouldn't have proof as to how we knew, which meant we'd still have to wait for the culprit— probably Penny—to try to kill someone so we could catch them at it.

James shifted his gaze to Will. "Do you need an extra agent in the van to replace Agent Cardinal?"

"No. We're fine. The three of us have good concentration, and then you have the extra eyes that go through the videos later. Imani has enough tech knowledge to solve any issues we might have as well." Will gave her a nod, and she smiled.

"Okay, good. I think we're done here, people." James and Millicent shared a loving smile before he made his doorway and disappeared.

There were still a few hours until we had to be in the van. "Olivia. Do you need any help with research?" I asked.

She shook her head. "No, but thanks for asking. Most of our searches haven't raised any red flags. And the ones that have are under control."

"Liv, I need you for another case that James is working on." Millicent came over. "Sorry, Lily, but I'm going to have to take her away."

I smiled. "It's okay. Maybe I'll go for a run or something." I wasn't into watching TV, and I was too antsy to sit and read. The longer Angelica stayed in that care home, the worse I felt. The time of her murder was fast approaching. My magic had never predicted a death more than twenty-four hours before it happened that I knew of. There was that guy at Sydney airport. I had no idea when he ended up dying, but the bride's father at the wedding I'd photographed and the older woman at Paris airport both died within hours of my camera predicting it.

Imani put her hand up. "I'll go with you. I run every day, and I haven't had one today."

"Really?"

"Yes, really." She smiled, revealing her straight, super-white teeth.

"Wow, thanks. Not that I mind running by myself, but

I'm supposed to have company." I wasn't sure how much I should tell her, but then Will jumped in.

"Years ago, Lily's parents went missing. We think the same people who took them are after her now. We don't know why, but it's just not safe for her to be out and about by herself."

"I'll stay alert, Will. It would be my pleasure to make sure she's safe."

I folded my arms. "Will, you didn't have to tell her. You know I can pretty much look after myself. My magic is way better now than it was when I got here." I thought back to when I'd arrived and knew absolutely nothing about magic. I really had come a long way, although I wasn't a superstar at it yet. I turned to Imani. "Sorry to put that pressure on you. If you don't want to come, it's okay."

"Don't be silly. I'm always alert when I run—you never know what weirdo might be waiting around the next corner." She winked.

I smiled. "Argh, so true. Okay, I'm going to pop home and get changed, and then we can meet somewhere. Where do you want to run?"

"Hyde Park? I love London. Don't get up there enough."

"Okay. I've never run there before. I'd love to."

"Here are the coordinates for the toilets next to the lake." Big golden numbers popped into my head. I took a mental photo and stored it in my "coordinates" folder. I was beginning to think of my brain in terms of a computer. It just made it easier to decide what to call things. Yes, I had a memory, but that had different compartments, I supposed.

"Awesome. I'll see you there in ten." I turned to Will. "And I'll see you in the van." I waggled my eyebrows.

He laughed. "If only it wasn't for work." He returned my eyebrow waggle. "I'll see you later. Stay safe."

"I will. Bye, everyone." I waved at my friends and left.

AFTER MY RUN, I WENT HOME, HAD A LATE LUNCH, showered, and dressed. I would have showered first, but knowing me, I would've spilled food all over my PIB uniform. I supposed I could have magicked it out, but I kept forgetting it was possible. Travelling had become second nature, but cleaning had not. How unusual for me....

Running in Hyde Park had been awesome. There were so many squee-worthy squirrels, and I'd gotten to know Imani a bit better. She was such a nice person, so bubbly, and she got my stupid sense of humour. I'd needed that outlet to banish my nervous energy. Each hour that passed ratcheted up my nerves. I'd be in a full-blown panic within two days. I didn't do suspense well. If there was a show on TV, and I knew something bad was going to happen, I usually had to get up and walk away. I just couldn't stand it.

When I wasn't in the van, I waited for the phone call telling me Angelica was dead. Nausea bubbled in my stomach and up my throat, disturbing my lunch. I mentally pulled up my big-girl pants, swallowed, and travelled to the van.

I slid the black curtain across. Three male agents I hadn't met were saying their farewells to Imani and Will. The new agents eyeballed me, but no one said hello. One by one, they disappeared through their doorways. "Friendly bunch."

Will smiled. "That lot are all about the job. They don't have time for chitchat. Even with someone as adorable as you." He gave me a hug, which was quite demonstrative for him in front of another agent, but I had a feeling Imani knew we were dating. I hadn't said anything, but maybe Will had, and she seemed like the kind of person who wouldn't care.

"Thanks for running with me today," I said to Imani.

"My pleasure, love. It was good to get out, and you kept a good pace. If you ever need anyone to run with, let me know. In fact, I'll give you my number."

Aw, how sweet. I'd definitely take her up on that. Will wasn't always available, and even though I felt confident I could at least pop away if anything happened, I was more relaxed having another agent around. Will sat in front of the monitors and started work, and I pulled out my phone. Imani gave me her number. I put it in and sent her a text so she had my details.

Imani and I sat at our places and observed. It was both a relief and a grim reminder of the situation when the teddy showed Angelica's see-through form. She was in the common lounge watching a small children's choir. I remembered doing that once when I was about nine. The teachers had taken our school choir to perform at the local old people's home. I'd been excited at the time, but I wondered if it was more torture than fun for the oldies. These kids weren't very talented, and I imagine we hadn't been either. A screechy high note stabbed through the din. I slammed my hands over my ears and winced. Yikes.

Apparently Angelica's patience lasted only so long, even when she was undercover. She stood, and her voice came through loud and clear. "I need the bathroom. Now!" she shouted. The choir stuttered but kept going. They got ten points for professionalism. I smirked. People thinking you were demented had its uses. You could be inappropriate, and no one would say a word.

Elizabeth—the real Elizabeth, not Penny the pretend Elizabeth—a scowl on her face, appeared at Angelica's side. She grabbed her arm. Although it looked gentle enough, Angelica said, "Ow! You're hurting me."

Elizabeth grinned through gritted teeth. "I'm hardly touching you." Then she whispered, "Do you want help to the bathroom or not? Because I can leave you here to soil yourself. And you can miss out on the Queen's visit tomorrow."

Angelica didn't respond, and I could no longer see her face, but she started moving slowly. Elizabeth's true nature was coming out. If we didn't have so much information on Penny, I would have pegged Elizabeth as the killer. She was probably just a mean person who had no patience. This was totally not the job for her. And what did she mean by the

Queen's visit? Surely Queen Elizabeth II had better things to do than visit a care home?

Something niggled at me. I looked at Will. "Does something seem off to you?"

He met my gaze. "Other than the fact she's being horrible to Angelica and I wonder if she was the same to my grandmother, no."

"That's it!" I knew something was familiar.

"What's it?" Will's brows drew down. He could practically have a conversation without using his mouth. His brows could do all the talking.

"Do you remember your gran mentioned the Queen visiting? I thought she was living in a fantasy land, but maybe she wasn't as bad as you thought."

Will stared at the screen for a minute. He turned to me. "You're right, Lily. But it might not mean anything. Maybe it's a thing they do for the residents, pretend the Queen is visiting to cheer them up. Didn't they give her chocolates or something?"

"I think so." My memory wasn't the best, but I was pretty sure chocolate was mentioned. I remembered that because, well, chocolate.

After going to the bathroom, Angelica insisted on going back to her room. Elizabeth saw her to the door before she was called to another incident in the common room. Angelica went into her room and shut the door. She whispered into her bear, "Let me know when the coast is clear. I'm going to visit Penny's room. She hasn't been around today, and she normally joins me for breakfast. It's a good excuse for me to visit, see if she's okay while I search for evidence."

"Okay." Will looked at the screen showing the hallway. "Coast is clear. I'll let you know when someone's coming."

Angelica wandered out, teddy in her arms. She must've been cuddling it to her chest with its head poking over her shoulder to give us a view behind her. Clever. No one could sneak up on her now.

"Still clear," said Will.

My heartbeat increased as she neared Penny's room. The camera in the common room near the plant didn't show the whole room. From what it did show, Penny wasn't there. I wasn't sure what the protocol on residents visiting each other was, but surely they were allowed?

Angelica reached the door and knocked. There was no answer. She opened the door and shuffled in, as if she had every right to be there. She quietly shut the door behind her.

Framed movie posters covered the walls—*Witches of Eastwick, Silence of the Lambs, Shrek, The Three Amigos,* and *The Lovely Bones.* Um, what an eclectic mix. It was the two serial-killer movies that worried me, though. Yeah, I was smart like that. I did wonder what she thought of the portrayal of witches in the *Witches of Eastwick,* though. Hmm, were there any witches in Hollywood? There probably were. Everyone deserved representation.

Angelica's gaze panned the room and finally rested on the empty bed. She whispered, "She's not here. She may have had a family day. They do take them out every now and then." She moved to the bedside drawers and opened them one by one. After finding nothing of note in any of the three drawers, she moved to the wardrobe.

Will said into the microphone, "Someone's coming down the hallway. One of the male nurses."

Angelica quickly shut the cupboard door and sat in a chair. She sure moved quickly for an old person. I chuckled.

"Okay, he's at the lift. Two residents are shuffling in your direction, but I think it's safe for you to finish what you were doing."

She hurried back to the wardrobe and slid the clothes across, then bent down and rifled through Penny's shoes. "I wondered where these went!" She pulled out a pair of white unicorn slippers with big eyes and multi-hued horns jutting out from the front. "They went missing yesterday. The people here are a bunch of kleptomaniacs. I'm keeping these. I'll tell her one of the nurses gave them back if she says anything." Angelica set the rest of the shoes to rights when she was done. She tapped on the back of the wardrobe, no doubt checking for a false wall. "Nothing," she whispered. "I could really use my magic about now."

She shut the cupboard, patted down the bed, and looked under the pillow. "Nothing." Her tone was jagged with frustration.

"Hallway is clear if you want to leave," said Will.

Angelica returned to her room without incident, and my shoulders relaxed as soon as she was safely inside. My neck ached, and I massaged it. Being a spectator was much more stressful than living it. When you were in it, you didn't have as much time to worry. Plus, I couldn't help from out here.

Someone knocked on Angelica's door but opened it without waiting for an answer. The old guy who had chatted to her at breakfast the other morning entered and shut the door behind him. My stomach dropped, and I gasped.

"Lily, what's wrong?" Will asked.

I almost blurted it out but caught myself in time. "I just have a *funny feeling* about old Winston. I hate when I can't see things *clearly*." If that wasn't enough of a hint for him, I didn't know what was. His eyes widened ever so slightly, and he gave me a nod.

Winston spoke with the good side of his mouth. "Sorry, didn't mean to alarm you. But I thought you'd like to hear the news."

"What news?" Angelica asked.

"They found Penny in the cool room."

"Well, that's silly of her. What was she doing in there?"

He hung his head before meeting Angelica's gaze again. "She's not silly. She's dead."

And there went our number-one suspect. And why hadn't she been ghostly when I'd seen her on the teddy-cam? Seemed my magic was fallible.

Angelica's next words summed things up nicely. "Oh dear. That was unexpected." She held up her teddy and looked into its eyes. "What are we going to do now, Mr Teddy?"

The teddy silently stared back at her.

What were we going to do, indeed?

# CHAPTER 12

Two hours later, and Angelica was having home-delivered pizza. The care home had to quarantine the cool room because someone had died in there. But had Penny died, or had she been murdered? Angelica did her best to find out, but she had to rely on overhearing news. Speaking to the residents wasn't helpful. Most of them were in their own little worlds and had no idea whether it was day or night, nor did they care.

Angelica sat at a table with her new friend, the old guy who'd spilled the news of Penny's death.

Winston swallowed his mouthful of pizza and laughed. "Best food I've had here in two years."

Angelica nodded. "I'm sad. Penny was nice to me."

Winston shrugged. "There are always casualties in a place like this. They think I don't know, but they sent me here to die."

"Who?"

"The government. They know I know what they're up to. They don't want to risk me telling everyone their secrets." He gave an exaggerated wink. "I was a spy in the war, you know."

Angelica didn't bother to comment on his revelation, which was probably a product of the fantasy land Winston resided in. Instead, she picked the teddy up and put it next to her ear. Her hair rustled through the microphone as it rubbed against the teddy's eyes. "Teddy wants to know how Penny died. Do you know?"

"No, but I have my suspicions." He looked around as if searching for eavesdroppers. He leaned forward, over his plate, and whispered loudly. "She might have just dropped dead, but how did she get to the cool room? It's downstairs, where we aren't allowed to go. I haven't been able to crack the lift code, and I doubt she could have either." He shook his head. "I don't have the clearance I used to."

"Hmm," was her only answer.

They finished dinner, and Angelica made her way to the common room to watch TV and likely listen for gossip. While she watched some British cop show, our dinner arrived. Lasagne and salad from the PIB cafeteria. Oh, and they'd brought me a large cappuccino. I inhaled my favourite scent and sighed.

"Careful, love, or you'll float into space." Imani laughed.

"What? Isn't this a normal reaction to caffeine?"

She lifted her cup. "Tea all the way, love. I don't like coffee."

I frowned. "Just when I thought you were awesome, you go and ruin everything." I sighed and slumped further down into my chair.

She laughed, and I couldn't hold my grumpy expression. I grinned. "I guess nobody's perfect."

"I'm close, though." She winked.

"Very true."

I took my first forkful of lasagne. Ooh, it was good. Mmm. I'd just taken my second bite when Beren showed up to see Angelica.

I tried swallowing and choked. Tears sprang to my eyes, but it wasn't from coughing. Will smacked my back till I stopped choking. I drew some much-needed breaths.

"Lily, what's wrong? It can't taste that bad." Will rubbed my back and bent slightly to stare at my downturned face.

This could not be happening. Could. Not. Be.

But it was.

I turned waterlogged eyes his way. "It's Beren."

Will's face drained of colour. He knew what I meant.

My eyes drifted back to the screen, drawn beyond my control. Beren and Angelica moved to her room and shut the door.

"Will, you have to tell him."

He stared at the screen. "What if it distracts him?"

"What's going on?" asked Imani.

Will and I both turned to her. I opened my mouth, not sure what to say. I shut it. Will, thankfully, jumped in. "Lily has a talent that works on and off. She can see if someone is in danger." He'd altered the truth, but it was good enough for now and vague enough that no one would hunt me down because of it.

Imani narrowed her eyes as she stared at me. Okay, so tears were extreme for just danger, but we couldn't risk telling her the truth. "Once before, someone died when I saw they were in danger. I'm paranoid. Beren's one of my best friends, so if it seems like I'm overreacting, that's why."

She nodded. Phew. Excuse believed.

Will grabbed his phone and texted someone. He finished and looked up. Imani and I were both focussed on him. "I texted Agent Cardinal. Asked him to be hypervigilant."

"Good idea," I said.

Beren's voice filled the van, and we all jerked our heads to watch the screens. He was looking at Angelica, answering a question we hadn't heard her ask. "That's too dangerous. If they catch me, our cover will be blown. We don't know who it is." He shook his phantasmal head.

I grabbed Will's arm—I didn't care if it was professional or not. I had begging to do. "You have to tell him. Nothing's changed. It's going to happen, Will. Tell him. Maybe it will be enough to save him." I bit my lip, another tear slipping from my eye.

Will gazed down at me, cupped my jaw with one hand, and wiped the tear away with his thumb. I wanted so badly to sink into his chest, have his arms around me, but that wasn't a line I'd cross at work, and why was I falling apart? I needed to fight for my friends, not trust everything to my talent. I'd given up before I'd even started. "You need to tell him. Put yourself in his shoes. What would you want?"

Will switched the microphone on. "Angelica, it's Will. Lily's seen *trouble* for Beren too." He could have texted Beren. Maybe he thought he needed Angelica's approval to give him such shocking information?

She must have been taken aback because she'd had some kind of reaction that Beren noticed. He leaned towards her. "What's wrong?" His brows drew down. "Angelica, talk to me?"

"I can't call off this investigation. You know that, Will."

Will shut his eyes, and his head fell forward. He massaged his forehead with one hand. So, he'd been hoping she'd get them both out of there.

"Dammit! Why not?" I knew I was out of line, but what the hell? I was ready to run in there and scream the place down, ruin it for them.

It was Will's turn to grab my arm. His sad eyes bored into mine, and he shook his head. "Arguing with her won't make any difference."

Angelica's voice filtered through. "Beren, dear, Lily's seen something. My fate is yours, but we must see this through. I'm sorry, but this will be our only chance to catch whoever's doing this."

"Is it worth your lives? Really? They're old people. You're both too valuable, too young," I pleaded, tears freely sliding down my face. "Surely there'll be another chance in a week or a month?"

The calm in Angelica's voice made me want to scream. "And how many others will die before then? Whatever happens to us, you'll have on camera. These people will be caught, and they won't be able to hurt anyone else."

"But what if it's all for nothing? What if you die and we still don't catch them?"

"That's nonsense, Lily. If you can't be quiet, you need to go home. I can't be having this conversation."

Someone knocked on the door. Beren turned. The door swung slowly inwards. There was a sharp intake of breath, and Beren said, "Will!" Then, before I could see who was coming in, our screens went black.

"What the hell?" Will growled and pressed some keys. His tapping noises turned to loud, keyboard-destroying finger pounds when it wouldn't work. "Shit, shit, shit!" He snatched his phone from the table and dialled. "What's going on in there, Cardinal? We've got nothing here." Will ran his hands through his hair as he listened. "Forget about fixing it. Get up there…. What do you mean the lights are out? Don't they have a generator…? Just get up there. We're coming in." Will hung up and shoved his phone into his top jacket pocket.

"Imani, we're going in." Will pulled out the "toolbox," mumbled a few words, and four handguns plus extra ammo appeared in mid-air. Imani grabbed two of each, and Will grabbed the rest. Will looked at me. "Call Millicent. Tell her we have a code red and that we've gone in. Then wait here. Do you understand?"

My mouth went dry, and my heart pounded a thousand beats per minute. I had to push the words out. "Call Millicent. Stay here."

Will slammed his lips against mine for an instant.

Then Imani hauled the van door open, and they both jumped out.

He was already gone when my words finally came.

"Stay safe, Will."

I bit my fingernail and called Millicent.

"Hi, Lily. What's up?" She sounded happy. I was about to ruin her day.

"Will and Imani have just stormed the care home, if two people can storm.... Will said to tell you it's a code red. Someone was walking into Angelica's room when Beren called out to Will and the transmission went black, and all the care-home lights went out. Will spoke to Agent Cardinal and told him to go to Angelica's room, but that's all I know." I shifted from foot to foot. I needed to get outside and see what was going on.

Millicent left me hanging for a minute. Her spritely tone had changed to serious and businesslike when she finally said, "Okay. You stay put. I'll have other agents there in a jiffy. You'll have to point out the care home."

"Okay."

"Bye, Lily." She hung up before I could say goodbye.

Despite being told to stay there, I jumped out of the van and ran around to take a look at the care home. All the lights were off. Evening had taken hold, so there was hardly any natural light either. It wouldn't have been impossible to see in there, but it wouldn't be easy. God, I hoped everyone was okay. What was happening inside? I resisted the urge to run in and help. I returned to the van in time to greet the six agents as they exited the cubicle one by one. Five beefy men and one super-fit-looking woman. They were in full black protective gear and heavily armed.

Things just got crazy serious.

"The care home is this way." I jumped out of the van and jogged to the middle of the road. I pointed. "There it is. The room you want is on the first floor. Third window from the right. That smaller one there." They'd likely been provided with a map of the place, but I wanted things to be as clear as possible.

"Thanks," an agent with a buzzcut said. He gestured to his comrades, and they bolted to the front doors, their boots slapping rhythmically on the bitumen as they crossed the road. Without even testing to see if the doors were unlocked first, they kicked them in and disappeared inside.

I stared at the care home, but there was no sign of what was going on inside. Were Angelica and Beren dead? I took a shaky breath and shook my head. There was no way I was going to stay here. Surely everyone knew I wasn't going to stay put just because they'd told me to. I mean, this was *me* we were talking about. Last time, though, when I'd ignored that order in Paris, I'd been kidnapped at gunpoint, and it had resulted in me killing one of the gang who was after me —not an ideal situation, and not one I wanted to repeat. But this time I hadn't started anything, and many of the people in there were people I loved. Losing one, let alone three of them, was not an option.

I didn't have a weapon, and I wasn't about to go and grab a gun from the van when I had no idea how to use it. I was likely to shoot myself or someone I was trying to save rather than a bad guy.

I went back inside the van and took a deep breath to calm myself. They'd told me to stay put. *Please do what they want, just once, Lily.* I clenched my hands into fists and looked at the black screens. I leaned over and pressed random keys on the keyboards, trying to get the screens to work. Argh, nothing!

That was it. I couldn't stand here in an empty plumbing van looking at equally empty screens when my friend's lives were on the line.

I leapt out of the van, a total failure at doing what I'd been told. I'd work on my dismal obedience skills later. After dashing across the street, I yanked a brick out of the edging of the care-home garden bed. Ooh, great! This would be ideal for bashing in someone's head. Hmm, since when had I gotten so happy about finding ways to hurt people? Angelica's influence had definitely rubbed off on me.

I rolled my shoulders back, bounded onto the front porch, and ran through the front entry.

I only hoped I got to them in time.

# CHAPTER 13

As I made my way down the entry hall, screams and shouts reached me. At least only non-dementia patients were on the ground floor. The staff would have better luck keeping them contained. Faint light filtered in from the front entry, but the further down the hall I went, the darker it became.

I reached the reception area. Squinting and blinking did nothing to help me see. But lighting on the walls, about five inches from the floor, stuttered to life—emergency lighting. Phew. That was definitely better than nothing.

No one manned the reception desk, whether it was because it was after hours or because of the unfolding drama, I couldn't tell. I was pretty sure the lift wouldn't be working, but I hurried over and tried it anyway.

Nope. The little button refused to light up when I pressed it. And I couldn't hear any noise indicating the car was moving. I jerked my head this way and that. Where were the stairs? Where would the stairs have been when it had been a house? Oh, there was a lit sign on the wall further down the corridor. I jogged to it. It was a map of the care home with all emergency exits shown in red, and there were the stairs.

I had to backtrack to the reception area, then keep going. Thumping came from above. This part of the building was the older section with timber floors. Looked as if all the action was upstairs. I hadn't seen a soul on the ground floor, which was eerie and worrying. Where had everyone gone?

I reached the small open area that held the original staircase. Emergency lights lit every third tread, and I could just make out the dark timber banister rising into the darkness.

As I warily climbed the stairs, a scream spilled down. Was that a resident or Angelica? Nah, I couldn't see her as a screamer. She was a battle-hardened PIB agent. She wouldn't scream—she'd be the reason someone else would scream. But what if in her moment of truth, when she was being murdered, she just let loose?

My heartbeat throbbed in my neck. Adrenaline had turned my legs to jelly, and my breathing came too fast. I did my best to slow it. I focussed on the brick, on its coarse texture, the comforting weight of it. I tightened my fingers around it till they ached. As I neared the top step, I was as ready as I ever would be.

I stopped and took a breath, held it to listen. A long, drawn-out but muffled groan followed by muted shouting made me clench my jaw. I remembered to breathe. The door to the top floor must be closed, which was a surprise. Why hadn't the agents kicked that in too? Maybe someone had opened it for them?

I tackled the final step to the landing. My eyes had adjusted to what little light existed. The door to the upper-floor hallway was in front of me. I reached out and tried the handle. It wouldn't budge. Damn! But it made total sense since it gave access to the fire stairs. It would likely open towards me from the other side. Should I knock, or would that distract the agents at the wrong time?

Maybe there was a different way to the first floor? Argh. I didn't have time to look. Would it matter if I broke this door down? "Ha ha. As if you're going to be strong enough to do that," I whispered to myself. *Stop being stupid and think, Lily.*

Maybe I could go outside and use magic to float to the top of the building and break a window to get in? I was pretty sure the magic ban only worked when you were inside the walls. But there was the little matter that I didn't know how to fly with magic.

Stuff it. I banged on the door.

No one answered. The door being fire-rated, my fist hadn't been loud against the solidness. I tried again, putting in enough effort that it hurt when I pounded. Still nothing. I growled, but I really wanted to scream. My friends could be being murdered right now.

I couldn't let it happen.

I ran down the stairs and out the front door, managing

not to trip in the gloom. The front yard held a couple of trees, some bushes, and grass. It wasn't too difficult to reach the part that was under Angelica's window. I tilted my head back and looked up. Nothing happening at her window, but she was in there, maybe dead already. No, I couldn't think like that, or I'd collapse into a crying heap. I blinked back tears and gritted my teeth.

I wouldn't give in.

So how was I going to get up there? There was nothing to climb on. Yes, I'd thought of floating up there, but I didn't even know if it was possible. Was I strong enough to support my weight with magic? Oh my God, I was so stupid! I slapped my forehead. Of course!

I mumbled a spell. "There's an extension ladder in Angelica's shed. Travel it to me now before everyone's dead." Hmm, that rhymed, but it was terrible. If everyone was dead, maybe it wouldn't turn up.

The aluminium ladder appeared at my feet. I wrestled with the extension function, but finally, I had it all stretched out and locked in. Now I just had to rest it against the wall. I grunted. It was heavy. I was such a crap witch. I rolled my eyes at my own stupidity.

I dropped the ladder on the ground, dipped into my magic, and said, "Ladder lying at my feet, rise to stand and lean against the wall, so that window up there I can reach." I pointed to Angelica's window. The spell didn't really rhyme, but whatever. I didn't have time to appease the poetic spell gods right now.

Tiredness swept through me as the ladder lifted and

settled in place. Once the ladder stopped moving, the drain on my powers stopped, and I felt okay. Except I yawned. There'd be plenty of time for a nap later… I hoped. For all I knew, I could be about to meet the same fate as Angelica and Beren. I hadn't taken any photos of myself lately, for good reason. I really didn't want to know when my time was up. I'd say it was the only surprise I approved of. Well, not the surprise of dying itself, just that I didn't want to know what was happening until it was all over. And even then, I wouldn't know it had happened because I'd be dead, so did that mean dying suddenly wouldn't even be a surprise? I shook my head. Going off on these tangents was slowing me down. And yes, it was a double standard that I had wanted Will to tell Beren he was going to die, but that was because I had a pretty good idea he was going to be attacked inside the care home, and maybe being forewarned could have helped.

I gripped the sides of the ladder and climbed using one hand and one elbow—the brick stayed in my left hand. Halfway up, I wobbled. My heart shot to my feet, but it eventually came back up, and I continued. Gah, I was not cut out for this stuff. I wasn't even an agent, for goodness' sake. Well, if I had been one, I would have been about to lose my job for ignoring orders.

And there it was. Angelica's window. The blind was down, which would protect anyone inside from flying glass. This brick was coming in handy. Who knew a brick could have so many uses? It deserved to win building material of the year, except there was no such competition. Lucky it didn't have feelings, or I imagine it would have been disappointed, not to mention the headache I was about to inflict on it.

I swapped the brick to my right hand, raised my arm behind my head, and before I could debate with myself about what a stupid idea this was, I wrenched my arm forward and smashed the brick against the middle of the window. It didn't give. In fact, it bounced, and I jerked back, almost losing my balance and falling. Gripping the ladder, I tried to slow my racing heart. I glanced down. I would probably survive if I fell since I'd be landing on grass, but it would likely result in broken bones. This was going to be harder than I thought.

I took a deep breath, gritted my teeth, and smashed the brick into it again, bracing for potential bounce back. But my aim was off, and instead of hitting the middle of the window, the brick connected lower down, which made an interesting *crunch* and no rebound. Hmm. I stepped down one rung and loaded my arm. I grunted as it connected with the window. *Crunch*. Cracks spiderwebbed out. I bashed it again and again. Finally, a hole! But that was just the first layer. Damn double-glazed windows.

On the other side of this glass was Beren and Angelica. I had to hurry.

I gripped the ladder with one hand and kept striking with my trusty brick. Eventually, the glass disintegrated into small beads.

Shrieking came from inside. I smacked more glass out,

until the hole was big enough, and jumped in, fighting with the blinds to gain access.

Shouting came from the hallway outside Angelica's room. I stood, brick poised in both hands, ready to strike anyone who came at me. The problem was, I couldn't see much. But if I couldn't see very well, neither could they. There looked to be three people in the room—one lying on the bed, which was probably Angelica—one taller than me and one shorter, both standing next to the bed.

"Who do we have here?" a woman's voice said. I recognised that voice.

Elizabeth.

Where was Beren? I blinked, hoping it would help me see better. Nope. Then I remembered my phone. I held the brick at the ready in my left hand and snatched my phone out of my back pocket with my right. I enabled torch mode and shone the light in their direction.

Elizabeth stood next to... was that her boyfriend from the other day? Yes, I was pretty sure it was. Angelica was lying on the bed, eyes closed. Elizabeth held up a syringe and grinned. "If you're here to save her, you're too late." And was that a crown on her head? *Queen Elizabeth*. So Will's gran hadn't imagined anything. Anger prickled every inch of my skin when I thought of how terrified she must have been. I dug my fingers into the brick and sized up whether I could run around the bed and smash Elizabeth's head in. That might be somewhat violent, but I would do anything to make sure she didn't get away.

Someone banged on the door. "Open up. If you

surrender without hurting anyone, we'll show you leniency."
Will! If he knew I was in here, he would rush in, and he
totally should. It was too late—Angelica was probably
already dead. There was nothing to lose.

Elizabeth yelled back. "Come in, and we'll kill them all."
Hang on, what did she mean: all? There had only been
Angelica, and now there was me, so didn't that make us a
"both?"

I looked down. My eyes widened. Beren lay on the floor,
face slack, eyes closed. Was that blood on his face? "What
did you do to him?" God, no. They couldn't both be
dead. No!

"And you're next." On her command, her boyfriend
slowly made his way around the bed, a solid-looking bar in
his hand. Well, I wasn't going to stay silent like those idiots
on TV that should have yelled when they were told to keep
quiet. Plus, keeping quiet or doing what I was told wasn't
my forte.

I opened my mouth and screamed. "Bash the door
down. They're dead, Will. They're dead!" Then I shrieked
as ear-piercingly as I could. Might as well make Elizabeth
and her evil partner suffer as much as possible.

My ears rebelled at the almighty thump and crack as the
door splintered inwards. I fell to the ground to avoid being
hit by flying debris, plus I could probably do some damage
with my brick. Elizabeth's boyfriend was distracted, so I
leaned across and smashed his shin as hard as I could. *Good
brick*.

He screamed and bent to clutch his shin. His head was

irresistibly close, so I drove the brick into it. He fell forward and collapsed on top of me. Booted feet shuffled into the room, and Will yelled, "Get down!"

"I'll never surrender! Death to all witches!" Elizabeth shrieked.

Will yelled, "She's got a knife!"

A gun went off, exploding my eardrums.

*Not again.* I curled into a ball and vowed that next time there was an assignment, I was wearing earplugs. The guy on top of me hadn't moved, and he was kind of heavy, but I wasn't game to leave the relative shelter of his body, but if he woke up, I could be in trouble. Decisions, decisions…

More stomping of booted feet. "Secure!" someone shouted. "Medics in here, now! Get Ma'am and Agent Bianchi out, now!"

"Lily? Lily, are you in here?" Will. He must have recognised my voice from before. It sounded as if things were relatively under control. I struggled but managed to squirm out from underneath Elizabeth's boyfriend.

I stood, and someone flashed a torch beam in my face. I squinted and put my hand in front of my eyes. "Hey. Do you mind?"

"Sorry," came the reply from some agent or other.

Before I could say okay, Will was at my side patting me down. "What the hell are you doing in here? I told you to stay put."

The lights flickered to life, power and full visibility restored. As much as I'd wanted light before, the scene it uncovered made me want to shut my eyes. Two agents lifted

Beren onto a stretcher. Blood matted his blonde hair, and he was deathly pale. Someone took Angelica's pulse, then gave Will a look and a slight head shake.

"Noooooooo!" I screamed and leapt to the bed. I started CPR, tears cascading down my face. Seemingly in the distance, I heard the screech of the bed as they raced Beren out. I counted the pumps. "One, two, three, f—"

Will grabbed me from behind, stopping me. "There's nothing we can do here. We'll take her outside and see if someone can heal her... see if there's anything we can do, but we don't know how they killed her. It might be something we can't reverse, and if she's been dead for too long, she'll have brain damage, like anyone would."

"But we have to keep oxygen going to her brain. Please, Will?"

"We have to wheel her out." He pulled me away from the bed, and two other agents lifted her onto a trolley bed and rushed her out. "Come on, Lily. We'll go downstairs. James will be waiting."

Imani spoke from behind Will. "That other guy's dead. Looks like someone hit him in the head with a brick." She held up my new friend.

Will looked at the brick, at Imani, then back at me. "Thanks, Agent Jawara. I'll follow it up later. Right now, I have to get Lily out of here."

I should have felt bad, but I had nothing left to give. Numbness was setting in, one inch at a time. What did that make this? Number three? My kill tally was really adding up.

Will released me before grabbing my arm and leading me through the corridor. Elderly people wandered the hallways, dazed, as staff tried to round them up. One man was saying, "I'm blind. I'm blind."

The carer leading him said in a dry tone, "Open your eyes, Walter."

He opened them. "It's a miracle! I can see!"

The carer rolled his eyes. If only I was as oblivious to reality as that guy.

Will took me via the emergency stairs—the lift was busy ferrying two people I loved. When we jogged to the lawn, James was already there, his hands on Beren's head. "He's dead," James's voice cracked. "They smashed his skull in. I'm doing my best." He refocussed, his brow creasing, his eyes shutting.

I looked at Angelica, agitation kicking my ribs and turning my stomach. I grabbed Will's hand and dragged him over. He didn't resist. I looked up at him. "You have to try."

"I'm not as good as Beren or James. She's been gone for too long."

"No! You have to try." I whispered, "I can lend you my power. You can't let her go without trying, dammit! I've already lost both my parents. I can't lose her too." I put his hands on her chest, and I placed my palms on top of them and opened myself to the river of power. I directed the flow into him.

His eyes widened, and he stared at me, his mouth falling open.

"Stop staring, and just do this. Please, Will. Every second counts."

His gaze lost the surprise and wonder, and he turned to Angelica. I shut my eyes and concentrated on giving him a steady flow of magic. As I fed him power, I silently chanted, "Heal Angelica. Heal Angelica." I imagined her heart beating, her lungs filling and emptying.

"There are two clots blocking her heart…. Ah, now they're gone." Will dropped the power and gave her CPR. I shut off my access to the river and ran around the other side of the trolley to breathe into her nose. I risked a glance back at James. His eyes were still closed, and sweat beaded his forehead.

James needed me. Beren needed me. "Someone here to help with CPR for Ma'am. Now!" I shouted. Stuff it. I wasn't in charge of anything, but we needed help.

"I'm here, Lily." Imani. Thank God. I nodded my thanks and hurried to James.

I grabbed his wrist. "I'm here. Take whatever you need." I opened up to the power again and let it slide through to James. He wasn't shy in taking it, and before long, my legs trembled with fatigue. I gritted my teeth and held on. We were trying to save a man who had become like a second brother during the last few months. I loved Beren, and my heart would break if we lost him.

I was barely aware of people hurrying past, hushed conversations, flashing lights. My groggy mind registered the fact that I was giving my magic out in the open—anyone could see. Would they realise what we were doing? Something that was apparently impossible, or had been for hundreds of years? But did it matter? Probably. It would mean whoever wanted me would likely kill me rather than keep me for their own purposes. This made me too much of a threat. But at least it was dark, and maybe no one would notice. Surely they couldn't see the light of my power filtering into James?

Heat scoured my face, my veins, and my skin itched.

I was burning up.

James's voice was strained, and he swayed, bumping me. I clung to the bed to keep from falling over. "Hang on, Lily. Just another minute. I'm almost done."

We were both at the edge of a precipice, at the limit of what we could endure.

But life without Beren wasn't worth contemplating. I visualised his gorgeous smiling face, warm eyes, contagious laugh. *Come on, Beren. You have to make it.*

"One last… thing," James panted.

An electrical jolt stunned me, ceasing the flow of power between James and me and ripping me from the source. I fell, landing on my bum on the grass. Gasping for air, I fell the rest of the way back and shut my eyes. God, the ground was amazingly comfortable. Sleep reached out, but then a voice swatted it away.

"Lily. Lily."

I opened my eyes.

James knelt next to me, tears coursing down his face. New tears burned my eyes. No. He couldn't mean he was gone.

Then a smile breached the exhaustion on his face, a ray of light dissipating the grief, like mist at the start of a sunny day. Someone coughed.

"Oh my God. Beren!" Ignoring my exhaustion, I jumped up.

James slowly stood and put his arm around my shoulders. "Welcome back, man."

Beren grinned, his eyes half shut. "Why do I feel like I've been hit by a truck?" He gingerly ran his fingers across the front of his head.

"Because you pretty much were. Someone smashed your noggin with an iron bar. You died." James shook his head, and my heart thudded. Even though he was here, knowing he'd been dead was horrific.

"But how am I still here?"

"James healed you." I smiled, the tears gathering in my eyes from relief and joy rather than pain.

"Lily helped, but I'll explain later."

"Is Angelica…?" Beren asked.

I swallowed. "Um. I don't know." I was too scared to look over my shoulder. Our nightmare wasn't over yet.

"I'll check. You stay here, Lily." James turned.

"I wouldn't bother asking her to stay anywhere. She never listens." Will had come up behind us. He stood next to me and raised a brow. I tensed, waiting for the lecture… which never came. "But if she had listened, I'm afraid this would have turned out a lot worse. Because of this infuriating woman, we got to you and Angelica in time." He grinned.

My mouth dropped open, and the new tears that had gathered in my eyes spilled over. I was going to be dehydrated after this. I spun around.

Imani was bent over Angelica, her ear close to her mouth, listening to something. "I'll be back!" I said and then ran to them.

Imani straightened and grinned. Angelica was pale, and dark circles marred the skin under her eyes. Her voice was quiet and raspy, but she was okay. "Thank you for disobeying orders. But if you tell anyone I said that, I'll deny it." Her smile wasn't any less wonderful for being wan and small.

"I promise I won't tell anyone, as long as you stay alive from now on. No more dying."

"I'll do my best."

I narrowed my eyes at her. "You know that's not good enough."

She shrugged. "It's the best I can do."

Two paramedics loaded their ambulance with a sheet-covered body. "Should they be removing that Elizabeth woman yet? Don't they need to photograph the scene and all that?"

"Yes, as a matter of fact, they do, love. Let me check it out." Imani approached the paramedics. After a quick conversation, one of them nodded, and Imani pulled back the sheet. Oh no. It was Winston. Had he died of natural causes or had Elizabeth taken care of him before visiting Angelica? My shoulders slumped.

Imani returned. "They said he was found in his bed. Probably natural causes."

I raised my brow and plonked my hands on my hips. "You really believe that, after everything we found out?"

She shrugged. "Not really, but what difference does it make? The outcome is the same. We got the bad guys, and we can't bring him back." She swivelled her head and watched as the ambulance drove away, no siren, but lights flashing. Yeah, he died because he didn't have people who loved him there when it happened—not like Angelica and Beren. Did he have family? Would someone miss him?

A crotchety but slightly stronger-than-before voice said, "Excuse me. Is it too much to ask to be taken home? I want a hot bath and bed. I've been lying out here for ages. It'll be winter soon."

I grinned. Angelica was back and in fine form. "I'll okay it with James, and then I'll take you home, Ma'am." I looked down at her. "Told you my magic wasn't faulty."

She rolled her eyes. Yep, she was fine. Now we just had to make sure she stayed that way. Which I had a feeling would be easier said than done.

I had to wait for James to stop talking to the buzz-cut-hair agent. And someone else was standing behind me, waiting for their turn. I yawned. Boy, would I be happy to get home, shower, and crawl into bed. It was hard to see, but I was pretty sure I had OPB on me—other people's blood. I shuddered and skipped past the thought that I'd killed another person. If I started thinking about it, I'd never stop.

James finally looked at me, bags under his eyes where before there'd been none. "Make it quick."

"Ah, Angelica wants me to take her home. Is that okay?" I was talking to Agent Bianchi, not James my brother, and that made me a tad nervous. I felt as if I could get in trouble at any moment. Plus, he looked drained after saving Beren's life. He needed bed as much as I did.

James rubbed his forehead, then held up his hand, palm towards me. "Just give me a sec." He turned to Will. "Can I get you to travel Angelica home and put her into bed? Maybe stay for half an hour, make sure she's okay, then get back here."

"Sure thing." Will clasped Beren's hand and bent down, so his mouth was close to his ear. I couldn't hear what he said, but I'd bet it was something akin to, "I'm so glad you're not dead." If so, he was speaking for all of us. Olivia was going to have a meltdown when she found out he'd died.

A dark shape noiselessly glided over me and alighted in a nearby branch. I stared at it. Oh, wow, it was an owl. I loved owls! It triggered a thought, but I had no idea why. My magic had been right—Angelica and Beren had died, but my magic wasn't definitive. We'd brought them back to life. Did that prove that knowing meant I could actually make a difference? Mind. Blown. Now I was never going to sleep.

"Lily… Lily, are you ready?"

I started and met Will's worried gaze. I licked my bottom lip. He was so good-looking, even now, with his hair mussed up and his jaw tense that it made me tongue-tied on occasion. I smiled. "Yep. Ready to take Angelica home. Plus, I need to shower my murdering arse. There's blood on me. I can smell it." I wrinkled my nose.

His tone was gentle when he said, "Hey, you did the right thing. You killed her accomplice, and he would have killed you, had you given him the chance. Never apologise for surviving, Lily. Losing Beren and Angelica would have broken my heart, but losing you…" He swallowed, his gaze intense. "Losing you would kill me." He gently ran the back of his hand down my cheek and stared at me, then said, "Come on. Our patient is rather *impatient*. The sooner we get her settled at home, the better for everyone."

"I heard that, Agent Blakesley. I'm tired, not deaf."

"Yes, Ma'am." He grinned, and I snorted. God, it was good to have her back.

I took a deep breath and set the coordinates for Angelica's reception room.

Finally, it was time to go home.

# CHAPTER 14

Three days later, and we were back at the bureau's conference room, with two additions to our group —Imani and Agent Cardinal. The biggest thing that made me smile was Angelica sitting in her usual spot at the head of the table, her bun immaculate and the dark circles under her eyes gone. James and I shared a grin—he'd enjoyed his stint in charge, but he admitted he was relieved to be back in his usual role.

Olivia and Beren were sitting next to each other, and whilst nothing had developed there... yet, his near-death experience had Olivia sticking close. No one had realised I had been giving James power to heal Beren—there was too much other stuff going on, and if anyone saw, they just thought I was giving him moral support. We hadn't even told Beren. As far as he knew, James was a superstar. I smiled—my brother totally deserved that accolade. We'd both nearly burned ourselves out healing Beren, but it was a price we were willing to pay. Thankfully, it hadn't come to that. Will and I had talked about me giving him power. He swore on losing his arm that he would never tell anyone, and it was kind of unnerving, the way he'd looked at me as if I was a freak. Thankfully, today he was looking at me normally. Maybe he'd just had to get used to the idea.

The thing I still didn't know was why. Why would someone who had devoted her life to helping people want to kill them?

Angelica clapped her hands twice in quick succession. Everyone turned to her. She smiled. "Firstly, I would like to say thank you to all of you for carrying out a successful mission. There were things we could have done better, but James and I will be reviewing everything, and we'll have recommendations within the next three weeks. At the end of the day, we caught the offenders, so we'll call this one a win." She took a sip of water from the glass in front of her. "I'd like to take a moment to especially thank Olivia and Agent Millicent Bianchi for their research efforts. Thank you, ladies." Millicent gave a nod—she was likely used to this stuff—but Olivia beamed. My mouth turned up at the corners. I loved that my friend had found a job she enjoyed and was being recognised for the awesome person she was.

"I'm sure you're all wondering about the motive behind the killings. Conveniently, the killer kept a diary, which we found at her flat. Her reasons, and that of her boyfriend, make for interesting and frightful reading."

The boyfriend I'd killed. So, he'd been in on it. Well,

good riddance to him. Still, I wish I hadn't killed him. My heart was gathering tattoos, written in scar tissue—numbers representing each of my victims. I hoped three was the last number that stained me. I didn't know if my heart could take any more.

Angelica continued. "They both belonged to a group called the Witch Extermination Society. They're an underground group we hadn't heard of. I don't need to give you all three guesses as to what they do. What matters to us, more than anything, is they discovered the Saint Catherine Laboure Care Home was for witches." She met everyone's gaze one by one, warning radiating from her. "They know witches exist and possibly how to distinguish who is and who isn't."

"But how?" I asked.

"That's what we have to discover. They either stumbled upon it accidentally, or another witch has clued them in without putting the appropriate spells in place to keep the information from spreading. I'm setting up a special task force to investigate. But more on that another time."

Olivia raised her hand.

"Yes, dear."

"So that other old lady, Penny. She wasn't involved in any of the murders?"

That would actually be interesting to know. I'm glad Olivia asked.

"We've yet to determine that. It's quite a coincidence that two murderers were in the same place, and if Elizabeth and her boyfriend had known of Penny's past, maybe they would have tried to pin these murders on her rather than kill her and risk discovery. We do know Elizabeth killed at least fifteen people—along with her diary, we found her hair trophies."

Ew, that was sick, although not surprising.

Will said, "I'd like to know why they chose that particular time to cut the power and make their move. Did they know we were closing in on them?"

Angelica took another sip of water, maybe composing herself before answering. She'd been through a lot, and we all forgot she was only human—albeit a witchy one—too. Even though she didn't show it, she would experience stress too. "Before they injected me in the neck, Elizabeth bragged, said they research every witch who comes in, and we'd been sloppy. Even though we used a different surname, they discovered who I was—but I'm not sure how. Now they're dead, it will be difficult to find out. As for how they killed me..." She looked down at her hands and took a moment before raising her head. "They forced me to eat two chocolates, which knocked me out, leaving them free to execute the next step. According to James, there was something blocking both my coronary arteries. He had to dissolve the blockages. We've tested my blood, but nothing has shown up. We have the syringe Elizabeth used. There are traces of magic on it."

Every intake of breath around the table echoed in the following silence.

Will and I looked at each other. His shocked expression

matched how I felt. How could a witch betray other witches this way?

Olivia raised her hand again and asked, "But I thought the care home was warded against magic use. How could the magic work?"

James answered, "Magic can't be drawn inside the ward, but a spell created beforehand and made to cause a reaction would work. Similar to how spelling the tea caused all that trouble last time. The ward was to prevent residents using magic, but it didn't prevent spelled items being brought in. As long as the spell didn't need to draw on extra magic to activate, it would work."

I leaned forward. "So, someone spelled whatever was in the syringe to give you two specific blood clots."

"Yes, Lily." Angelica nodded.

It still didn't make total sense. "But why do that when they could have injected you with air, like with Will's grandmother?"

James looked at me. "They wanted to be sure. They knew Angelica was a threat. We just can't figure out how, but we'll get to the bottom of it."

"And Penny was just another random victim?" I asked, not that she was a total victim. She'd gotten off lightly, considering how many people she'd murdered.

Angelica gave Will a nod, indicating he should answer. "We're yet to get the autopsy results, but the manager's going to forward them as soon as they're done. Let's just say he was shocked down to his purple underwear when he found out what was going on in his care home. He's being very cooperative."

"I should hope so." I folded my arms. Many witches had died because of his incompetence. "Do we know why Elizabeth hated witches so much? She was invested enough to die for her cause. Surely she knew that attacking Angelica would be the last thing she did. At the very least, she must have known she'd go to jail."

Angelica pressed her lips together. Her voice was sad when she answered, "Her two-year-old son died in suspicious circumstances ten years ago. The police called it misadventure, but she wouldn't let it go. During her own investigations, she met someone she later names in her diary as Vargore. It looks like he was a real witch, and he convinced her that witches had murdered her child. He introduced her to the man you killed, Lily."

"But why would a witch do that to their own kind?"

Angelica shrugged. "Your guess is as good as mine. Does anyone have any other questions?"

Everyone looked around the table at each other, but no one put up their hand.

Angelica stood. "This meeting is over. I'll see Agents Bianchi"—she nodded at both Millicent and James—"Cardinal and Jawara here tomorrow at nine. You're on my task force for this one." She turned to James. "I'll see you in my office in ten."

He nodded.

Angelica left the normal non-witch way by walking out the door. Conversation broke out around the table, everyone discussing what we'd just found out. Will turned to me. "We're supposed to go to lunch in a few days. I'm not really feeling up to it. Is it okay if we change the booking to Friday the twenty-sixth? I'm just a bit distracted, and after everything that's happened in the last week and a half, I won't be the best lunch companion. I'm also thinking you might need a break too, especially since that hospital visit."

He didn't say too much, likely because Imani and Cardinal were there. "Sounds good. I could do with a break from all things magic-related, well, except for the magic that makes my life easier." I smiled. Plus, with almost losing two of my favourite people, I wasn't in the mood to face images of my long-disappeared parents. There was only so much emotional turmoil I could take, and I still had a hangover from three days ago.

"What about we see a film tonight? There's a couple of good ones showing at Everyman Oxted. I'll even throw in popcorn and Maltesers."

"I'm in. But you had me at what." I snorted.

He wrinkled his brow, and I couldn't resist placing my fingertips on it to smooth it out. He grabbed my wrist, brought my hand to his lips, and kissed my palm. "What do you mean, I had you at what?"

"It was the first word that came out of your mouth."

"Are you saying you'd pretty much do whatever I asked?" He raised his brows.

I smiled. "Maybe…"

His gaze darkened. "I distinctly remember asking you to stay in the van."

Oops. How had I managed to steer the conversation towards my own demise? My grin was overly huge. "Sorry." I shrugged.

He sighed and shook his head, but his mouth turned up at the corners, revealing his sexy dimples. "What am I going to do with you?"

"Last time I checked, you were taking me to the movies."

"That I am. I suppose I should get back to work so I can finish in time to pick you up. See you at Angelica's reception room at seven?"

"it's a date." I grinned.

After Will left, I looked at Beren and Olivia chatting, their heads close together. My heart swelled with affection for both of them. Despite the horrible week we'd all had, it had turned out okay, but I had one last thing to do before I could move on.

I turned to Imani. "Are you ready?"

"Yes." She gave me a sad smile.

IT TURNED OUT THAT WINSTON DIDN'T HAVE FAMILY WHO cared. The day after he died, I contacted the care home and asked about him. He'd never had children, and his partner of forty years had died a few years ago. Whether he had nieces or nephews, who knew, but if he did, they didn't care.

A blackbird swooped past, and the day darkened as a cloud covered the sun. Imani and I stood at Winston's graveside. Four men in dark suits waited, hands folded in front, to lower Winston's casket into the maw that would claim his body for eternity. I shuddered. Death and I didn't see eye to eye. It scared me, and as far as I was concerned, there wasn't anything peaceful or beautiful about not existing. Frankly, it was terrifying.

But enough about me. We were here to farewell a kind soul, a man who had taken Angelica under his wing. A tear trickled down my cheek as the minister spoke. "...and we return Winston Alfred Baker to the earth. Ashes to ashes, dust to dust. May he be eternally at peace in the arms of our Lord."

My tears increased, despite my attempts at stopping them—they were more stubborn than me, apparently. My sorrow was for everyone I'd lost, and for people I didn't know who had recently lost someone. The death of one person somehow became the death of every person. Sorrow and loss were universal, and while Imani and I watched, a scene that would be played out millions more times unfolded in front of us.

I hoped Winston somehow knew that Imani and I had come to say goodbye, to acknowledge that his life mattered. Imani and I both threw dirt on his coffin as it was lowered into the ground.

At least the killers had been caught—whether Winston's death was because of murder or natural causes, it no longer mattered. The end result, as Angelica had said, was the same.

"Goodbye, Winston. Thank you for watching out for Angelica."

As Imani and I walked away, I let the tears fall freely. My grief was for my parents, myself, my brother, and for every forgotten soul who had died quietly, without fanfare, alone.

We reached the car—there were no toilets here we could travel to, and appearing and disappearing in a cemetery might give someone a heart attack. Imani looked at me over the roof of the car.

"We did good today, Lily. Winston is watching from somewhere. Don't be sad, love."

"Do you believe in that stuff?"

"I believe in God, but not the Bible. I'd call myself spiritual rather than religious, and I think Winston's spirit is happy we came." She stared at me, and it seemed like she'd come to a decision about something at that very moment. "Did Will mention what my talent was?"

The hairs on my nape stood on end. I wasn't sure where this was going, but it didn't look good. "Ah, no." She obviously wanted me to ask, but I wasn't game—not because I didn't want to know her talent, but it would be what came after that I was bound not to like.

She smiled. "You have good senses, Lily. I can tell you don't want this conversation to progress, but I have to tell you. My talent will bug me until I do."

Hmm, that was weird. "Okay, but do you want to do this in the car?"

"Sure."

We both got in, Imani in the driver seat, me in the front

passenger seat. I took a deep breath and turned to her. "Okay. Just give it to me. I'm a Band-Aid ripper offer."

"I know." *Huh?* "You're braver than you realise, Lily. My talent is knowing things about people, even things they don't know about themselves. I can't see things about everyone, and never at will, but I get flashes of images and feelings. I never know when it will happen, but just now, at the grave, I saw some things about you that you need to know."

"And?" I bit my nail.

"You have a special talent, a talent people will kill to own. I can't tell what it is, but you need to know that you're in grave danger. I can also tell you that there is trouble brewing in the witch world, and you're at the centre of it. If anything happens to you, evil will win."

"What evil?" Could she be talking about the snake group?

"I see you're not surprised."

"Um, maybe not. There was something you said.... Why would evil win just because I wasn't here?"

"I don't know, Lily, but maybe you should try and find the answer. Something sinister is coming. We'll be fighting for our existence. It may not be next month, or even next year, but a shadow darkens my dreams. And I don't know why or how, but you're the key for good to triumph over evil." Her eyes were locked on mine, and she wouldn't look away.

"Are you sure you're not overstating things?" I asked casually, trying to lighten the mood. And good versus evil?

This wasn't a medieval novel. There were shades of good and evil in most people.

"I'm afraid not, love. Anyway, nothing for you to worry about right now, but I think you should talk to Angelica about it. And, love, just so you know, I'm in your corner." She started the car, and I clicked my belt in as we drove away.

"Thanks, Imani. I appreciate it." I huffed a laugh and shook my head. How could I not worry? I sighed. But at least she was on my side. Maybe we should add her to our little group of snake catchers. At least one thing was true: I would definitely talk to Angelica about this.

If the last week had taught me anything, it was to live each day as passionately as I could—with no fear, and no regrets. Who knew when my time here would be done?

The sun burst out from behind the clouds, and I smiled. Tonight, I had a date with a handsome witch who had promised me popcorn and Maltesers. I was going to enjoy every second of my date because tomorrow would come soon enough, and I'd just deal with it when it arrived. And maybe, just maybe, the universe would bring me more good than bad. I thought about all my friends: Olivia, Beren, Angelica, my brother and Millicent, and of course Will, and I realised it already had.

# ABOUT THE AUTHOR

USA Today bestselling author, Dionne Lister is a Sydneysider with a degree in creative writing, two Siamese cats, and is a member of the Science Fiction and Fantasy Writers of America. Daydreaming has always been her passion, so writing was a natural progression from staring out the window in primary school, and being an author was a dream she held since childhood.

Unfortunately, writing was only a hobby while Dionne worked as a property valuer in Sydney, until her mid-thirties when she returned to study and completed her creative writing degree. Since then, she has indulged her passion for writing while raising two children with her husband. Her books have attracted praise from Apple iBooks and have reached #1 on Amazon and iBooks charts worldwide, frequently occupying top 100 lists in fantasy. She's excited to add cozy mystery to the list of genres she writes. Magic and danger are always a heady combination.

# ALSO BY DIONNE LISTER

### *Paranormal Investigation Bureau*

*Witchnapped in Westerham #1*

*Witch Swindled in Westerham #2*

*Witch Undercover in Westerham #3*

*Witchslapped in Westerham #4*

*Killer Witch in Westerham #6 (out April 2019)*

### *The Circle of Talia*

(YA Epic Fantasy)

*Shadows of the Realm*

*A Time of Darkness*

*Realm of Blood and Fire*

### *The Rose of Nerine*

(Epic Fantasy)

*Tempering the Rose*

Printed in Great Britain
by Amazon

28937381R00133

# INTERMIT...
# FASTING
## THE COMPLETE
# KETOFAST
## SOLUTION

# INTERMITTENT FASTING THE COMPLETE KETOFAST SOLUTION
THE KETOGENIC DIET COOKBOOK GUIDE TO HELP UNLOCK YOUR WEIGHT LOSS, REVERSE DISEASE & ILLNESS

**ISBN 9781913005368**

## DISCLAIMER

# CONTENTS

## KETOFAST DINNERS

## KETOFAST SOUPS & SALADS

## KETOFAST SAUCES & SEASONING

## KETOFAST DESSERTS, SNACKS & SMOOTHIES

# INTRODUCTION

*Intermittent fasting combined with a ketogenic approach to living can yield previously unachievable results in weight loss, well-being and relieving the symptoms of, and sometimes even reversing, disease and illness.*

## PRACTICE OF KETOSIS AND INTERMITTENT FASTING

If you are reading this book it's likely you want to learn what ketosis and intermittent fasting really means and are no doubt interested in the many potential health benefits which can include weight loss and diabetes management.

Lets start by explaining what Ketosis actually is.

## WHAT IS KETOSIS? HOW DOES IT AFFECT THE BODY?

The body typically gets its energy from carbohydrates through a process called glycolysis. If the body does not have carbohydrates to use, another metabolic process kicks in. This metabolic process is called ketosis(1).

Ketosis is a metabolic state/process where the body burns fat at a high rate, converting fatty acids into ketones(1). It is a normal metabolic process. When the body does not have enough glucose for energy, it burns stored fats instead; this results in a build-up of acids called ketones within the body. Ketosis describes a condition where fat stores are broken down to produce energy, which also produces ketones, a type of acid. This aids weight loss as it forces the body to burn fat stores.

In recent times nutritionists have become increasingly concerned with the intake of too much fat. The first Dietary Guidelines for Americans, published in 1980, listed, *"Avoid too much fat, saturated fat, and cholesterol"* (3). Likewise, in the UK, the NHS publication titled *"Fat: the facts"* advises against the intake of too much fat. The publication quoted *"Too much fat in your diet, especially saturated fats, can raise your cholesterol, which increases the risk of heart disease. Current UK government guidelines advise cutting down on all fats and replacing saturated fat with some unsaturated fat."*(4)

This advice however doesn't differentiate strongly enough between good/unsaturated fats and bad/saturated fats. Consuming good fats can actually help our metabolic system and is a key component in the success of the Keto Diet.

The body can be forced to enter a state of ketosis through the consumption of ketogenic low-carbohydrate diets especially to lose weight. The key principles of the ketogenic approach to eating are based on the **Atkins Diet** and the **Paleo Diet**.

The Atkins Diet is a low-carb diet, usually recommended for weight loss. This diet has evolved since its introduction in 1972 by a physician, Dr Robert C. Atkins in his best-selling book "Dr Atkins' Diet Revolution". It encourages losing weight by eating low-carbohydrate (low-carb) diets that contain proteins, vegetables, and healthy fats.

The Paleo Diet popularised by Loren Cordain, PhD is literally based on the idea that if we eat like our prehistoric ancestors, we will be leaner and less likely to get diabetes, heart disease, cancer, and other health problems. It promotes consumption of high-protein and high-fibre promising the loss of weight without rigorous calorie counting. It is these two principles that form the basis of the Ketogenic Diet (or Keto Diet). Put simply the Keto Diet is a low-carb, high-fat diet. In this diet, carbohydrate intake is significantly replaced with fat.

Various research has revealed that Ketogenic diets can cause a massive reduction in weight, cardiovascular disease and diabetes(5). Calories are derived from three major compositions fats, proteins, and carbohydrates (or carbs). Fats composition is the highest (usually more than 50 per cent), followed by protein and carbs are the lowest usually below 10 per cent of the composition. The reason for high consumption of fats is to force the body to source energy from fats instead of carbohydrate. Protein is also consumed in significant quantities to avoid the loss of muscle mass and at the same time facilitate the loss of body mass(5).

**There are different classification of ketogenic diets depending on the result you are trying to achieve.**

**The Standard Ketogenic Diet (SKD)** contains high-fat (75%), moderate-protein (20%) and very low-carb (5%). It is the most used Keto diet plan and very effective in reducing weight (2).

**The Targeted Ketogenic Diet (TKD)** is dubbed a Traditional Approach. It is usually combined with exercise to lose weights. Carbs are eaten 30-60 minutes prior exercise. It's advisable to choose easily digestible carbs with high Glycemic Index ranking to avoid stomach upset. The carbs consumed before exercise are assumed to burn out during exercise.

**Cyclic Ketogenic Diet (CKD)** involves periods of higher-carb refeeds, such as eating low-carb diets for 5 days and high-carb diets for two days.

**High-protein ketogenic Diet (HPKD)** is similar to SKD but contains more protein. The composition is usually 60% fat, 35% protein and 5% carbs.

**Restricted Ketogenic Diet (RKD)** are special Keto diets for therapeutic treatment of diseases like cancer. The carb intake is restricted below 20 grams per day(6).

Ketogenic diets do not have to be unpalatable. As with our recipes, they can include different delicious, tasty, versatile and nutritious foods that allows you to maintain your low-carb goal daily(7).

The best tasting and most effective Keto meals should include some of the following;

- Fish and seafood
- Low-carb vegetables
- Meats
- Natural fat
- High-fat sauces
- Nuts and seeds
- Cheese
- Avocados
- Meat and poultry
- Eggs
- Plain Greek yogurt & cottage cheese
- Olives and olive oil
- Coconut oil
- Butter and cream
- Dark chocolate

These foods offer numerous health benefits such as reduced risk of diseases, improved mental health and eye health, anti-ageing benefits and maintenance of body mass(8,9,10).

High-carb foods which should be avoided include:

- Sugar
- Starch
- Beer
- Margarine
- Sugary alcoholic drinks
- Processed foods
- Grains
- Milk
- Farm-processed meats
- Artificial sweeteners
- Legumes except peanuts
- Soy products
- Tropical fruits
- High-carb fruits

## INTERMITTENT FASTING:

For optimal results from Keto diets, it is logical to combine it with Intermittent Fasting (IF).

### What is Intermittent Fasting?

Intermittent fasting is a pattern of eating. It is not focused on dietary restriction, instead, it is a timeline of when you eat. Just like Keto Diets, IF kicks the body into ketosis a process whereby the body breaks down fat for energy. It should not be compared to starvation. Starvation is involuntary, while IF is voluntary. A concern some people have is the fact that this method may involve skipping breakfast which many consider the most important meal of the day. However studies have shown that short-term repeated fasting in mice increased lifespan(11).

There are 6 major types of Intermittent Fasting. All of them can be successful but the best choice for you will depend on the type of result you desire and how the fasting schedule fits in which your lifestyle.

### 16/8 Method

This IF method, just as its name implies, involves a daily fasting of 14-16 hours with a restricted eating timeframe of 8-10 hours. Following this method of fasting can actually be as simple as not eating anything after lunch and skipping breakfast. If for example, you finished your last meal at 2pm you are not expected to eat another meal until after 6am the next day. It is acceptable for women to only fast 14-15 hours since they can respond better with shorter fasting hours(12).

### 5:2 Diet

This IF method was popularised by British journalist and doctor, Michael Mosley. It involves eating normally for 5 days of the week and reducing intake on two days of the same week. On the fasting days, it is recommended that women consume 500 calories, and men 600 calories. Although there has been no scientific research on the use of this method so far, there have been many studies confirming the benefits of intermittent fasting(12).

## Eat-Stop-Eat

The Eat-Stop-Eat proposes 24-hour fasting once or twice in a week. You may decide to commence your fasting after breakfast, lunch, or dinner. For example if you started fasting at lunch, you will complete the 24-hour at lunch the next day.

## Alternate-Day Fasting

This fasting method involves fasting for every other day. It requires enormous will power and is not recommended for anyone trying IF for the first time.

## The Warrior Diet

After a long day fasting or low carb consumption, you are allowed to eat a huge meal at night. You will eat small amounts of raw fruits and vegetables during the day, then 'feast;' at night(12).

## Spontaneous Meal Skipping

Skip meals occasionally, when you don't feel hungry or are too busy to cook and eat. Our bodies are well equipped to handle missing one or two meals from time to time. Just be sure to eat healthy balanced food groups in the meals you do have.

Please note that the approach to intermittent fasting is a personal one and we do not recommend one approach over another. Some methods are considered more 'extereme' than others. We recommend prior to emabarking on any diet that you seek the advice of a health professional .

To help make Intermittent Fasting more tolerable there are some drinks you could occasionally consume during the fasting period to help you remain well and active during the period:

## Liquids

- Water should be top of your list whilst fasting. It's important to stay hydrated.
- Herbal teas; these taste great and can help stave off hunger. Some also have useful detoxifying benefits.
- Coffee (ideally black); drinking coffee helps suppress hunger and the caffeine it contains can also provide an energy boost. Don't drink too much though. Two cups a day is probably the maximum.
- Cider vinegar; This is a great ingredient which can be added to sparkling water to make a refreshing drink. Although it is acidic it actually helps to balance your body's pH levels. It contains almost no calories and is perfect for fasting as it helps keep your electrolytes in check and prevent deficiencies.

## Food

What you can eat during fasting depends on the type of fasting you are undertaking. Some methods like 5:2 term fasting as an intake of 500/600 calories or less per day whilst other forms of IF may mean short periods of absolutely no food at all. If however you are taking in some food during IF the best sources of energy include: Low carb veg, whole grains, healthy fats (avocados and nuts), and small amounts of meat and dairy.

To maximise your weight loss program, it makes sense to combine KETO & IF. It's like effectively having two solutions to one problem. If however your health will not allow you to fast, stick solely to Keto foods.

Our delcious and easy to follow collection of high protein, high-fat, low-carb breakfasts, lunches, dinners, smoothies and snacks will help you adopt a new and exciting approach to dieting with results you'll be proud of.

## Notes
- All nutritional measurements are approximate, you can use your trusted recipe measurement method.
- Carbs represent total carbs, sections where net carbs are included are tagged "net carbs"

## References
1. Medical News Today. (2017). Ketosis: What is ketosis?. Available at *https://www.medicalnewstoday.com/articles/180858.php*
2. Freeman JM, Kossoff EH, Hartman AL. (2017). The ketogenic diet: one decade later. US National Library of Medicine National Institutes of Health, PMID: 17332207 DOI: 10.1542/peds.2006-2447 Available at *https://www.ncbi.nlm.nih.gov/pubmed/17332207*
3. U.S. Department of Health and Human Services and U.S. Department of Agriculture. (1980). Nutrition and Your Health: Dietary Guidelines for Americans. 1st Edition. Available at *https://health.gov/dietaryguidelines/1980thin.pdf*
4. National Health Service. (2018). Fat: the facts. Available at *https://www.nhs.uk/live-well/eat-well/different-fats-nutrition/*
5. Bueno NB, de Melo IS, de Oliveira SL, da Rocha Ataide T. (2013). Very-low-carbohydrate ketogenic diet v. low-fat diet for long-term weight loss: a meta-analysis of randomised controlled trials. US National Library of Medicine National Institutes of Health, 110(7):1178-87. doi: 10.1017/S0007114513000548. Available at *https://www.ncbi.nlm.nih.gov/pubmed/23651522*
6. Giulio Z, Norina M, Anna P, Franco S, Salvatore V, et al. (2010). Metabolic management of glioblastoma multiforme using standard therapy together with a restricted ketogenic diet: Case Report. US National Library of Medicine National Institutes of Health, doi:  10.1186/1743-7075-7-33.
7. Franziska S. 2017. 16 Foods to Eat on a Ketogenic Diet. HealthLine. Available at *https://www.healthline.com/nutrition/ketogenic-diet-foods#section1*
8. Morris MC, Evans DA, Tangney CC, Bienias JL, Wilson RS. Fish consumption and cognitive decline with age in a large community study. US National Library of Medicine National Institutes of Health. 88(6):1618-25. doi: 10.3945/ajcn.2007.25816.
9. Andreas E. 2018. Ketogenic diet foods – what to eat. Diet Doctor. Available at *https://www.dietdoctor.com/low-carb/keto/foods*
10. Martina S. 2015. Complete Keto Diet Food List: What to Eat and Avoid on a Low-Carb Diet. Ketodiet. Available at *https://ketodietapp.com/Blog/lchf/Keto-Diet-Food-List-What-to-Eat-and-Avoid*
11. Sogawa H, Kubo C (2000). Influence of short-term repeated fasting on the longevity of female (NZB x NZW) F1 mice. US National Library of Medicine National Institutes of Health, PMID: 10854629.
12. Kris G (2017). 6 Popular Ways to Do Intermittent Fasting. Health Line. Available at *https://www.healthline.com/nutrition/6-ways-to-do-intermittent-fasting#section1*

# BREAKFASTS

# KETO CINNAMON ROLLS

calories: 320
fat: 29g
carbs: 5g
fibre: 0g
protein: 11g

## Ingredients

For the dough:
- 12½oz/360g almond flour
- 12½oz/360g mozzarella
- 3oz/75g cream cheese
- ½ tsp cinnamon (more to taste)
- 1 egg, whisked

- 2 squeezes of liquid stevia (more to taste)

For the filling:
- 3 tbsp melted butter
- 2 tsp cinnamon
- Icing:

- 4 tbsp cream cheese
- 2 tbsp vanilla extract
- 2oz/60ml butter at room temperature
- 1 tbsp lemon juice
- 3 squeezes of liquid stevia

## Method

**1** Preheat oven to 200C/400F/GAS6.

**2** In a bowl, add mozzarella and cream cheese. Put in the microwave for one minute, take out and stir.

**3** Put in the microwave for another minute, stir again.

**4** Add in the almond flour, stevia, cinnamon and the egg. Mix to combine well.

**5** The dough will be a little wet but if it's too wet that you can't get it to stop sticking to your fingers then add a little more almond flour.

**6** Roll the dough out flat with a rolling pin or with a piece of plastic wrap on top and use a wine bottle.

**7** Once you've rolled it out, spread on the melted butter and sprinkle on the cinnamon.

**8** Roll it up long ways until you have a long cylinder. Use a knife or pizza cutter and cut into pieces. Place these on a baking sheet lined with parchment paper.

**9** Bake at 200C/400F/GAS 6 for 10-12 mins.

**10** While they're baking, make the icing. You can do this with a mixer. Add cream cheese and butter and mix until creamy. Add in the vanilla extract and lemon juice. Mix until well combined.

**11** Once cinnamon rolls are done, put on icing. If you put it on immediately, it will melt a little into the actual cinnamon roll. Instead allow the rolls to cool for ten minutes before spreading over the top.

# INDIAN BREAKFAST DISH

calories: 252
fat: 21g
carbs: 8g
fibre: 4g
protein: 7g

## Ingredients

- 1 head cauliflower
- 2 tbsp olive oil
- 1 tbsp yellow mustard seeds
- 1 tbsp cumin seeds
- 1 red onion, chopped

- 5 curry leaves
- 1 tsp fresh grated ginger
- 1 green chilli pepper
- 10 peanuts, chopped
- Fresh Coriander, for garnish

## Method

**1** Break cauliflower into large florets. Transfer into a food processor and pulse until completely broken down into couscous-sized pieces.

**2** Heat the olive oil in a frying pan and add the mustard seeds and cumin.

**3** Once they start to sizzle, add chopped onion, curry leaves, ginger, green chillies and peanuts.

**4** Fry on low-medium heat until the onions get translucent.

**5** Salt to taste.

**6** Add the couscous-sized cauliflower, combine well and fry for a few minutes.

**7** Add a little water so it almost covers the mixture.

Cook for 10 mins with the lid on.

**8** Keep checking and stirring every few minutes to ensure that nothing sticks to the bottom of the pan.

**9** Cook until the water evaporates.

**10** Finish with adding the fresh Coriander.

### CHEF'S NOTE
You can replace the olive oil with ghee or butter.

# KETO MEXICAN SCRAMBLED EGGS

calories: 229
fat: 18g
carbs: 2g
fibre: 1g
protein: 14g

## Ingredients

- 6 eggs
- 3 spring onions
- 2 pickled jalapeños
- 1 tomato
- 3oz/75g grated cheese
- 2 tbsp butter, for frying
- Salt and pepper

## Method

**1** Finely chop the spring onions, jalapeños and tomatoes.

**2** Fry in butter for 3 minutes on medium heat.

**3** Beat the eggs and pour into the frying pan. Scramble for 2 minutes.

**4** Add cheese and season to serve.

## CHEF'S NOTE

You can also serve with avocado and shredded crisp lettuce.

# NO-BREAD KETO SANDWICH

calories: 334
fat: 20g
carbs: 2g
fibre: 0g
protein: 20g

## Ingredients

- 2 tsp butter
- 4 eggs
- 4 slices smoked ham slices
- 2oz/50g cheddar cheese or provolone cheese, cut in thick slices
- Salt and pepper

## Method

**1** Add butter to a frying pan and place over medium heat.

**2** Add eggs and fry. until the yolk is firm

**3** Add salt and pepper to taste.

**4** Use two of the fried eggs as the base for each sandwich.

**5** Place the ham slices on each base and then add the cheese to the bases.

**6** Top off each base with the other fried eggs. Leave in the pan, on low heat and allow the cheese to melt before serving.

## CHEF'S NOTE

Sprinkle a few drops of Tabasco or Worcestershire sauce if you're in the mood, and serve immediately.

# KETO WAFFLES

calories: 280
fat: 26g
carbs: 4.5g
fibre: 2g
protein: 7g

## Ingredients

- 5 eggs
- 4 tbsp coconut flour
- 4 tbsp granulated sweetener
- 1 tsp baking powder
- 2 tsp vanilla
- 3 tbsp full fat milk or cream
- 125g/4oz butter melted

## Method

**1** Prepare two bowls.

**2** In first bowl: Whisk the egg whites until firm and form stiff peaks.

**3** In second bowl: Mix the egg yolks, coconut flour, sweetener, and baking powder.

**4** Add the melted butter to the egg yolks slowly mixing to ensure it is a smooth consistency.

**5** Then add the milk and vanilla to the yolks and mix well.

**6** Gently fold spoons of the whisked egg whites into the yolk mixture. Try to keep as much of the air and fluffiness as possible.

**7** Place enough of the waffle mixture into the warm waffle maker to make one waffle. Cook until golden.

**8** Repeat until all the mixture has been used.

## CHEF'S NOTE

The waffles be frozen in between sheets of baking paper placed inside an airtight container.

# BLUEBERRY COCONUT PORRIDGE

calories: 405
fat: 34g
carbs: 8g
fibre: 7g
protein: 10g

## Ingredients

- 250ml/1 cup almond milk
- 2oz/50g ground flaxseed
- 2oz/50g coconut flour
- 1 tsp cinnamon
- 1 tsp vanilla extract
- 10 drops liquid stevia

- 1 pinch salt
Toppings
- 2 tbsp butter
- 75g/3oz blueberries
- 2 tbsp pumpkin seeds
- 1oz/25g shaved coconut

## Method

1 Gently warm the almond milk in a pan on a low flame.

2 Add in flaxseed, coconut flour, cinnamon and sal, using a whisk to break up any clumps.

3 Heat until slightly bubbling. Add in liquid stevia and vanilla extract.

4 When the mixture is as thick as you want it to be,

5 Remove from the heat and add in the toppings: butter, blueberries, pumpkin seeds and shaved coconut!

## CHEF'S NOTE
If you want additional fat and protein slowly add a beaten egg into the cooking porridge.

# LOW-CARB PUMPKIN & MUSHROOM RISOTTO

calories: 312
fat: 24g
carbs: 10g
fibre: 4g
protein: 12.9g

## Ingredients

- 14oz/400g pumpkin
- 2 tbsp extra virgin olive oil
- 800ml chicken or vegetable stock (about 3 ½ cups)
- 2 garlic cloves, crushed
- 1 onion

- 2 heads cauliflower
- 5oz/150g mushrooms, sliced
- 1 tbsp butter
- 3 tbsp cream
- 6 sprigs of fresh thyme
- ¼ tsp sea salt, or to taste

- ¼ tsp cracked black pepper
- 2oz/50g pumpkin seeds
- 2oz/50g grated parmesan cheese

## Method

1 Preheat oven to 190C/375F/GAS5. Peel the pumpkin, remove the seeds and chop into small chunks (¾ inch). Place on a baking tray and toss with 1 tbsp of the oil and a pinch of salt. Roast in the oven for 20 minutes until soft.

2 Add the stock to a pot and simmer on a medium heat until the volume reduces to about 500 ml (this concentrates the stock and really adds to the flavour.)

3 Whizz the cauliflower in a high-speed food processor until it resembles a rice consistency.

4 Peel and finely dice the onion. Fry the onion in the rest of the olive oil on a medium heat for a few minutes until translucent. Add the garlic and cauliflower rice and fry for a further 2-3 minutes.

5 Add the stock, salt, pepper, thyme and simmer on a medium heat until all the stock is absorbed.

6 Place the seeds on a baking tray and roast in the oven for 5-6 minutes until golden. Remove from the oven and allow to cool.

7 Heat the butter in a pan and fry the mushrooms on a medium heat for 2-3 minutes.

8 Stir through the mushrooms, cream, pumpkin and half of the cheese. Taste and add more seasoning if required.

9 Spoon the Pumpkin, Mushroom and Thyme Cauliflower Rice Risotto into bowls and top with pumpkin seeds, the remaining cheese and a sprinkling of fresh thyme leaves.

# KETO MORNING HOT POCKETS

calories: 455
fat: 38g
carbs: 5g
fibre: 2g
protein: 25g

## Ingredients

- 7oz/200g mozzarella
- 2½oz/60g almond flour
- 2 eggs

- 2 tbsp unsalted butter
- 4 slices streaky bacon cooked

## Method

**1** Preheat the oven to 200C/400F/GAS6

**2** On a gentle heat melt the mozzarella & add the almond flour. Stir until well-combined into a soft dough and remove from the heat.

**3** Roll the dough out thinly to approx 15cm square between 2 sheets of parchment paper.

**4** Quickly scramble the eggs in a frying pan in melted butter and lay them with streaky streaky bacon slices along the centre of the dough.

**5** Fold over and seal the dough. Add some holes on the dough surface using a fork. This helps release the steam while baking.

**6** Bake for about 20 mins or until it turns golden brown and firm to the touch. Remove from oven and enjoy!

## CHEF'S NOTE

One ounce of mozzarella has 183 milligrams of calcium, which is over 18 per cent of the recommended daily intake.

# CHEWY MUESLI BAR

calories: 180
fat: 17g
carbs: 2g
fibre: 0.5g
protein: 4g

## Ingredients

- 12½oz/360g sliced almonds
- 4oz/125g flaked coconut (unsweetened)
- 4oz/125g pecans
- 4oz/125g sunflower seeds
- 4oz/125g dried, unsweetened cranberries (chopped)

- 4oz/120ml butter
- 4oz/125g powdered erythritol
- ½ tsp vanilla extract
- 1 pinch salt

## Method

**1** Preheat the oven to 150C/300F/GAS2 and line a square baking dish with parchment.

**2** Combine the almonds, coconut, pecans, and sunflower seeds in a food processor.

**3** Pulse the mixture until it is finely chopped and crumbed..

**4** Pour the mixture into a bowl and stir in the cranberries and a pinch of salt.

**5** Melt the butter in a saucepan over low heat then whisk in the erythritol and vanilla extract.

**6** Pour the mixture over the muesli and stir until well combined.

**7** Press the mixture into the prepared dish, compacting it as much as possible, and bake for 20-25 minutes.

**8** Cool the mixture in the pan completely then remove and cut into 16 bars.

### CHEF'S NOTE
Pack into the dish very tightly and let cool after baking to stick properly.

# ONION CHIVE CAULIFLOWER HASH BROWNS

calories: 93
fat: 6g
carbs: 4g
fibre: 2g
protein: 5g

## Ingredients

- 15oz/425g riced cauliflower
- 1 egg
- ¼ tsp salt
- Couple pinches of cracked black pepper
- 1 finely diced onion
- 1 finely diced red pepper
- 2 tbsp onion & chive cottage cheese
- ½ tbsp olive oil

## Method

**1** In a bowl, mix the cauliflower rice, egg, salt & pepper, onions and red peppers until thoroughly combined.

**2** In a small pan over medium-high heat, add olive oil.Once the pan is hot and olive oil rolls around easily in the pan, use a large spoon to scoop half the cauliflower mix into the pan.

**3** Use the spoon to flatten the cauliflower down to about 1/3 inch thick, and also to smooth around the side so that it's in a round or rectangle shape.

**4** Let sit and cook until brown and crispy underneath, about 4-5 minutes.

**5** Use a spatula to flip the hash brown.

**6** Let the hash brown cook until crispy underneath (another 3-4 minutes)

**7** Remove from your pan with a spatula, and repeat with the second half of the "batter".

**8** pile a tablespoon of ottage cheesd on top to serve.

### CHEF'S NOTE
Calcium and vitamin D found in cottage cheese reduces the risk of breast cancer.

23

# CHEESY SCRAMBLED EGGS

calories: 353
fat: 33g
carbs: 1.2g
fibre: 1g
protein: 19g

## Ingredients

- 2 eggs
- 1 tbsp butter
- 1oz/25g cheddar cheese

- 2 tbsp chopped chives
- 1 red pepper, sliced

## Method

1 Heat a frying pan on the stove, adding the butter and saute the peppers for a few minutes untl softened.

2 Crack the eggs into the pan and add the chives..

3 Let the eggs cook cook and move them arounf the pan until just about to set.

4 Add the cheese and and serve.

### CHEF'S NOTE
Cheddar cheese contain vitamin A which is essential for proper functioning of organs, good vision and cell growth.

# CHEESY FRITTATA MUFFINS

calories: 205
fat: 16.1g
carbs: 1.3g
fibre: 0g
protein: 13.6g

## Ingredients

- 8 eggs
- 120ml/ ½ cup cream
- 4oz/125g streaky bacon, pre-cooked and chopped
- 4oz/125g cheddar cheese
- 1 tbsp butter
- 2 tsp dried parsley
- ½ tsp pepper
- ¼ tsp salt

## Method

1 Preheat the oven to 190C/375F/GAS5.

2 Whisk the eggs and cream in a bowl.

3 Fold in the streaky bacon, cheese, and oter ingredients.

4 Grease a muffin tin with butter.

5 Pour the mixture, filling each cup about ¾ way.

6 Place in the oven for 15-18 minutes, or until puffy and golden on the edges.

7 Remove from the oven and let cool for 1 minute.

## CHEF'S NOTE

Use whichever type of full fat cheese you prefer in these delicious muffins.

# BAKED DENVER OMELETTE

calories: 252
fat: 15g
carbs: 4g
fibre: 2g
protein: 19g

## Ingredients

- 1 chopped red pepper
- 1 chopped green pepper
- 1 onion
- 2 tsp olive oil
- 8oz/225g chopped cooked ham

- 8 eggs
- 1 tbsp milk
- Salt and freshly mince black pepper
- 4oz/125g grated cheddar cheese

## Method

**1** Preheat oven to 200C/400F/GAS6.

**2** Grease the baking dish with a little oil. Sprinkle the ham into an even layer in bottom of baking dish.

**3** Heat the oil in a frying pan over medium-high heat. Once hot, add the peppers and onion and cook until softened for about 4 minutes.

**4** Evenly pour the pepper mixture over the ham then sprinkle evenly with cheese.

**5** In a large mixing bowl whisk together eggs and milk until well blended. Season with salt and pepper and stir, then pour over mixture in baking dish.

**6** Bake in preheated oven for approx 20 minutes until puffy and set.

**7** Cut and serve warm.

## CHEF'S NOTE

You can add sliced avocados, chopped chives and hot sauce for serving.

# BLACKBERRY EGG BAKE

calories: 114
fat: 10g
carbs: 4g
fibre: 2g
protein: 8.5g

## Ingredients

- 5 eggs
- 1 tbsp butter, melted
- 3 tbsp coconut flour
- 1 tsp grated fresh ginger
- ¼ tsp vanilla
- ⅓ tsp fine sea salt
- Zest of half an orange
- 1 tsp fresh rosemary
- 4oz/125g fresh blackberries

## Method

**1** Preheat oven to 180C/350F/GAS4 and grease four ramekins.

**2** Place all of the ingredients except the fresh rosemary and blackberries into a blender and process about one or two minutes on high until the mixture is completely combined and smooth.

**3** Add the rosemary and pulse a few times until rosemary is just combined.

**4** Divide the egg mixture between the four ramekins and add blackberries to each ramekin.

**5** Place the filled ramekins on a baking sheet and bake for fifteen to twenty minutes until the egg mixture puffs and is cooked through.

**6** Cool on a rack a few minutes before indulging. Can be eaten in or popped out of the ramekins.

### CHEF'S NOTE

You can replace orange zest with lemon zest, and add cinnamon and blueberries instead of ginger, blackberries.

27

# BLUEBERRIES & CREAM CREPES

calories: 390
fat: 32g
carbs: 7g
fibre: 3g
protein: 13g

## Ingredients

**Crepe Batter**
- 2oz/50g cream cheese
- 2 eggs
- 10 drops liquid stevia
- ¼ tsp cinnamon
- ¼ tsp baking soda
- Sea salt, to taste

**Filling**
- 4oz/125g cream cheese
- ½ tsp vanilla extract
- 2 tbsp erythritol
- 2½oz/60g blueberries

## Method

**1** Combine the cream cheese and eggs in a bowl and beat them with an electric hand mixer until completely smooth.

**2** Add in the stevia, cinnamon, baking soda and sea salt. Combine that all together.

**3** Heat up a medium-sized, nonstick pan on medium heat. Add in some butter or coconut oil to grease it lightly.

**4** Pour in a bit of batter (about ¼ cup at a time) while swirling the pan to help it spread to the edges. Cook until the edges start to crisp up (about 3 minutes per crepe). Wiggle a spatula around the edges to loosen them, then under the crepe gently and flip.

**5** While the crepes are cooking, prepare your filling by combining the filling cream cheese, vanilla extract and powdered erythritol in a bowl. Beat with an electric hand mixer until smooth and creamy.

**6** When the crepes have finished cooking, add a bit of the filling down the centre of each crepe. Add some fresh blueberries and wrap it up.

## CHEF'S NOTE
You can microwave the berries for 30 seconds to soften.

# STREAKY BACON, EGG & CHEESE CUPS

calories: 201
fat: 14g
carbs: 2g
fibre: 0g
protein: 16g

## Ingredients

- 12 eggs
- 4oz/125g frozen spinach, thawed and drained
- 12 strips streaky bacon
- Handful of grated cheddar cheese
- Salt and pepper, to taste

## Method

**1** Preheat the oven to 200C/400F/GAS6.

**2** Fry the streaky bacon in a frying pan and set aside on a cooling rack to drain excess oil.

**3** Grease muffin pan generously with coconut oil or olive oil then line each cup with one slice of streaky bacon.

**4** Press the slice down, it will stick up on either side (these are your handles!)

**5** In a large bowl, crack and lightly beat eggs.

**6** Wring out any extra water from the spinach beforehand with a clean kitchen towel or paper towel. Stir the spinach into the eggs,

**7** Scoop egg mixture into each muffin well, filling them up about ¾ of the way.

**8** Sprinkle the tops evenly with the shredded cheese and season with salt and pepper.

**9** Bake on the middle rack for 15 minutes.

## CHEF'S NOTE

Store in an airtight container in the refrigerator. Heat up in a microwave for better taste.

# BRIE & APPLE CREPES

calories: 411
fat: 37g
carbs: 6g
fibre: 2g
protein: 14g

·········· *Ingredients* ··········

**Crepe Batter**
- 4oz/125g cream cheese
- 4 eggs
- ½ tsp baking soda
- ¼ tsp sea salt

**Toppings**
- 2oz/50g chopped pecans
- 1 tbsp unsalted butter
- ¼ tsp cinnamon
- 1 gala apple
- 4oz/125g brie cheese
- Fresh mint leaves, for garnish

·········· *Method* ··········

**1** Begin by combining the batter ingredients in a Nutribullet or blender. Blend until smooth.

**2** Heat up a small amount of unsalted butter in a non-stick pan on medium heat.

**3** Ladle some of the crepe batter into the pan and swirl the contents around so that the batter is thin and spread out evenly.

**4** Let cook until the top looks dry (about 2-3 minutes), then flip gently with a large spatula and cook the other side for a few seconds.

**5** Repeat this step until you have about 8 crepes. Layer them on top of each other on a plate while you prep the toppings/fillings.

**6** Melt a tbsp of butter in a small pan and toast the chopped pecans until fragrant. Sprinkle with cinnamon and mix. Then, transfer them to a plate to cool.

**7** Slice the apple & brie thinly. .Arrange the apple slices and brie on 1 crepe and top with some of the toasted pecans. Repeat for all the crepes until all the toppings have been used.

**8** Garnish with mint and enjoy with a fork and knife or rolled up

## CHEF'S NOTE
You can roll each crepe into delicious little cigars and pack away for lunch later. You can also store in a refrigerator.

# HAM & CHEESE WAFFLES

calories: 626
fat: 48g
carbs: 5g
fibre: 3.2g
protein: 45g

## Ingredients

- 4 eggs
- 2½oz/60g unflavored whey protein powder
- 1 tsp baking powder
- 6 tbsp melted butter
- ½ tsp sea salt

- 2 slices ham, chopped
- Handful of cheddar cheese, grated
- A few pinches of paprika
- 1 tbsp fresh basil

## Method

**1** Start by separating eggs into two mixing bowls. Into the bowl with the egg yolks, add the protein powder, baking powder, melted butter and sea salt. Whisk to combine.

**2** Add the finely chopped ham and grated cheddar cheese to the egg yolk mixture and carefully fold.

**3** Whisk the egg whites and a pinch of salt with an electric hand mixer until stiff peaks form. Gently fold in half the stiff egg whites into the egg yolk mixture. Try not to let the egg yolk deflate. Fold in the other half once the egg yolks have aerated a bit.

**4** Add ¼ cup of batter to a well-greased waffle maker and cook on medium heat for about 3-4 minutes each. (or according to manufacturer's instructions.

**5** Cook only until they're lightly golden. The residual heat will continue to cook the waffle even once it's out of the waffle maker.

**6** Sprinkle with a little paprika and fresh basil.

## CHEF'S NOTE

Paprika contains vitamin E which helps control blood clot formation and promotes healthy blood vessel function.

31

# THE PERFECT SCRAMBLE

calories: 444
fat: 35g
carbs: 9g
fibre: 4g
protein: 25g

## Ingredients

- 6 eggs
- 2 tbsp butter
- 2 tbsp sour cream
- 2 stalk green onion
- 4 strips streaky bacon

- ½ tsp salt
- ½ tsp garlic powder
- ½ tsp onion powder
- ¼ tsp black pepper
- ¼ tsp paprika

## Method

**1** Crack the eggs into a cold, ungreased pan and add the butter. Only start mixing the eggs once they're on the heat. This ensures no areas of the egg starts to cook before the others. We are saving the seasoning for after the eggs are cooked. Adding salt will only break the eggs down and create a watery finish; we want creamy!

**2** Place the pan on a medium-high heat and begin stirring the eggs and butter together with a silicone spatula. As the butter melts slowly, it'll give the eggs extra creaminess and will also prevent the eggs from sticking to the pan.

**3** While stirring the eggs, let some streaky bacon strips cook to your desired crispiness in another pan (or bake them!).

**4** Alternate stirring the eggs on the heat and off the heat. If you see the eggs starting to cook in a thin, dry layer at the bottom of the pan, take it off the heat! Scrape it with your silicone spatula and that layer should integrate back with the rest of the eggs and regain some creaminess.

**5** Stir alternatively on and off the flame  a few seconds on the flame, a few seconds off.

**6** The eggs should start coming together slowly. When they're almost done cooking to your liking, turn the flame off. The eggs will continue cooking a little more from the residual heat from the pan.

**7** Add sour cream, salt and paprika to serve.

**8** To add some contrasting flavor, add stalks of srping onions, chopped.

# SHAKSHUKA

calories: 490
fat: 39g
carbs: 4g
fibre: 3g
protein: 35g

## Ingredients

- 250ml/1 cup marinara sauce
- 1 chilli pepper
- 4 eggs
- 1oz/25g feta cheese
- Pinch of ground cumin
- Salt and pepper, to taste
- Fresh basil

## Method

**1** Preheat the oven to 200C/400F/GAS6.

**2** Heat a small frying pan on a medium flame with a cup of marinara sauce and some chopped chilli pepper. Let the chilli pepper cook for about 5 minutes in the sauce.

**3** Crack and gently lower your eggs into the marinara sauce.

**4** Sprinkle feta cheese all over the eggs and season with salt, pepper and cumin.

**5** Using an oven mitt, place the frying pan into your oven and bake for about 10 minutes. Now the frying pan should be hot enough to continue cooking the food in the oven instead of heating itself up first.

**6** Once the eggs are cooked, but still runny, take the frying pan out with an oven mitt. Chop some fresh basil and sprinkle over the shakshuka.

### CHEF'S NOTE
You can make your sauce from scratch instead of using marinara sauce if you have the time.

# LUNCHES

# BLT CHICKEN SALAD STUFFED AVOCADOS

**SERVES 6**

calories: 291
fat: 23g
carbs: 13g
fibre: 6g
protein: 25g

## Ingredients

- 12 slices of streaky bacon
- 12½oz/360g shredded roasted/rotisserie chicken
- 2 large roma tomatoes, chopped
- 14oz/400g cottage cheese
- 2 shredded Romaine lettuce
- 3 avocados

## Method

**1** Preheat your oven to 200C/400F/GAS 6

**2** Lay the streaky bacon out on a foil lined baking sheet

**3** Bake for 10 minutes and, when cooked, lay the streaky bacon out over several sheets of paper towels to cool before crumbling.

**4** In a large bowl, combine the chicken, cottage cheese, lettuce , tomatoes, crumbled streaky bacon, and mix together

**5** Season to taste with salt and pepper

**6** Half your avocados, remove the pits, and season lightly with salt and pepper.

**7** Pile the the chicken salad over the top of of each avocado half to serve.

**CHEF'S NOTE**
The recipe is gluten free.

# VEGETARIAN KETO CLUB SALAD

calories: 330
fat: 26g
carbs: 5g
fibre: 2g
protein: 17g

## Ingredients

- 2 tbsp sour cream
- 2 tbsp mayonnaise
- ½ tbsp garlic powder
- ½ tbsp onion powder
- ½ tbsp dried parsley
- 1 tbsp milk

- 3 boiled eggs, sliced
- 4oz/125g cheddar cheese, cubed
- 2 Romaine lettuce, shredded
- 4oz/125g cherry tomatoes, halved
- 1 cucumber, diced
- 1 tbsp dijon mustard

## Method

**1** Mix the sour cream, mayonnaise, and dried herbs together until combined.

**2** Add one tbsp of milk and mix to make a dressing..

**3** Layer your salad with the salad vegetables, cheese, and sliced egg. Add a spoonful of Dijon mustard in the centre.

**4** Drizzle with the prepared dressing, about 2 tbsps for one serving, then toss to coat.

## CHEF'S NOTE

Cucumber contains antioxidants which prevent the accumulation of harmful free radicals reducing the risk of chronic disease.

# KETO BAKED GARLIC PARMESAN SALMON

**calories: 318**
**fat: 24g**
**carbs: 1g**
**fibre: 0.3g**
**protein: 25g**

## Ingredients

- 1lb/453g wild caught salmon fillet (preferably frozen)
- 2 tbsp butter (pasture raised, grass fed)
- 2 cloves garlic, minced or pressed
- 2oz/50g parmesan cheese, grated
- 2oz/50g mayonnaise (made with avocado oil)
- 2 tbsp organic dried parsley
- Sea salt and pepper

## Method

**1** Preheat oven to 180C/350F/GAS4 and line baking pan with parchment paper.

**2** Place salmon on a baking tray and lightly season with sea salt and pepper. Set aside while preparing the topping.

**3** In a medium-sized frying pan, melt butter and lightly saute garlic over medium heat. Once the garlic has softened, reduce the heat to low and add in the remaining ingredients, stirring until combined and melted.

**4** Spread this mixture over the salmon fillets, place in the oven and bake for 10-15 minutes or until cooked through.

**5** Check salmon with a fork. Don't overcook to remain slightly translucent.

### CHEF'S NOTE
Sea salt provides the body with minerals like zinc, iron and potassium which helps prevent your body from "keto flu" majorly caused by electrolyte deficiencies.

# KETO BEEF STUFFED PEPPERS

calories: 410
fat: 31g
carbs: 11g
fibre: 3g
protein: 21g

## Ingredients

- 1 tbsp of olive oil
- 2 slices streaky bacon, finely chopped
- 1 onion, peeled and finely chopped
- 15 white button mushrooms, finely chopped
- 11oz/300g minced beef
- 1 tbsp smoked paprika
- 3 large sweet peppers
- Salt and freshly mince black pepper, to taste

## Method

**1** Preheat the oven to 180C/350F/GAS4.

**2** Cut the top off the peppers and remove all seeds. Lightly brush olive oil on the entire pepper, inside and out. Set aside.

**3** Heat the olive oil in a pan. Cook the streaky bacon until crispy. Remove streaky bacon, keeping as much oil in the pan as possible.

**4** Add the onions and mushrooms to the oil and cook until soft. Then add the beef and paprika. Cook until the beef is browned. Season with salt and pepper. Remove from heat.

**5** Scoop the beef and mushroom mixture into the peppers.

**6** Place the peppers on a baking tray and bake for 20-25 minutes.

**7** Garnish with chopped parsley.

### CHEF'S NOTE
You can also enjoy with a batch of keto hummus and some veg sticks.

# KETO EASY TACO BOWLS WITH CAULIFLOWER RICE

calories: 459
fat: 38g
carbs: 9g
fibre: 3g
protein: 21g

## Ingredients

For taco bowl
- 450g/1lb of minced beef
- 3 cloves of garlic, minced or finely diced
- 1 onion, finely diced
- 6 cherry tomatoes, finely diced

- 1 pepper, diced
- 1 tsp of fresh ginger, grated
- 2 tsp of cumin powder
- Dash of chilli powder, to taste
- 2 tbsp avocado oil
- Salt and pepper, to taste

For the cauliflower rice
- 11oz/300g cauliflower rice
- 2 tbsp of coconut oil, to cook cauliflower with
- Chilli powder and salt, to taste

## Method

**1** In a large frying pan, heat avocado oil and garlic. Add minced beef and cook until almost completely browned.

**2** Add onion, tomatoes, and pepper. Cook until vegetables are soft.

**3** Add ginger, cumin, chilli powder, salt, and pepper, to taste. Mix well to combine.

**4** To make the cauliflower rice, sauté the cauliflower pieces in the coconut oil on high heat for 5 mins until softened. Season with chilli powder and salt, to taste.

**5** Serve taco meat over the cauliflower "rice."

### CHEF'S NOTE
Cauliflower rice is made by pulsing cauliflower florets in a food processor.

40

# KETO CURRIED TUNA SALAD

calories: 626
fat: 37g
carbs: 14g
fibre: 2.6g
protein: 47g

## Ingredients

- 6oz/175g tuna, drained and flaked
- 2 tbsp mayo
- 2 tsp curry powder
- ½ red onion, sliced
- 1 tsp dried parsley
- 5 black pitted olives, sliced
- Salt and pepper, to taste

## Method

1 Drain and flake the tuna in a bowl.

2 Mix with the mayo, curry powder, and dried parsley.

3 Combine with the olives and red onion.

4 Season with salt and pepper, to taste.

5 Serve with a spinach salad or cauliflower rice.

## CHEF'S NOTE

Curry powder is a great 'cheat' ingredient to have in the cupboard.

# BEANLESS PUMPKIN KETO CHILLI RECIPE

calories: 189
fat: 9g
carbs: 6g
fibre: 3g
protein: 17g

## Ingredients

- 1lb/450g grass fed minced beef
- 1 onion
- 1nred pepper
- 500ml/2 cups tomato passata/sieved tomatoes
- 1¾lb/800g tomatoes, diced
- 15oz/425g pumpkin, diced
- ½ tbsp chilli powder
- 1 tsp cayenne pepper
- 1 tsp cumin

## Method

1 Brown the meat in a large pan over medium heat.

2 Chop the onion and pepper, then add into the pan with the meat. Cook until the onions become translucent (3-5 minutes)

3 Add in the rest of the ingredients and let simmer on low for 30 minutes.

4 Taste your chilli, adjust seasonings as you like and cook for another 30 minutes.

### CHEF'S NOTE

Tomatoes contains antioxidants that have been proven to be effective against many forms of cancer.

# KETO SOUTHERN FRIED CHICKEN TENDER

calories: 365
fat: 21g
carbs: 3.5g
fibre: 4g
protein: 38.5g

## Ingredients

- 4 chicken breasts
- 5oz/150g almond flour
- 1 egg
- ½ tbsp cayenne pepper
- ½ tbsp onion salt
- ½ tbsp garlic powder
- ½ tbsp dried mixed herbs
- 1 tsp salt
- 1 tsp black pepper

## Method

**1** Preheat the oven to 180C/350F/GAS4

**2** Slice up chicken into strips, about 5-6 pieces per breast. Lay chicken strips out on a plate.

**3** Mix all dry ingredients, except the almond flour to make a spice mix.

**4** Using half of the spice mix, coat the chicken evenly. Turn over the chicken and coat the other side.

**5** Combine the rest of the spice mix with almond flour in a bowl. In a separate bowl, whisk your egg well.

**6** Take the chicken one piece at a time, and dunk it into the egg, and then dunk it straight into the almond flour mixture. Roll it around in the flour to make sure it is evenly coated.

**7** Place the coated chicken on a greased baking tray.

**8** Place in the oven for about 20-25 mins or until cooked through.

## CHEF'S NOTE

Be careful, so that the coating doesn't stick to the rack and come away from the keto fried chicken.

# BAKED STREAKY BACON COATED CHICKEN TENDERS

calories: 320
fat: 20g
carbs: 2g
fibre: 0g
protein: 29g

## Ingredients

- 2 tsp salt flakes
- 2 tsp cayenne pepper
- 2 tsp paprika
- 2 tsp garlic powder
- 1 tsp onion powder

- 1 tsp oregano
- 1 tsp thyme
- 2lb/900g chicken min breast fillets
- 16 slices streaky bacon

## Method

**1** Preheat oven to 220C/425F/GAS7. Line a large rimmed baking tray and top with metal rack.

**2** In large plastic zipper bag, dump in all the herbs and spices. Close bag and shake to blend.

**3** Place each chicken tender in the zipper bag, close, and shake bag to coat the chicken in the spice blend. Once coated wrap in streaky bacon being sure to tuck in the ends and then place on rack in prepared pan.

**4** Bake for 35 minutes or until cooled through. Streaky bacon should be crispy. If streaky bacon isn't crispy, you can place under the grill for a minute or two.

### CHEF'S NOTE
Serve with a fresh green salad.

# KETO CHICKEN BROCCOLI CASSEROLE

calories: 445
fat: 27.3g
carbs: 14g
fibre: 4.9g
protein: 39.6g

## Ingredients

- 2 tbsp coconut oil divided
- 1½pint/1 litre fresh broccoli florets
- 1 onion, diced
- Sea salt
- Pepper
- 8oz/225g mushrooms sliced
- 750g/1lb 11oz cooked chicken shredded
- 9oz/250g chicken stock
- 8½oz/250ml full fat coconut milk
- 2 eggs

## Method

**1** Preheat the oven to 180C/350F/GAS4. Grease a casserole pan with half the coconut oil and set aside.

**2** Steam the broccoli until just barely cooked and set aside, uncovered.

**3** In a sauce pan melt the coconut oil, brown the onions and season with salt and pepper. Add the mushrooms, saute until cooked and move the pan off the heat.

**4** Transfer the broccoli, mushroom, onions, and shredded chicken into the casserole pan distributing evenly.

**5** Mix the stock, coconut milk and eggs with a pinch of salt & pepper in a bowl and pour over the contents of the casserole dish.

**6** Place the casserole in the oven and cook for 35 to 40 minutes or until cooked through.

**7** Remove from the oven and serve.

### CHEF'S NOTE
Serve with a pile of steamed greens.

# KETO CHICKEN CURRY

calories: 357
fat: 27g
carbs: 6g
fibre: 3g
protein: 22g

## Ingredients

- 1lb/450g chicken or turkey mince
- 14oz/400ml coconut milk
- 1 tbsp curry powder
- ½ cauliflower head, broken into small pieces
- 2 tbsp coconut oil, to cook with
- Salt and pepper, to taste

## Method

1 Add coconut oil to a small pot and cook the mince chicken until slightly browned.

2 Add coconut milk, curry powder, and salt and simmer with the lid on for 15 minutes.

3 Then add in the cauliflower and cook for another 5 minutes.

4 Season with additional salt and pepper, to taste.

## CHEF'S NOTE

Curry powder increases metabolism and aids pain relief.

# KETO ASIAGO CAULIFLOWER RICE

calories: 250
fat: 22g
carbs: 5.6g
fibre: 2.2g
protein: 7g

## Ingredients

- 2 cauliflower heads
- 8oz/225g asiago cheese*, shredded
- 4oz/120ml double cream

## Method

**1** Whizz the cauliflower in a food processor to make cauliflower rice.

**2** In a large saute pan, add the riced cauliflower and 2 tbsp of water. Cover and cook for 5 minutes.

**3** Add the cream and cheese and mix until cheese is melted.

**4** Taste to see if the cauliflower is done.

**5** Take off the heat and serve.

## CHEF'S NOTE

Calcium in asiago cheese helps maintain heart rhythm and muscle function.

# AVOCADO FRIES

calories: 587
fat: 51g
carbs: 12g
fibre: 5g
protein: 17g

## Ingredients

**For the fries:**
- 3 avocados
- 1 egg
- 12½oz/360g almond meal
- 12½oz/360g sunflower oil

- ¼ tsp cayenne pepper
- ½ tsp salt

**For the spicy mayo:**
- 2 tbsp homemade mayonnaise
- 1 tsp sriracha

## Method

**1** Break an egg into a bowl and beat it. In another bowl, mix your almond meal with some salt and cayenne pepper.

**2** Slice each avocado in half and take out the seed. Peel off the skin off every half. and slice each avocado vertically into 4 or 5 pieces (depending on the size of the avocado).

**3** Start heating your deep fryer (or deep pan with lots of oil) to about 350°F. If you don't have a cooking thermometer, try sticking a wooden spoon into the oil when it's been heating for about 7-8 minutes. If bubbles arise from the spoon, your oil is hot enough for deep frying.

**4** Coat each slice of avocado in the egg. Roll each coated slice in the almond meal until covered.

**5** Carefully lower each avocado slice into the deep fryer (or pan) to avoid splashing. It will hurt!

**6** Allow each piece to fry from 45 seconds to a minute until a light brown. Dark brown means they've been in there a few seconds too long.

**7** Transfer quickly to a plate lined with a paper towel to soak up the excess oil.

**8** Mix some sriracha sauce and mayonnaise to serve as a dip.

### CHEF'S NOTE
You can use coconut oil instead of sunflower oil.

48

# FRIED CHICKEN AND STREAKY BACON PATTIES

calories: 415
fat: 23g
carbs: 4.5g
fibre: 3g
protein: 39g

## Ingredients

- 4 slices streaky bacon
- 2 red peppers, seeded
- 5oz/150g chicken
- 2oz/50g grated parmesan cheese
- 3 tbsp coconut flour
- 1 egg
- 2 tbsp coconut oil
- Salt and pepper, to taste

## Method

**1** Cook the streaky bacon until crisp then drain on paper towels and chop well.

**2** Place the peppers in a food processor and pulse until coarsely chopped.

**3** Add the chicken and cooked streaky bacon then pulse until it comes together in a smooth mixture.

**4** Pulse in the parmesan cheese, coconut flour, and egg then season with salt and pepper.

**5** Melt the coconut oil in a large frying pan over medium-high heat.

**6** Shape the mixture into 9 patties and fry for 2 to 3 minutes on each side until browned.

**7** Drain on paper towels and repeat with the remaining mixture.

## CHEF'S NOTE
Streaky bacon contains vitamin B-12 which is important for healthy red blood cells.

# CHICKEN STRIP SLIDER

**SERVES 4**

calories: 625
fat: 51g
carbs: 4.3g
fibre: 2g
protein: 34.8g

## Ingredients

Almond flour buns
- 1oz/25g almond flour
- 2oz/50g flax seed
- 3 tbsp parmesan cheese
- 2 eggs
- 4 tbsp butter

- 1 tsp baking soda
- 1 tsp southwest seasoning
- 1 tsp paprika
- ½ tsp apple cider vinegar
- 4 chicken breasts

## Method

**1** Preheat oven to 180C/350F/GAS4.

**2** Mix together all dry ingredients in a large mixing bowl.

**3** Melt butter in the microwave, then add eggs, vinegar, stevia and butter to mixture.

**4** Mix everything well and spread the mixture out between 8 muffin top slots in a pan.

**5** Bake for 15-17 minutes. Once baked, let cool for 5 minutes, then cut buns in half.

**6** Whilst the buns are baking cook the chicken breasts on a grill until cooked through.

**7** Cut the cooked breast lengthways to make 8 pieces.

**8** When the buns are ready place a piece of chicken in each to serve.

### CHEF'S NOTE
Serve with crisy green lettuce and some BBQ sauce.

# DINNERS

# CHICKEN ENCHILADA CASSEROLE

calories: 406
fat: 24g
carbs: 7g
fibre: 1g
protein: 37g

## Ingredients

- 1lb/450g boneless skinless chicken breasts trimmed & pounded
- 14oz/400g of enchilada sauce store bought or from scratch
- 7oz/200g finely crumbled feta cheese
- 4 green chiles, chopped
- 3 tbsp chopped fresh coriander

- Pinch of salt
- Pinch of pepper
- Olive oil spray or use olive oil in a little bowl with a brush
- 15oz/425g shredded cheddar cheese

## Method

**1** Preheat oven to 230C/450F/GAS8.

**2** Pat the chicken dry and season with salt and pepper.

**3** Combine the chicken and enchilada sauce in a medium saucepan & simmer for 15-20 minutes over medium-low heat until cooked through.

**4** Remove chicken from pan and shred into bite-sized pieces. Combine shredded chicken, the enchilada sauce, feta cheese, chiles and coriander in a bowl.

**5** Spray a casserole dish with olive oil (or use a brush) and coat the entire bottom and sides.

**6** Evenly spread cheddar cheese on the bottom of the dish. Add the chicken mixture, then add the rest of the cheddar cheese on top.

**7** Cover with foil and bake for about 10 minutes. Remove foil and bake an additional 3 to 5 minutes to melt the cheese.

## CHEF'S NOTE
You can serve with lime wedges and sour cream.

# ROASTED PECAN GREEN BEANS

calories: 240
fat: 20.8g
carbs: 5.3g
fibre: 2g
protein: 4.7g

## Ingredients

- 8oz/225g green beans
- 2 tbsp olive oil
- 2oz/50g chopped pecans
- 2 tbsp parmesan cheese
- ½ lemon zest
- 1 tsp minced garlic
- ½ tsp red pepper Flakes

## Method

**1** Preheat oven to 230C/450F/GAS8,

**2** Blitz the pecans in a food processor until they are roughly chopped.

**3** In a large mixing bowl, mix together green beans, pecans, olive oil, parmesan cheese, the zest of ½ lemon, minced garlic, and red pepper flakes.

**4** Spread everything out on a foiled baking sheet.

**5** Roast the green beans in the oven for approx 20 minutes or until cooked through.

**6** Let cool for 4-5 minutes, then serve!

## CHEF'S NOTE

Try pairing this lovey dish with steak too.

# LOW CARB KETO LASAGNA

calories: 364
fat: 21g
carbs: 12g
fibre: 7g
protein: 32g

## Ingredients

- 1 tbsp butter
- 8oz/225g spicy Italian sausage
- 15oz/425g ricotta cheese
- 2 tbsp coconut flour
- 1 egg
- 1½ tsp salt
- ½ tsp pepper

- 1 tsp garlic powder
- 1 clove garlic, finely chopped
- 12½oz/360g mozzarella cheese
- 3½oz/100g parmesan cheese
- 4 courgettes quatered lengthways

- 500ml/2 cups marinara sauce
- 1 tbsp mixed Italian herb seasoning
- ½ tsp red pepper flake
- 2 tbsp chopped fresh basil

## Method

**1** Heat butter in a large frying pan over medium-high heat. Crumble and brown Italian sausage. Remove from heat and let cool.

**2** Preheat oven to 190C/375F/GAS5 and coat a 9×9" baking dish with cooking spray or butter.

**3** Add ricotta cheese, mozzarella cheese, parmesan cheese, egg, coconut flour, salt, garlic, garlic powder, and pepper to a small bowl and mix until smooth. Set aside. Add Italian seasoning and red pepper flakes to a jar of marinara, stir well. Set aside.

**4** Add a layer of sliced courgette to the bottom of greased dish. Spread of cheese mixture over courgette, sprinkle with Italian sausage and then add a layer of sauce.

**5** Repeat process 3-4 times until ingredients are all gone, ending with a layer of sauce. Add remaining mozzarella cheese and sprinkle with remaining parmesan cheese.

**6** Cover with foil and bake for 30 minutes. Remove foil and bake for an additional 15 minutes until golden brown. Remove from oven and let sit for 5-10 minutes before serving. Sprinkle with fresh basil if desired.

### CHEF'S NOTE
Marinara is a simple Italian/American sauce now widely availible in the UK.

# KETO BUFFALO WINGS

calories: 391
fat: 33g
carbs: 1g
fibre: 0g
protein: 31g

## Ingredients

- 12 chicken wings
- 4 tbsp butter
- 2oz/60ml hot sauce
- 1 clove minced garlic

- 1 tsp paprika
- 1 tsp cayenne pepper
- 1 tsp salt
- 1 tsp black pepper

## Method

**1** Preheat oven to 200C/400F/GAS6. Using a wire rack, with a baking dish or sheet underneath, spread wings evenly. The wire rack will keep them from getting soggy on the bottom. Rub some olive oil and season generously with salt and pepper.

**2** Bake for about 45 minutes or until crispy and at 140C/275F/GAS1.

**3** While your chicken wings are baking (or frying, cook whichever way you prefer), add your garlic and butter to a small saucepan over medium-low heat until hot and melted.

**4** Once melted, add the rest of the ingredients and mix together.

**5** When your wings are cooked, toss them in a bowl with sauce, until coated.

**6** Serve with salad and celery, or coated with blue cheese crumbles.

## CHEF'S NOTE

Cayenne pepper helps increase the amount of heat your body produces, making you burn more calories per day.

# PORTOBELLO BUN CHEESEBURGERS

calories: 336
fat: 22.8g
carbs: 4g
fibre: 1.2g
protein: 29.g

## Ingredients

- 1lb/450g grass fed minced beef
- 1 tbsp Worcestershire sauce
- 1 tsp pink Himalayan salt
- 1 tsp black pepper
- 1 tbsp avocado oil
- 8 portobello mushroom caps, destemmed, rinsed and dabbed dry
- 4 slices sharp cheddar cheese

## Method

**1** In a bowl, combine minced beef, Worcestershire sauce, salt, and pepper.

**2** Form beef into burger patties.

**3** In a large pan, heat avocado oil over medium heat. Add portobello mushroom caps and cook for about 3-4 minutes on each side. Remove from heat.

**4** In the same pan, cook burger patties for 4-5 mins on either side or until cooked through.

**5** Add cheese to top of burgers and cover with a lid and allow cheese to melt, about 1 minute.

**6** Layer one portobello mushroom cap, then cheeseburger, desired garnishes, and top with remaining portobello mushroom cap.

### CHEF'S NOTE
You can garnish with sliced dill pickles, romaine, sugar-free barbecue sauce, and spicy brown mustard.

# KETO CHINESE ASPARAGUS CHICKEN STIR-FRY

calories: 240
fat: 41g
carbs: 10g
fibre: 4g
protein: 24g

## Ingredients

- ¼ onion, diced
- 16 spears of asparagus, chopped
- 1 chicken breast, diced
- 4oz/120g avocado oil
- 2 tbsp gluten-free tamari sauce or coconut aminos
- 1 tsp sesame oil

## Method

**1** Add avocado oil to a hot frying pan or wok on a medium heat.

**2** Add the diced onion and cook until it turns translucent.

**3** Add in the diced chicken and stir-fry until the chicken is cooked. Set aside.

**4** Then add the asparagus into the frying pan and stir-fry for 5 minutes on high heat.

**5** Add the chicken back in, season with tamari sauce and sesame oil. Cook until piping hot then serve.

### CHEF'S NOTE
Sesame oil is good for maintaining blood sugar levels.

# LOW CARB MINI MEXICAN MEATZAS

calories: 418
fat: 24g
carbs: 5.5g
fibre: 2g
protein: 39.8g

## Ingredients

- 1lb/450g minced beef
- 1 onion
- 1 egg
- 1 head cauliflower
- 2 tsp chilli powder
- 1 tsp cumin
- 1 tsp salt
- ½ tsp pepper
- 1 tsp garlic powder
- ¼ red onion, sliced thin
- 9oz/250g cheddar cheese, shredded
- 4oz/125g sweet pepper slices

## Method

**1** Preheat oven to 180C/350F/GAS4.

**2** Add onion to a food processor and pulse until finely chopped.

**3** Place in a large bowl and then add cauliflower to food processor and pulse until it looks like grains of rice.

**4** Add that to the large bowl along with meat, a beaten egg, chilli powder, cumin, salt, pepper and garlic powder.

**5** Mix well and split meat into 4.

**6** Take each piece and make into a very thin, round pizza looking shell. Place on a lined baking tray.

**7** Bake for 20 minutes or until meat is cooked.

**8** Take out of the oven, sprinkle cheese and add onions and peppers on top.

**9** Return to the oven until the cheese is melted.

### CHEF'S NOTE
Serve with avocado slices and sliced tomatoes.

# EASY STEAK FAJITA

calories: 415
fat: 27g
carbs: 5.5g
fibre: 3g
protein: 36g

## Ingredients

- 2oz/60ml olive oil
- 2oz/60ml fresh lime juice
- 1 tbsp chilli powder
- 1 tsp mince cumin
- 1 tsp paprika
- 1 tsp minced garlic

- 1lb/450g beef flank steak cut into strips
- 2 tbsp coconut oil
- 1 yellow onion, sliced
- 1 red pepper, sliced
- 1 green pepper, sliced
- Salt and pepper, to taste

## Method

1 Whisk together the olive oil, lime juice, chilli powder, cumin, and paprika in a bowl to make a marinade.

2 Add the garlic and red pepper flakes, stirring to combine.

3 Season the steak with salt and pepper then place it in a freezer bag and pour in the marinade.

4 Shake to coat then seal and chill for 2 to 4 hours.

5 Preheat a grill to high heat and oil the grates.

6 Add the steak strips to the grill and cook until done to the desired level then set aside.

7 Heat the coconut oil in a large frying pan over medium heat.

8 Add the peppers and onions then season with salt and pepper – sauté until they are just tender, about 5 minutes.

### CHEF'S NOTE
You can add ½ tsp chilli flakes if you prefer it more spicy and serve in lettuce cups with sour cream.

# SHAKE AND BAKE PORK CHOP

calories: 350
fat: 14g
carbs: 1g
fibre: 0.5g
protein: 52g

## Ingredients

- 8 small boneless pork loin chops
- ½ tbsp psyllium husk powder
- ½ tsp paprika
- ½ tsp salt
- ¼ tsp garlic powder
- ¼ tsp onion powder
- ¼ tsp dried oregano

## Method

**1** Preheat the oven to 180C/350F/GAS4 and line a baking sheet with parchment.

**2** Rinse the pork chops in cool water then pat dry.

**3** Combine the psyllium husk powder and spices in a zippered freezer bag.

**4** Add the pork chops one at a time and shake to coat.

**5** Place the pork chops on the baking sheet and bake for 20-30 or until cooked through.

### CHEF'S NOTE
Psyllium is a soluble fibre particulalry good for gut health

# EASY COCONUT CHICKEN

calories: 286
fat: 20g
carbs: 3g
fibre: 0g
protein: 23g

## Ingredients

- 1 tbsp coconut oil
- 5 cloves garlic, crushed
- 4 tbsp apple cider vinegar
- 1lb/450g boneless skinless, chicken thighs cut into bite sizes pieces
- ½ tsp black pepper
- ½ tsp Sea Salt
- 2oz/60ml water
- 250ml/1 cup tinned coconut milk

## Method

**1** In a sauce pan over medium/low heat add the coconut oil and diced chicken thighs.

**2** Cook for 2 -3 minutes and then add the apple cider vinegar, water and garlic cloves and cook for 3 minutes.

**3** Add the black pepper and Sea Salt and cook until the liquid all boils down. This should take roughly 10 minutes.

**4** Stir in the coconut milk and simmer for 5 to 10 minutes until your liquid thickens slightly and you have a gravy.

### CHEF'S NOTE
Serve with cauliflower rice or courgette noodles.

# LOW CARB MEATBALLS ITALIAN STYLE

calories: 204
fat: 14g
carbs: 4g
fibre: 2g
protein: 16g

## Ingredients

- 1lb/450g minced beef
- 2oz/50g grated parmesan cheese
- 2oz/50g golden flaxseed meal
- 1 tbsp Italian seasoning
- ¾ tsp sea salt
- ½ tsp black pepper
- 2oz/60ml unsweetened coconut milk

- 1 onion, finely chopped
- 1 egg
- 3 cloves garlic, minced
- 2 tbsp fresh parsley, chopped
- 250ml/1 cup tomato passata/sieved tomatoes

## Method

**1** Preheat the oven to 220C/425F/GAS7. Line a baking sheet with parchment paper.

**2** In a large bowl, stir together the grated Parmesan cheese, golden flaxseed meal, Italian seasoning, sea salt, and black pepper.

**3** Whisk in the milk, onion, egg, garlic, and fresh parsley. Let the mixture sit for a couple of minutes.

**4** Mix in the minced beef using your hands, until just incorporated. (Don't over-mix to avoid tough meatballs.

**5** Form the mixture into 1-inch balls and place on the lined baking sheet. (don't pack the meatballs too tightly).

**6** Bake for 10-12 minutes, or until the meatballs are cooked through.

**7** Meanwhile warm the passata through in a pan. Add the cooked meatballs and cook until pipting hot.

**8** Garnish with additional fresh parsley and serve.

### CHEF'S NOTE
This is good served with courgette noodles.

# ASPARAGUS STUFFED CHICKEN PARMESAN

calories: 317
fat: 26g
carbs: 11g
fibre: 4g
protein: 23g

## Ingredients

- 3 chicken breasts
- 1 tsp garlic paste
- 12 stalks asparagus, stalks removed
- 4oz/125g cream cheese
- 1 tbsp butter
- 1 tsp olive oil
- 125ml/½ cup tomato passata/sieved tomatoes
- 9oz/250g shredded mozzarella
- Salt and pepper, to taste

## Method

**1** Butterfly the chicken (slice it in half without slicing it all the way through. The chicken breast should open out like a butterfly with one end still intact in the middle).

**2** Remove the hardy stalks of the asparagus and set aside.

**3** Rub salt, pepper and garlic paste all over the chicken breasts (inside and outside).

**4** Divide cream cheese between the chicken breasts and spread it on the inside. Place four stalks of asparagus and then fold one side of the breast over the other, tucking it in place with a toothpick to make sure it doesn't come open.

**5** Preheat the oven and set it to grill. Add butter and olive oil to a hot frying pan and place the chicken breasts in it. Cook the breasts on each side for 6-7 minutes until the chicken is cooked through.

**6** Meanwhile pre heat the grill.

**7** Top each breast with passata sauce and divide the shredded mozzarella on top. Place under the grill until the cheese melts.

### CHEF'S NOTE
Cooking times may slightly differ depending on the size of the chicken breast.

# SAUSAGE AND EGG MEATLOAF PIE

calories: 408
fat: 29g
carbs: 1g
fibre: 0g
protein: 34g

## Ingredients

- 1lb/450g mince pork
- 15oz/425g shredded mozzarella cheese
- 6 eggs
- 1 tsp mixed herbs
- Large pinch salt & pepper

## Method

**1** Preheat oven to 180C/350F/GAS4.

**2** Brown the pork mince..

**3** Whisk together eggs, seasonings and shredded cheese.

**4** Drain the pork and allow to cool.

**5** Blend the pork and egg mixture and pour into a 9" pie pan.

**6** Bake for 45-55 minutes or until firm and cooked through.

## CHEF'S NOTE

This simple meatloaf style dish is great served with steamed broccoli.

# SOUPS & SALADS

# LOW-CARB PUMPKIN SOUP WITH CHORIZO CRUMB

calories: 254
fat: 18.9g
carbs: 9.1g
fibre: 1.4g
protein: 12.7g

## Ingredients

- 2 tbsp virgin coconut oil
- 1 brown onion, chopped
- 1lb/450g chopped pumpkin
- 1 garlic clove, minced
- 1 tbsp fresh grated ginger
- Pinch of garam masala

- ½ tsp cumin
- ½ tsp paprika
- 1.5l/6 cups chicken stock
- 1 Mexican chorizo sausage
- Salt and pepper, to taste

## Method

**1** Place the stock in a pan on a medium heat and simmer for 10 minutes until the stock reduces in volume by about a third.

**2** Preheat the oven to 180C/350F/GAS4.

**3** Slice the pumpkin in half, remove the seeds and peel. Cut into cubes, toss in a little olive oil, bake for 20 -25 mins in the oven until tender and then set aside.

**4** Meanwhile, heat the coconut oil in a pan on a medium heat. Peel and finely chop the onion and garlic. Gently fry the onion on a medium heat for 3 mins until soft. Add the garlic and fry together for 1 further minute.

**5** Add the cumin, ginger, garam masala, paprika, salt and pepper to the onions and garlic and fry for 4 minutes on a medium-low heat.

**6** Add the roasted pumpkin and concentrated stock. Simmer on a medium heat for about 5 minutes. Place in a high-speed blender and process until smooth. Add a little more stock or water if needed to reach your desired consistency.

**7** Remove the skin from the chorizo sausage. Finely dice the chorizo meat and fry on a medium heat in a dry non-stick pan for about 5 minutes until cooked through and crispy.

**8** Ladle the pumpkin soup into bowls, top with the chorizo crumb and optionally, top with yoghurt, sesame seeds and watercress.

# SLOW COOKER PUMPKIN & COCONUT SOUP

calories: 234
fat: 21.7g
carbs: 11.4g
fibre: 1.5g
protein: 2.3g

## Ingredients

- 1 onion, diced
- 1 tsp fresh ginger, grated
- 1 tsp garlic, crushed
- 2 tbsp butter
- 1lb 2oz/500g pumpkin chunks
- 750ml/3 cups vegetable stock
- 500ml/2 cups coconut milk
- Salt and pepper, to taste

## Method

1 Place all the ingredients into slow cooker dish and combine.

2 Cook on HIGH for 4-6 hours OR Cook on LOW for 6-8 hours.

3 Puree until smooth using a stick/immersion blender.

4 Check the seasoning and serve.

**CHEF'S NOTE**
You can also cook on stove top for 30 - 45 mins.

## SERVES 6

# KETO PHO STYLE CHICKEN SOUP

calories: 152
fat: 7.2g
carbs: 6.6g
fibre: 5.2g
protein: 17.4g

## Ingredients

- 4 chicken thighs , boneless
- 1 garlic cloe, crushed
- 1 fresh ginger root
- 1 onion
- 2 tbsp fish sauce

- 1.5 litre/6 cups chicken stock
- 300g/11oz shirataki noodles

## Method

**1** Peel ginger and cut into large chunks.

**2** Slice the onion.

**3** Add chicken stock, garlic, fish sauce & chicken thighs. Reduce heat and simmer for 20-30 mins until the chicken is tender.

**4** Remove chicken and discard ginger root chunks. Let chicken cool until you can shred it. You can discard the skin or shred it to up too.

**5** Return shredded chicken to soup along with the noodles. Warm through and serve.

### CHEF'S NOTE
Shiritaki noodles (also called Miracle noodles) are very low carb.

# KETO BROCCOLI SOUP WITH TURMERIC & GINGER

calories: 439
fat: 36g
carbs: 17g
fibre: 4g
protein: 8g

## Ingredients

- 1 onion
- 3 cloves garlic
- 500ml/2 cups coconut milk
- 1 tsp salt

- 1 tsp turmeric powder
- 2 tsp fresh ginger, chopped
- 2 broccoli heads, chopped into florets
- 500ml/2 cups vegetable stock

## Method

**1** Pour half of the coconut milk in a pan and place on low heat.

**2** Add the onion and garlic and cook for 5 minutes until soft.

**3** Once cooked, add the salt, turmeric, ginger, broccoli florets, stock and remaining coconut milk.

**4** Simmer for 20 mins, stirring occasionally and mashing the broccoli.

**5** Let the mixture cool, before placing in a food processor and blending into a puree.

### CHEF'S NOTE
You can serve with yoghurt, roasted almonds, fresh greens and sesame seeds.

# TACO SOUP CROCKPOT

calories: 505
fat: 32g
carbs: 8.5g
fibre: 0g
protein: 44g

## Ingredients

- 900g/2lb lean minced beef
- 450g/16oz cream cheese
- 15oz/425g diced tomatoes
- 3 tbsp taco seasoning

- 1.5 litre/6 cups chicken broth
- 4oz/125g shredded cheddar cheese
- 2oz/60ml sour cream

## Method

**1** Brown the minced beef in a large saucepan until cooked through then drain the fat off and add the meat to the slow cooker.

**2** Sprinkle in the chopped cream cheese along with the diced tomatoes and taco seasoning.

**3** Pour in the chicken broth then cover and cook on low heat for 4 hours or on high for 2 hours.

**4** Stir everything together then adjust seasoning with salt and pepper to taste.

**5** Spoon into bowls and serve with shredded cheese and sour cream.

### CHEF'S NOTE
Riboflavin in sour cream has antioxidant properties which help fight free radical damages in the body.

# KETO GREEK MEATBALLS SALAD

calories: 399
fat: 36g
carbs: 2g
fibre: 0g
protein: 20g

## Ingredients

For the meatballs
- 1lb/450g minced lamb or beef
- 2 tsp dried oregano
- 2 tbsp fresh mint, finely chopped
- 2 cloves garlic, peeled and crushed
- Salt and pepper, to taste

- 4 tbsp olive oil

For the salad
- 1 tomato, cut into wedges
- Few lettuce leaves, to serve with
- 1 lemon, cut into wedges
- 4 tbsp flat leaf parsley, chopped

## Method

**1** Preheat oven to 180C/350F/GAS4.

**2** Mix the mince lamb with the dried oregano, mint, garlic, salt and pepper. Form small meatballs from the mixture.

**3** Add olive oil to a large pan and fry the meatballs in batches until browned. Transfer to a lined baking tray and bake in the oven for 10 minutes to ensure the centre of the meatballs cook through.

**4** Serve the meatballs over a salad made of lettuce and tomato wedges. Generously squeeze over the lemon and garnish the salad with chopped parsley.

## CHEF'S NOTE
Lemon helps balance your body's pH and optimise overall health.

# BLTA PESTO CHICKEN SALAD

calories: 375
fat: 27g
carbs: 3g
fibre: 0g
protein: 27g

## Ingredients

- 1lb/450g chicken, cooked and cubed
- 6 slices streaky bacon
- 1 avocado, cubed
- 10 vine ripened tomatoes, quartered
- 4oz/125g mayonnaise
- 2 tbsp green pesto
- 1 red onion, sliced
- 1 romaine lettuce, shredded

## Method

**1** Cook the bacon until very crisp. When it cools crumble into small pieces.

**2** In a large mixing bowl, combine together the chicken, streaky bacon pieces, avocado, tomatoes, mayonnaise, lettuce, red onion and pesto.

**3** Toss gently to coat well. Loosen with a little olove oil if needed.

**4** Check the seasoning and serve.

### CHEF'S NOTE
Feel free to add some cubed cucumber and spinach leaves to this salad too.

# STEAK & CHIMICHURRI SALAD

calories: 438
fat: 32g
carbs: 7g
fibre: 2g
protein: 30g

## Ingredients

- 1 romaine lettuce, shredded
- ¼ head red cabbage, shredded
- 2 radishes, sliced thinly
- 2 tbsp fresh coriander, coarsely chopped
- 1 tbsp house vinaigrette salad dressing
- 3 tbsps Chimichurri Sauce
- 4oz/125g great steak

## Method

1 Toss the first five ingredients together with House Vinaigrette.

2 Flash fry your steak until cooked to your perference (medium rare is best)

3 Thinly slice the steak and serve with the salad and the Chimichurri Sauce. on the side.

## CHEF'S NOTE

Chimichurri sauce is an Argentinian sauce which is readily availble in US & UK supermarkets.

# LOADED CHICKEN SALAD

calories: 430
fat: 29.36g
carbs: 12.86g
fibre: 6.12g
protein: 31.73g

## Ingredients

- 4 boneless chicken breasts,
- 1 tbsp extra virgin olive oil
- ¼ tsp Himalayan salt
- ¼ tsp black pepper
- 1 avocado
- 3½oz/100g mozzarella balls
- 1 tomato

- 1 jar artichoke hearts, chopped
- ½ red onion
- 4 asparagus spears
- 20 leaves basil
- 200g/7oz baby spinach

Dressing
- 2 tbsp extra virgin olive oil
- 1½ tbsp balsamic vinegar
- 1 tsp dijon mustard
- 1 clove garlic
- Pinch Himalayan salt
- Pinch black pepper

## Method

**1** Peel and dice the avocado. Slice the red onion. Dice the tomato. Pile the basil leaves together, roll them up and slice. Cut the stems off the asparagus and slice in half. Crush the garlic.

**2** Slice the chicken breasts in half lengthwise. Sprinkle salt and pepper on each side. Heat the 1 tbsp of olive oil in a cast iron frying pan and place the chicken breasts in. Fry on each side, about 3 until they have a nice golden brown colour and are cooked through. Add the asparagus beside the chicken breasts and cook a few minutes until soft and grilled. Take out the chicken and slice.

**3** In a small bowl, combine the crushed garlic, olive oil, balsamic vinegar, dijon, and salt & peper.

**4** Add the baby spinach to plates.

**5** Pile the grilled chicken, avocado, mozzarella, tomatoes, artichoke, red onions, asparagus and basil leaves on top. Pour the dressing over and serve.

## CHEF'S NOTE
Sundried tomatoes could be used in place of artichokes if you prefer.

# KETO CEASAR SALAD

calories: 527
fat: 22.75g
carbs: 1.8g
fibre: 0.5g
protein: 13g

## Ingredients

- 1 egg yolk
- 2 tbsp avocado oil
- 1 tbsp apple cider vinegar
- 1 tsp dijion mustard
- 4 anchovy filets, finely chopped

- 2 garlic cloves
- 1 tbsp grated parmesan
- 1 romain lettuce shredded
- 2oz/50g crispy bacon, chopped
- 1 tbsp parmesan, shavings

## Method

**1** Create a mayonnaise by gently blending together the egg yolk, apple cider, mustard, vinegar and avocado oil.

**2** Once the base mayo is ready add the anchovies, garlic and grated parmesan to the cup.

**3** Blend slowly until all ingredients are well blended together and create a smooth mayonnaise-like dressing.

**4** Lay the lettuce out on a plate and drizzle the dressing over the top.

**5** Sprinkle the bacon pieces over and garnish with the shaved parmesan.

### CHEF'S NOTE
Add chicken and prawns if you wish to this tasty salad.

# SHRIMP AVOCADO SALAD

calories: 255
fat: 13g
carbs: 4g
fibre: 1g
protein: 27g

## Ingredients

- 1lb/450g cooked shrimp (peeled and deveined)
- 2oz/60ml fresh lime juice
- 1 tsp olive oil
- Salt and pepper

- 1 avocado, pitted and diced
- 1 small tomato, diced
- 2oz/50g red onion, diced
- 2 tbsp fresh chopped coriander

## Method

**1** Chop the shrimp into bite-sized pieces.

**2** Whisk together the lime juice, olive oil, salt, and pepper in a bowl.

**3** Toss in the shrimp, avocado, tomato, red onion, and coriander.

**4** When well combined, cover and chill until ready to serve.

## CHEF'S NOTE
You can add 1 jalapeno (seeded and minced) if you like.

# SAUCES & SEASONING

# ENCHILADA SAUCE

calories: 53
fat: 2g
carbs: 2g
fibre: 0g
protein: 2g

## *Ingredients*

- 500ml/2 cups tomato passata/ sieved tomatoes
- 1 chicken stock cube
- 3 tbsp tomato puree
- 1 bay leaf
- 2 tbsp mild chilli powder

- 1 tbsp sweet paprika
- 2 tsp ground cumin
- 1 tsp dried oregano
- ½ tsp salt
- ½ tsp granulated garlic
- ½ tsp onion powder

- ¼ tsp instant coffee powder
- Pinch ground clove
- Pinch ground cinnamon

## *Method*

**1** Put all of the ingredients into a medium to large frying pan on medium heat.

**2** Simmer gently for 20 minutes, stirring occasionally, until the r sauce has reduced a little.

**3** The sauce will be thin but flavorful.

**4** It will thicken-up in the oven as the enchiladas cook..

### CHEF'S NOTE
Add a ltitle sweetener if the sauce is a bitter, it will help balance the flavours. Discard the bay leaf before using.

# HOMEMADE WORCESTERSHIRE SAUCE

calories: 10
fat: 0.1g
carbs: 1.6g
fibre: 0g
protein: 1g

## Ingredients

- 4oz/125g apple cider vinegar
- 2 tbsp water
- 2 tbsp soy sauce
- 1 tbsp brown sugar
- 1 tsp mustard powder

- ¼ tsp onion powder
- ¼ tsp garlic powder
- ¼ tsp mince cinnamon
- Mince black pepper, to taste

## Method

1 Combine apple cider vinegar, water, soy sauce, brown sugar, mustard powder, onion powder, garlic powder, mince cinnamon, and black pepper together in a saucepan.

2 Bring to a boil and cook until fragrant, about 45 seconds.

3 Cool to room temperature and store in the fridge.

## CHEF'S NOTE

Sodium plays an important role in the removal of any excess carbon dioxide that has accumulated in the body.

# HOMEMADE KETO MAYONNAISE

calories: 95
fat: 11g
carbs: 0g
fibre: 0g
protein: 0g

## Ingredients

- 4 egg yolk
- 12 tbsp apple cider vinegar
- 2 lemons, juiced
- 2 tsp sea salt

- 1 tsp paprika
- 1 tsp garlic powder
- 2 tbsp avocado oil

## Method

**1** Gently blend together the egg yolk, apple cider vinegar, lemon juice, sea salt, paprika and garlic powder

**2** Add the avocado oil to emulsify.

**3** transfer to a clean jar to store.

## CHEF'S NOTE
You can refrigerate and keep for up to 2 weeks.

# SOUTHWESTERN SEASONING MIX

calories: 2
fat: 0g
carbs: 0g
fibre: 0g
protein: 0g

## Ingredients

- 2oz/50g chilli powder
- 2oz/50g onion powder
- 2 tbsp ground cumin
- 2 tbsp ground coriander
- 2 tbsp dried oregano
- 2 tbsp dried basil
- 1 tbsp dried thyme
- 1 tbsp garlic powder

## Method

**1** lay all your dry ingredients out.

**2** Add each in turn to a pestle and mortar and grind together to form a combined powder.

**3** Adjust the seasonign to suit your taste.

## CHEF'S NOTE

Store in an airtight container. Use as a seasoning for cooked vegetables, grilled meats or chip dips.

# MARINARA SAUCE

calories: 159
fat: 10.5g
carbs: 10.7g
fibre: 3g
protein: 2g

## Ingredients

- 2 tbsp of olive oil
- 1 clove of garlic, crushed
- 2 tsp of onion flakes
- 2 tsp fresh thyme, finely chopped
- 2 tsp fresh oregano, finely chopped
- 1 tsp each salt & pepper
- 1lt/4 cups tomato passata/sieved tomatoes
- 2 tsp erythritol
- 1 tsp salt
- 1 tsp red wine vinegar
- 2 tbsp fresh parsley, finely chopped

## Method

1 In a saucepan, place the oil, garlic, onion flakes, thyme and oregano. Saute over medium heat for 3 minutes.

2 Add the tomato passata and stir well.

3 Add the erythritol, pepper, salt and red wine vinegar and bring to a simmer.

4 Turn off the heat and stir through the parsley.

5 Cool the sauce.

**CHEF'S NOTE**
Scoop into an airtight jar and store in fridge.

# DESSETS
# SNACKS &
# SMOOTHIES

# EASY KETO CHOCOLATE MOUSSE

calories: 227
fat: 24g
carbs: 3g
fibre: 1.5g
protein: 4g

## Ingredients

- 2oz/60ml unsalted butter
- 2oz/50g cream cheese
- 3oz/75g double cream, whipped
- 1 tbsp cocoa powder
- Stevia, to taste

## Method

**1** Soften butter and combine with sweetener, stirring until completely blended.

**2** Add cream cheese; blend until smooth.

**3** Add cocoa powder and blend completely.

**4** Whip double cream and gradually add to the mixture.

**5** Spoon into small glasses and refrigerate for 30 minutes.

### CHEF'S NOTE
For extra smoothness add coconut oil.

# COCONUT DROP SCONES

calories: 280
fat: 16g
carbs: 3.5g
fibre: 1g
protein: 8g

## Ingredients

- 2 eggs
- 2oz/50g cream cheese
- 1 tbsp almond flour
- 1 tsp cinnamon

- ½ tbsp erythritol
- 1 pinch salt
- 2oz/50g unsweetened shredded coconut
- 2 tbsp sugar free Maple Syrup

## Method

1 Crack the eggs into a mixing bowl and whisk.

2 Add in cream cheese and whisk until completely combined and creamy.

3 Whisk in the almond flour, cinnamon, erythritol and salt to complete the scone mixture.

4 On a pan on medium heat, add in half the drop scone batter. Cook until the edges start to brown and look dry (about 3-5 minutes). Flip carefully and cook the other side for up to a minute.

5 Transfer the drop scones onto a plate and sprinkle with the shredded coconut.

6 Drizzle with maple syrup to serve.

## CHEF'S NOTE
Make sure your heat is not too high, otherwise the drop scone will burn before the centre cooks.

# ALMOND LEMON CAKE SANDWICHES

calories: 180
fat: 17.5g
carbs: 1g
fibre: 0.8g
protein: 2.8g

## Ingredients

**Almond Lemon Cakes**
- 4oz/125g almond flour
- 4oz/125g coconut flour
- 4oz/120ml butter
- 3 eggs
- 4oz/125g erythritol
- 1 tbsp lemon juice

- 1 tbsp coconut milk
- 1 tsp cinnamon
- ½ tsp almond extract
- ½ tsp vanilla extract
- ½ tsp baking soda
- ½ tsp apple cider vinegar
- ¼ tsp liquid stevia

- ¼ tsp salt

**Sandwich icing**
- 2oz/50g powdered erythritol
- 4oz/120g cream cheese
- 4 tbsp butter
- 2 tbsp double cream

## Method

**1** Preheat your oven to 170C/325F/GAS3.

**2** Sift and mix the coconut flour, almond flour, cinnamon salt, and baking soda.

**3** Combine eggs, erythritol, vanilla extract, almond extract, lemon juice, melted butter, coconut milk, vinegar, stevia, and food colouring.

**4** Mix the wet ingredients into the dry ingredients, using a hand mixer until it is fluffy.

**5** Divide batter between muffin top pan and bake for 17-18 minutes or until cooked.

**6** Remove from the oven and cool on a cooling rack for 10 minutes.

**7** Slice cakes in half and fry them in butter until crisped. Allow to cool on the rack again.

**8** Mix together the butter, cream cheese, double cream, and erythritol until fluffy.

**9** Divide icing in between middle of the cakes and make a sandwich.

**10** Garnish with lemon zest and pistachios.

## CHEF'S NOTE
Lemon zest contain limonene, which protects against skin cancer.

# SMOKED SALMON EGG STUFFED AVOCADOS

calories: 480
fat: 39g
carbs: 18g
fibre: 14g
protein: 20g

## Ingredients

- 4 avocados
- 8 slices smoked salmon
- 8 eggs
- Salt
- Black pepper
- Chilli flakes
- Fresh dill

## Method

**1** Preheat oven to 220C/425F/GAS7.

**2** Halve the avocados, remove the seed. If the hole looks small, scoop out a small bit at a time until it can hold an egg.

**3** Arrange the avocado halves on a baking tray and line the hollows with strips of smoked salmon. Crack each of the eggs into a small bowl, then spoon the yolks and however much white the avocado will hold.

**4** Add salt and fresh cracked black pepper on top of the eggs, to taste.

**5** Gently place the baking tray in the oven and bake for about 15-20 minutes.

**6** Sprinkle chilli flakes and fresh dill on top.

**7** Serve warm.

### CHEF'S NOTE
Avocados are a great source of vitamins C, E, K, and B-6, as well as riboflavin, niacin, folate, pantothenic acid, magnesium, and potassium.

# SALTED CARAMEL CASHEW SMOOTHIE

calories: 181
fat: 19g
carbs: 1g
fibre: 0g
protein: 2g

## Ingredients

- 8½oz/250ml unsweetened cashew milk
- 3 tbsp double cream
- 5 ice cubes
- 2 tbsp sugar-free salted caramel syrup
- Pinch of nutmeg to garnish

## Method

**1** Put all the ingredients, except the nutmeg, into a blender.

**2** Blend until smooth.

**3** Pour into a glass to serve and sprinkle with nutmeg.

## CHEF'S NOTE
Almong milk also makes a good base for this smoothie.

# KETO HUMMUS WITH CAULIFLOWER & TAHINI

calories: 124
fat: 11g
carbs: 4g
fibre: 2g
protein: 2g

## Ingredients

- ½ head of cauliflower, broken into florets
- 1 tbsp olive oil
- 2 tbsp mayo
- 3 cloves of garlic, peeled
- 2 tbsp lemon juice
- 1 tbsp white tahini
- Sea salt and freshly mince black pepper, to taste
- 1 tsp fresh parsley, finely chopped for garnish

## Method

**1** Steam the cauliflower until softened. Drain the water well.

**2** Place into a blender and blend really well with the rest of the ingredients (except for the parsley).

**3** Drizzle with a little more olive oil and garnish with chopped parsley.

**4** Serve with vegetable sticks like carrot or celery sticks.

## CHEF'S NOTE
Take the time to blend your ingredients well, so the end result is nice and smooth.

# TURKEY BANGER FRITTATA

calories: 240
fat: 16.7g
carbs: 5.5g
fibre: 0g
protein: 16.7g

## Ingredients

- 12oz/350g turkey mince
- 2 peppers
- 12 eggs
- 8oz/225g sour cream

- 1 tsp pink Himalayan salt
- 1 tsp black pepper
- 2 tsp kerry gold butter

## Method

**1** Preheat your oven to 180C/350F/GAS4.

**2** Crack all your eggs into a blender, add in the sour cream, salt and pepper. Blend on high for 30 seconds. Set aside.

**3** Heat a large oven proof frying pan on medium heat. When it comes to temperature add in the butter.

**4** Slice your peppers into strips. Add it to the frying pan. Sauté until browned and tender. Remove the peppers from the frying pan.

**5** Add the turkey mince to the pan and cook until browned.

**6** Flatten the turkey to the bottom of the frying pan. Add the peppers over it, evenly distributed. Pour the egg mix over everything.

**7** Place the frying pan in the oven and bake for 30 mins until cooked thorugh.

**8** Cut into wedges to serve.

### CHEF'S NOTE
If you want to add cheese, sprinkle over as soon as it's out of the oven

# TACO TARTLETS

calories: 241
fat: 19.4g
carbs: 1.7g
fibre: 0g
protein: 13.1g

## Ingredients

For the pastry:
- 8½oz blanched almond flour
- 3 tbsp coconut flour
- 5 tbsp butter
- ¼ tsp salt
- 1 tsp xanthan gum
- 1 tsp oregano

- Pinch of paprika & cayenne

For the filling:
- 2½oz/60g cheese
- 400g/14oz minced beef
- 3oz/75g mushroom
- 3 spring onions
- 2 tbsp tomato paste

- 1 tbsp olive oil
- 2 each tsp mustard & garlic
- 1 tsp each cumin & salt
- 1 tsp worcestershire
- ¼ tsp each cinnamon & pepper

## Method

1 Combine all the dry ingredients of the pastry and put them into a food processor.

2 Chop cold butter into small squares and add it to your food processor. Pulse the dough together until crumbly, adding 1 tbsp of ice water until pliable.

3 Chill your dough in the freezer for 10 mins.

4 Roll the dough out between 2 pieces of clingfilm using a rolling pin. Cut out circles using a cookie cutter or a glass.

5 Put the dough pieces into your a muffin trays to make tartlets.

6 Put the oven on to heat to 170C/325F/GAS3.

7 Prepare all the filling ingredients by chopping the spring onions, mince garlic, and slice mushrooms.

8 Saute the onions and garlic in olive oil. Add minced beef to the mixture and sear it well – adding the dry spices and Worcestershire.

9 Add mushrooms and mix together. Then add tomato paste and mustard right before finishing.

10 Spoon minced beef mixture evenly into the pastry tartlets. Cover with cheese and bake for 20-25 minutes.

11 Allow to cool a little and remove the pastries to serve.

# PUMPKIN CHEESECAKE BARS

calories: 273
fat: 25g
carbs: 5g
fibre: 1g
protein: 4g

## Ingredients

For the crust:
- 14oz/400ml whole pecans
- 1 tsp cinnamon
- 1 tbsp coconut oil
- 12 drops liquid stevia
- 1 pinch sea salt
- For the filling:

- 8oz/225g cream cheese
- 2oz/60ml double cream
- 10oz/275g pumpkin puree
- 2 tsp vanilla extract
- 20 drops liquid stevia
- Pinch of nutmeg
- 1 tsp cinnamon

- 1 pinch salt
- 2 eggs
For the icing:
- 2oz/50g cream cheese
- 2 tbsp double cream
- 2oz/50g erythritol
- ½ tsp vanilla extract

## Method

**1** Preheat the oven to 180C/350F/GAS4. Combine all the crust ingredients in a food processor and pulse until the pecans are a fine crumb texture.

**2** Line a 9 x 6 inch baking dish with parchment paper, letting two sides spill over for easy removal. Press the crust into the dish, making one even layer. Bake for 12 minutes, then let cool.

**3** Make the filling by beating in the cream cheese and double cream until fully combined.

**4** Add in the pumpkin puree, vanilla extract and liquid stevia and combine.

**5** Add in the nutmeg, cinnamon and a pinch of salt then combine.

**6** Add in one egg at a time, incorporating each before adding another to make a batter.

**7** Once the crust has cooled a bit, pour the pumpkin cheesecake batter into the baking dish. Reduce the heat in the oven to 325°F and bake for 25-30 minutes. The middle of the pumpkin cheesecake should be a bit wobbly after baking. Refrigerate for 6 hours or, ideally, overnight.

**8** To make the icing, combine all the icing ingredients and beat with an electric hand mixer until light and fluffy.

**9** Frost the top of the cheesecake bars or add a dollop to each one after slicing.

# KETO CHEESECAKE STUFFED BROWNIES

calories: 144
fat: 13g
carbs: 4g
fibre: 2g
protein: 4g

## Ingredients

For the Filling
- 8oz/225g cream cheese
- 2oz/50g granulated erythritol
- 1 egg

For the Brownie
- 3oz/75ml low carb milk chocolate

- 5 tbsp butter
- 3 eggs
- 4oz/125g granulated erythritol
- 2oz/50g cocoa powder
- 4oz/120g almond flour

## Method

**1** Heat oven to 180C/350F/GAS4 and line a brownie pan with parchment. Make the cheesecake filling first by beating softened cream cheese, egg for the filling, and granulated sweetener smooth. Set aside.

**2** Melt the chocolate and butter at 30-second intervals in the microwave, frequently stirring until smooth. Let cool slightly while you prepare the brownie.

**3** Beat remaining eggs and sweetener on medium until the mixture is frothy.

**4** Sift in the cocoa powder and almond flour and continue to beat until thin batter forms.

**5** Pour in melted chocolate and beat with the hand mixer on low for 10 seconds. The batter will thicken to a mousse-like consistency.

**6** Pour ¾ of the batter in the prepared pan, top with dollops of the cream cheese, then finish with the remaining brownie batter.

**7** Using a spatula, smooth the batter over the cheesecake filling in a swirling pattern.

**8** Bake for 25-30 minutes or until the centre is mostly set. It may jiggle slightly but once you remove it from the oven it should firm completely. Cool before slicing!

### CHEF'S NOTE
Temperatures and cook times varies depending on oven. Watch these carefully and bake them until they are firm on the edges but just slightly soft at the centre.

# EASY ALMOND BUTTER FUDGE

calories: 120
fat: 11g
carbs: 2.5g
fibre: 1g
protein: 3.5g

## Ingredients

- 8oz/225g cream cheese, softened
- 8½oz/250ml butter, softened
- 8½oz/250ml natural almond butter (softened)

- 9oz/250g powdered erythritol
- 4oz/120g almond flour
- Liquid stevia extract, to taste

## Method

**1** Line a square 9x9-inch baking pan with foil or parchment paper.

**2** Melt the cream cheese and butter in a small saucepan over medium heat.

**3** Stir in the almond butter and cook until it melts.

**4** Remove from heat then stir in the powdered erythritol and peanut flour.

**5** Adjust sweetness to taste with liquid stevia extract and stir smooth.

**6** Spread the mixture in the prepared baking pan as evenly as possible.

**7** Chill until set then cut into squares to serve.

## CHEF'S NOTE

Do not overheat the cream cheese and butter mixture. Heat in small intervals until you can mix the two together and then remove from the heat.

# PECAN SOFTIES WITH SEA SALT & DARK CHOCOLATE

calories: 128
fat: 13g
carbs: 4.43g
fibre 2.16g
protein: 2.7g

## Ingredients

- 4oz/120g almond flour
- 9oz/250g pecan halves
- 1½ tbsp butter, melted
- 1 tsp baking powder

- 2oz/50g erythritol
- ½ tsp sea salt
- 1 egg white
- 1oz/25g low-carb dark chocolate, melted

## Method

**1** Heat oven to 180C/350F/GAS4 and line a baking tray with parchment paper.

**2** Combine the dry ingredients in a blender or food processor and pulse until the pecans are a coarse mince.

**3** Add the butter, salt, and egg white into the blender and pulse a few times to combine. The cookie dough should like wet and feel sticky but still chunky.

**4** Using a spoon or small scoop, portion out 10 rounded cookie dough balls onto the parchment. Flatten the tops of the balls until you have evenly round, flat biscuits.

**5** Bake for 15 minutes or until the edges begin to brown.

**6** Melt the chocolate by placing in a microwave safe bowl for 45 seconds. Stop it every 15-20 seconds to stir.

**7** Drizzle each cookie with chocolate and sprinkle with extra sea salt.

## CHEF'S NOTE

You can pack in a plastic container and store in the freezer.